FASHIONING THE DUKE

Suddenly a Duke Series
Book Five

Alexa Aston

ARE YOU SIGNED UP FOR DRAGONBLADE'S BLOG?

You'll get the latest news and information on exclusive giveaways, exclusive excerpts, coming releases, sales, free books, cover reveals and more.

Check out our complete list of authors, too!

No spam, no junk. That's a promise!

Sign Up Here

www.dragonbladepublishing.com

Dearest Reader;

Thank you for your support of a small press. At Dragonblade Publishing, we strive to bring you the highest quality Historical Romance from some of the best authors in the business. Without your support, there is no 'us', so we sincerely hope you adore these stories and find some new favorite authors along the way.

Happy Reading!

CEO, Dragonblade Publishing

Additional Dragonblade books by Author Alexa Aston

Suddenly a Duke Series
Portrait of the Duke
Music for the Duke
Polishing the Duke
Designs on the Duke
Fashioning the Duke

Second Sons of London Series
Educated By The Earl
Debating With The Duke
Empowered By The Earl
Made for the Marquess
Dubious about the Duke
Valued by the Viscount
Meant for the Marquess

Dukes Done Wrong Series
Discouraging the Duke
Deflecting the Duke
Disrupting the Duke
Delighting the Duke
Destiny with a Duke

Dukes of Distinction Series
Duke of Renown
Duke of Charm
Duke of Disrepute
Duke of Arrogance
Duke of Honor
The Duke That I Want

The St. Clairs Series
Devoted to the Duke
Midnight with the Marquess
Embracing the Earl
Defending the Duke
Suddenly a St. Clair
Starlight Night (Novella)
The Twelve Days of Love (Novella)

Soldiers & Soulmates Series
To Heal an Earl
To Tame a Rogue
To Trust a Duke
To Save a Love
To Win a Widow
Yuletide at Gillingham (Novella)

The Lyon's Den Series
The Lyon's Lady Love

King's Cousins Series
The Pawn
The Heir
The Bastard

Medieval Runaway Wives
Song of the Heart
A Promise of Tomorrow
Destined for Love

Knights of Honor Series
Word of Honor
Marked by Honor
Code of Honor
Journey to Honor
Heart of Honor
Bold in Honor
Love and Honor
Gift of Honor

Path to Honor
Return to Honor

Pirates of Britannia Series
God of the Seas

De Wolfe Pack: The Series
Rise of de Wolfe

The de Wolfes of Esterley Castle
Diana
Derek
Thea

Also from Alexa Aston
The Bridge to Love
One Magic Night

PROLOGUE

London—February 1812

D ELANEY COLEBOURNE THANKED her last customer and saw the woman out the door, turning the sign to indicate Delaney's Designs was now closed for the day. She and Fanny, her salesclerk, went about the store, straightening things up, before Delaney bid the girl goodnight.

She went to the back of the store, where two milliners brought her designs to life. Once, she had toiled creating hats herself. For five long years, she had apprenticed with a top milliner in London. Those years were behind her now, thanks to the Earl of Kinnison, who had bought the building Delaney's Designs was located in four years ago when she turned five and twenty. It had taken close to a year for her to outfit the building, make a stock of hats, and hire the right people. Now, the *ton* flocked to her millinery shop, raving about her original creations.

Not a one of them knew that Lord Kinnison was her father.

It wasn't something she deliberately hid from her clients. The subject simply never came up. Ladies of Polite Society came in to find new hats and bonnets for themselves. While they admired Delaney's work, it wasn't as if they engaged in personal conversations with her. They simply talked to her about colors they liked or the preferences they held. Sometimes, they would ask her opinion, but they never spoke to her of anything other than hats.

Her father also did not keep it a secret, but it wasn't something that came up in everyday conversation. Now, the people back in Devon knew. Lord Kinnison had immediately claimed paternity of Delaney, even insisting that her surname be Colebourne, as his was. Growing up, they had spent long hours together. Though he had a son and two other daughters, he devoted more time to Delaney than his three legitimate children combined, calling his children with the countess useless and spoiled. Their mother had died with the birth of their final child, the Kinnison heir, and everyone from relatives to friends to the servants had coddled and pampered the three motherless Colebourne children.

Delaney's mother had been the wife of a dairy farmer, wed to him less than a year when he ran off with the local clergyman's daughter. Neither was heard from again. It left her mother to run the farm herself. Lord Kinnison had come to visit with the woman and see if she needed any help, financially or otherwise. Sparks had flown at their meeting, and they had begun a long, torrid affair that continued until her mother's death. Delaney was the product of their love.

The earl had still been wed to his shrewish wife when the affair began. After the countess' death, Delaney's mother had refused to marry Kinnison, despite his frequent pleading. Instead, she had continued running the dairy farm. Her only request was that he take time to get to know his out-of-wedlock daughter.

Delaney had worshipped Lord Kinnison as a child and still thought him the best man she had ever known. He had seen she had a good education and when her mother died unexpectedly, the earl brought Delaney to London, placing her in the care of the expert milliner, who began with the basics and over time taught Delaney the intricacies of millinery. Her father had encouraged her artistic bent, which had emerged at a young age. Delaney had been fascinated by clothes and sewed them for her dolls. Later, her interest had turned to hats. Her father recognized his bastard was bright, industrious, and creative and told her she would need all three to make her way in the world.

He had opened his estate's ledgers and taught her about business, preparing her for the day when she would own and run her own shop. He marveled that she had good business sense, balanced with her creative side, telling her that was rare. It was Kinnison who had encouraged Delaney to be very selective about whom she took on as a client, telling her to always receive a personal recommendation before she accepted someone new.

Her father had set her up to apprentice with the best-known millinery in London. Delaney had spent five years under the woman's tutelage, learning everything she could. When she believed the time was right, she went to her father and told him she was ready to strike out on her own. He encouraged her to follow her dreams, knowing the *ton* would not accept the bastard daughter of an earl. He told her to make the *ton* come to her.

And she had.

She told Ruth and Dilly, her milliners, that they could finish what they were working on tomorrow and locked up after them. Her business would soon be booming, with Polite Society returning to town for the upcoming Season, her busiest time of year. Delaney had not heard from her father in over a week, which was unusual. He spent most of his year in London now, and they would see each other often, dining in his home, going to a museum, or taking a ride through Hyde Park, either on horseback or in his phaeton. She decided she would leave now and call upon him so they might make plans to see one another in the coming days.

As she slipped her shawl about her, she heard a knock at the door. Knowing she had posted the closed sign, she wondered who might be calling. She claimed her reticule and went to the front, seeing Papa's coachman at the door.

Opening it, she said, "I was just coming to see his lordship."

The driver shook his head, looking at her strangely. Immediately, Delaney knew something was wrong.

ALEXA ASTON

"What is it?" she demanded.

"Lord Kinnison is seriously ill, Miss Colebourne. The doctor said it is apoplexy, and he hasn't long to live. You must come now."

Cold fear pooled in her belly. Apoplexy often rendered those it struck with paralysis. Victims rarely could speak. She blinked away the tears that formed in her eyes and locked the door to her store.

She accompanied the coachman to the earl's carriage, dread filling her with every step. She wondered if the attack had occurred today or if several days had passed before she had been notified. Papa had told her that his son was coming to town. The heir apparent loathed Delaney, though the pair had never been introduced, and it wouldn't surprise her if he had kept the news from her of their father's illness.

"Breathe," she told herself, closing her eyes and taking slow, deep breaths, trying to calm herself as they traveled to the Kinnison townhouse in Mayfair.

The carriage halted, and Delaney bounded from it, rushing to the front door and knocking.

The butler answered her knock and loudly said, "You are not welcomed here, Miss Colebourne."

That was her first clue. He always called her Miss Delaney. She knew her half-brother must be lingering nearby.

Knowing now the servant was putting on an act, she said, "But I must see Papa. I beg you to please tell him that I am here."

"Lord Kinnison is not home to you now—or ever," the butler said ominously.

As he closed the door, however, he thrust a note at her. She took it and quickly opened it. It told her to go to the kitchen door, and she would be taken up the back staircase to see the earl.

Delaney hurried down the block and descended the stairs. Before she could knock, the door flew open and Cook latched on to her wrist, pulling her in from the cold.

"He's in a bad way, Miss Delaney," Cook said. "Go to him

4

now."

She did, passing servants in the kitchens and others in the hallway upstairs. All looked at her with sympathy.

Reaching her father's rooms, she saw the butler waiting there for her.

"I apologize for not sending word sooner, Miss Delaney. The viscount constantly hovered. He wants his father dead." The servant paused. "And now that the earl is near his end, the viscount is holding a party in the drawing room for his friends." Disgust filled the servant's face. "The lot of them are already drunk."

Anger sizzled through her. She knew from stories Papa shared that her half-brother was lazy, thoughtless, and self-centered. He lived in rooms with a friend of his, visiting gaming hells nightly, spending most of his time drinking. Of her two half-sisters, one had died in childhood, and the other had wed a Scottish laird years ago. She had never returned to London after her marriage.

"Thank you for sending for me."

"Of course, Miss Delaney. His lordship favors you for a reason. You are the only one of his children who ever loved him."

She swallowed the lump in her throat and entered the room, crossing it and stepping inside Papa's bedchamber. His valet sat next to the bed and now rose, nodding deferentially at her and leaving in order to give the two of them some privacy. Delaney went to the bed and took her father's hand.

He smiled at her, an odd, crooked smile. She realized one side of his face must be paralyzed.

"Everything . . . worth it . . . because of you," he rasped from one side of his mouth. "I loved your mother and . . . you, my sweet." He paused. "Sorry couldn't . . . make you . . . legitimate."

Delaney knew the effort he must be expending to speak. She cradled his cheek. "Don't speak, Papa. Rest. I know you loved Mama and me."

He frowned. "Hated . . . wife. Forced to . . . wed her. You . . .

taken care of."

She tried to alleviate his worries. "I know you have taken care of me, Papa. You have already provided my shop's building. My business is thriving. All because of your belief in me and my talents."

"Not . . . enough," he protested weakly, closing his eyes, his breathing becoming more labored.

She took the seat the valet had vacated and clasped his hand in both of hers, no words necessary. After some time, he opened his eyes again.

"You . . . in will. Inherited unentailed . . . estate. Solicitor has it. You . . . get . . . ten thousand pounds."

Shock filled her. Ten thousand pounds was a huge fortune. She need never work again if this were true. And that did not include this estate he had mentioned.

"You know I love to work, Papa. I live to work."

He grinned crookedly again, hope in his eyes. "Could . . . slow down. Marry."

Delaney had seen what his marriage was like and determined long ago that marriage wasn't for her. Her mother, though wed less than a year, had spoken of the beatings doled out to her by her husband before he ran away with his lover. Mama had constantly preached to Delaney never to wed—and especially never to wed a member of the *ton*. Despite Mama's feelings for her lover, she despised the upper crust of society.

No, marriage was not for her. Besides, if she ever did wed, Delaney would lose her business, along with whatever Papa had left her in his will. English law made certain that a wife's property and monies became that of her husband's upon marriage. Delaney would not be stripped of everything she had worked so hard and long for, not to mention the other things Papa would leave her. She would keep her name and everything she owned. Marriage was for fools.

Delaney Colebourne was no fool.

Papa shut his eyes again and mumbled to himself before

falling silent. His breathing grew more labored. Knowing nothing could be done for him, she remained at his side, holding his hand, stroking his hair, willing him to let go and be at peace.

When he passed, a smile graced his face. She sat another few minutes, his hand growing cold in hers, savoring these last few moments with him.

Finally, she rose, kissing his brow and leaving his bedchamber. Both his valet and the butler lingered in the corridor.

"He is gone now. He went peacefully." She paused, her head high. "I will go out the front door this time."

She descended the stairs, hearing the raucous noise coming from the drawing room, thinking it a pity that such a wonderful man hadn't been loved by his other children, especially his heir.

It didn't matter. Delaney would honor him. Mourn him. She would create what would rival any millinery shop in London. She knew she would not be allowed to attend his funeral or burial in Devon.

But she would hold him dear in her heart forevermore.

CHAPTER ONE

Spain—February 1813

MAJOR-GENERAL NIGEL FOXWELL listened as Wellington walked his senior staff through the next campaign.

"Thanks to Bonaparte's invasion of Russia being such a dismal failure last summer, we finally have The Little Corporal on the run," the commander said. "Intelligence reports reveal that French armies in eastern Europe will soon fall back to the Elbe."

"What of Prussia?" someone asked.

Wellington smiled. "From all accounts, it looks as if Prussia intends to reenter the war as early as next month." The commander paused, letting that information be digested before continuing. "It means Bonaparte will not be able to spare any fresh troops in the Peninsula because he must prepare for a counterattack in the east. In the meantime, I have been assured by the War Office that reinforcements will be shipped to me throughout the spring."

For the first time in a long time, Fox smiled. Things had been going well, for the most part, for Wellington's troops in Spain, especially after the Battle of Salamanca the previous year. With Bonaparte's main forces tied up, it would be increasingly difficult for the French commanders in Spain to mount much of an offensive. That meant England and her allies would be on the move, striking north at Burgos.

Perhaps an end to this war might occur someday, after all.

War was all Fox had known as an adult. He had been an officer in His Majesty's army for thirteen years now, a seasoned veteran. Wellington was by far his favorite of the commanders he had served under. If more commanders had Wellington's guts and keen intelligence, they would have made mincemeat of the French years ago.

He wondered if peace would truly ever come. Even with Bonaparte on the defensive now, the wily Corsican might continue to fight for many years. Still, Fox believed the end was in sight, and Bonaparte's days were numbered.

And then what?

He would always be a part of the army. He had risen through the ranks due to his intelligence and charisma. In battle, he was physical. Daring. Colorful. Known for taking calculated risks. His men followed him because of his leadership and their loyalty to him. It seemed when they engaged their enemy, a calm came over Fox, a supreme confidence that made him fearless. He knew his place and where he was headed.

If England were finally at peace, though, would he be happy?

Of course, no man truly enjoyed war. Fox certainly hated the killing and waste of men. Still, he had risen through the ranks and even if sent home if the war ended, he would command a garrison somewhere in England, keeping the mother country safe.

The meeting ended, and Fox left with a few of his fellow officers, heading first to the stewpots for something to fill their bellies. Then he went to the medical tent to visit the men under his command who were injured. One had already been discharged and told to report for duty again. Another was on the mend, and Fox gave him encouraging words. The final soldier, though, would not make it.

He went and took a seat beside Lieutenant Garrison. The young officer's face was flushed with fever. He had a gut wound and had lasted two agonizing days.

Placing his hand on Garrison's brow, Fox felt the fever burning up the man.

"Can I get you something to drink, Lieutenant?"

Garrison looked at him with eyes bright from the fever. "No. What would be the point, Major-General? It would be wasted on a dying man."

He sat silently, not knowing what words of comfort to offer, the first time in a long time he hadn't been able to provide solace to a soldier.

"Might I ask a favor?"

"Anything," Fox said fervently.

"When this is over—this war—will you go see my widow, Major-General? She lives with her parents now, she and our little boy. He's but two years old. I will die never having seen him." Garrison choked on this last word.

Frankly, he thought it foolish that the man had thought to wed, much less have a child, with a war going on. Though he liked Garrison, who was personable and had shown true leadership qualities, the man should not have married before he became an officer. Yet he looked down at the feverish soldier, who wouldn't last another day, and pity filled him.

"I will do as you ask, Lieutenant Garrison. I will tell both your wife and your son of your bravery on the battlefield and how you represented England well."

Garrison shook his head, wincing with pain. "No. Don't do that. All you need to say is that I love them. That they were in my thoughts always, especially at the very end."

He stiffened. "If that is your wish, Lieutenant."

The officer blew out a long breath. "It is. I have missed them every day I have been in Spain. Oh, I know it sounds mad, to love someone you have never seen. I do love my boy with all my heart. And my wife. More than words could ever convey. Please, let her know they were in my heart . . . always."

Garrison choked, and his head dropped to the side. Fox touched two fingers to the pulse point in his neck.

Dead.

Though he thought it absurd to convey a message of love, he would do it. He would also make certain the widow knew her husband was a brave man.

Rising, he motioned for a private and said, "Lieutenant Garrison has passed."

"Thank you for letting me know, Major-General," the soldier responded.

As Fox slowly returned to his tent, he tried to comprehend something such as the love the lieutenant had known for his wife and a son he had never seen. Fox had never known love.

He was the product of a second marriage. His father died when Fox was only two, and he had no recollection of the man. His mother became the Dowager Duchess of Abington, and he had grown up in the dower house at Crosshaven. Mama had spent most of her time in London, while Fox was left alone in Hertfordshire, brought up by nannies, the housekeeper, and a tutor before he had gone away to school. He only saw his mother sporadically before he left for his army training. She had remarried when he was twelve, and her husband did not want his new wife's son from another man around. He had learned of her death five years ago in the only letter he had received since leaving England.

The new Duke of Abington, his half-brother, was twenty years Fox's senior. He had seen Abington out and about at Crosshaven a few times during his childhood, but the duke never made a point to come see Fox. Abington also spent the bulk of his time in London, only returning to Crosshaven for a couple of weeks at Christmas each year. Fox learned from servants' gossip that the duke had wed, and his duchess had given birth to two girls a year apart. After that, he left for the Continent with his regiment. Perhaps more children had come. He had no idea. All he knew was that his mother, in effect, abandoned him to the care of servants and teachers. He had raised himself. His half-brother had never bothered to meet him, much less extend friendship.

The idea of love was foreign to Fox. Yes, he did care for his men a great deal. He had also had friends at school and university, particularly the Earl of Morton, whom he had shared rooms with at Oxford. But love?

He knew nothing of it—and decided he was better off without it.

Returning to his tent, he went straight for his makeshift desk. He would write to Mrs. Garrison and her son and notify them of her husband's death.

Fox found himself struggling as he wrote, which was odd. He had written hundreds of these types of letters over the years. Yet the thought of a weeping Mrs. Garrison and her toddler bothered him. He had lost his own father near the same age. He wondered if Mrs. Garrison would marry again. If she would tell her son stories of his father, or if Garrison would be forgotten and the new husband would become the father the boy knew.

Finally, he finished the letter and sealed it, glad to have completed the task. He would have it posted in the morning.

The flap to his tent opened. "Major-General?"

"Come."

A young private entered, so young that Fox doubted he needed to shave. "Yes?"

The man produced a folded parchment. "A letter for you, sir."

A letter?

"Thank you," he said brusquely, accepting it and watching the private leave before he turned his eyes to it.

Who could have written him?

He glanced at the front, seeing his name and rank. Clearly, someone from home knew of him. Perhaps it was from someone in the War Office.

Turning it over, he broke the seal and opened it to read.

Dear Major-General Foxwell —

My name is Hodgkins, and I am the Foxwell family solicitor. I am writing to inform you of the death of the Duke of

Abington. His Grace died with only two daughters and no son. That means you have succeeded to the title.

I am aware of the fact that you and His Grace never met. He was a bit resentful when his father married again, having been close to his mother. He knew, however, that having had no legitimate sons, you would become his heir.

I know this news may come as a great shock to you, as you left England shortly after university and have never been in contact with His Grace. I do believe you should now be told that your army commission was purchased at His Grace's request, because it was your father's fondest wish for you to enter the military, something he always had longed to do.

My best advice is for you to sell out as quickly as possible and return to England to assume your title. You are now the guardian of your two nieces. They lost their parents a day apart, both from the pneumonia, and are a bit forlorn. They are, however, of an age to make their come-outs, so once they wed, they will no longer be your responsibility.

My condolences to you, Your Grace. Please come to my office in London, the address of which I have listed below. We can talk of Crosshaven and the girls, who are named Eliza and Grace, and make certain you understand your new responsibilities now that you are the Duke of Abington.

I look forward to meeting you and thank you for your service to our great country.

Sincerely,
G. Hodgkins

The page fluttered from Fox's hand, falling to the floor.

He was a duke. A bloody duke. Responsible for two young women he had never met, ones grieving for their parents. How was he supposed to step in and make things right?

Bloody hell.

CHAPTER TWO

London—March 1813

FOX'S HEAD SWIRLED with the amount of information Mr. Hodgkins had dumped upon him. He knew it would take several more meetings with the solicitor before he felt comfortable with everything he had been told today. One thing he knew— he was an incredibly wealthy man. He supposed dukes, being on the highest social rung of Polite Society, had vast fortunes. It was never something he had given a thought to before. Life in the dower house had been comfortable, and then he had gone away to some of the best schools in the land, as well as graduating from Oxford. He had no one to send his soldier's pay home to, and so he had merely banked it, the army providing for all his needs in the meantime while he had been at war. But what he had saved over the years was a mere pittance compared to the funds now at his disposal.

"Do you have someone who can teach you the finer things about being part of the titled nobility, Your Grace?" Hodgkins asked. "Someone who could guide you as to finding the right tailor. How to acquire your membership at White's. The manner in which you take your seat in the House of Lords."

"I was close friends with the Earl of Morton at university, but we have not spoken since our time at Oxford," he volunteered.

"Then I would do my best to get in contact with this Lord Morton. He, along with your valet, will be invaluable in easing your way into Polite Society."

"I have no valet," Fox replied.

"The previous duke did," the solicitor pointed out. "Most likely, he has remained on the payroll, awaiting the new duke's arrival." Hodgkins paused. "As for your nieces, I suggest you allow them to make their come-outs as soon as possible and find husbands for the pair. I find girls to be rather bothersome."

"Won't they still be in mourning?" he asked. "After all, they lost both parents only this past November."

Hodgkins shrugged. "True, but these circumstances are more than unusual. They are strangers to you and you to them. I would do my best to encourage them to step into society this year. As I mentioned earlier, they do have substantial dowries, which will attract a good number of suitors. If your friend, Lord Morton, has wed, it might be possible for his wife to sponsor the girls. Many things go into a young lady's come-out Season. Things which you will have no knowledge of, Your Grace. If you could find a woman to help guide you through his process, it would be that much easier."

Fox rose. "You have given me much food for thought, Hodgkins. I would like to digest it and return tomorrow for us to continue our discussion. What time is convenient?"

The solicitor called in his clerk, who said the duke would be welcome to return at two o'clock tomorrow afternoon.

"Then I will see you tomorrow at that time."

"Until tomorrow, Your Grace," Hodgkins said.

Fox left the solicitor's office, the address of his townhouse on a slip of paper in his pocket. He had never visited London, much less this residence, but Hodgkins had said it was located in Mayfair. He asked the clerk how far Mayfair was and decided to walk to the square instead of traveling by hansom cab once he received directions to it. He told himself it was because he wanted to see a bit of the city. In actuality, he dreaded arriving there. He knew the names of his nieces. That information had been provided to him by Hodgkins. Eliza was the elder by a year at nine and ten. Grace was eight and ten. Hodgkins had never met either girl so he knew nothing else to share with Fox. It surprised him that he could have been in charge of hundreds of men, and yet the thought of being the guardian to two young ladies terrified him.

He had to stop twice for directions but finally arrived at his destination. Awe filled him as he gazed upon his house, which took up one entire side of the square. He could not begin to venture a guess as to how many rooms lay inside the townhouse, much less the number of servants it took to maintain it. Hodgkins had allowed Fox to see a list of every servant in his employ and their salary. It went on for so many pages that he lost count. He hoped he had an efficient butler and housekeeper. He would look at this as the army. He had been in charge of a large number of men and had to put his faith in the officers of a lesser rank under his command, hoping they would do their jobs and guide the men according to Fox's orders. The same might be true of his London staff, with the butler and housekeeper doling out responsibilities and overall managing the servants.

At least that was what he hoped. He would not be someone to come in and begin dismissing servants left and right. He would observe how his household worked. If it ran smoothly, then he would keep with the status quo and make no changes.

As he approached the front door, his chief concern lay with his guardianship of Eliza and Grace. He would sound them out to see if they were comfortable making their come-outs this year or if they would prefer to remain in mourning and come out next year instead. He wondered if his half-brother had kept to the schedule he had set when he became the Duke of Abington and continued to only visit Crosshaven for the two weeks at Christmas. If so, the girls might prefer staying in town if they were more comfortable being here. He thought of so many choices and decisions that must be made in the coming days and weeks.

Fox rapped on the door. Immediately, a footman answered, and he realized the servant had been stationed next to the door.

"May I help you, sir?" the footman asked.

"I am the Duke of Abington," he announced, causing the footman's eyes to widen considerably.

"Please, come in, Your Grace," was the response, spoken in a deferential manner.

The servant stepped back, and Fox entered what would be his new home. He gazed up at the crystal chandelier, which probably cost more than he had earned his entire time in the army. The foyer was wide and circular, containing bits of furniture for others to sit upon, most likely when they were waiting for their carriage to be readied. A large painting of his half-brother graced one wall, and Fox walked to it, studying it carefully.

The previous duke had been captured most likely soon after Fox had left for university, because this image was close to his last memories of his blood relative. The duke's dark hair was tinged with a bit of gray at the temples.

Turning, he saw a tall, lean man with an air of authority about him and knew the servant to be his butler.

"I am Abington," he said, knowing the servant would take things in hand.

The butler bowed. "Welcome home, Your Grace. I am Driskell, your butler. My wife, Mrs. Driskell, serves as your housekeeper here in town." The butler paused. "We were both in the household as a footman and maid when your father was alive, God rest his soul. We are happy to have you here."

"I would like to meet with you and Mrs. Driskell later. First, I want to speak with my nieces. Are they at home?"

"Yes, Your Grace. Lady Eliza and Lady Grace are in the music room finishing their weekly pianoforte lesson. If you wish, I can take you to the drawing room, and you can meet with them there."

"Very well."

"If you will follow me, Your Grace."

It still sounded foreign to his ears, being called Your Grace by everyone. He supposed just as he would never be known as Major-General Foxwell ever again, no one would call him Fox. The thought saddened him. He had known his place in the world for so many years, as an officer in His Majesty's army. Now, it was as if he were plucked from the army and dropped into a foreign country, where he knew neither the language nor the rules. He would need to seek out Morton as soon as possible. If his old friend was nowhere to be found, Fox would truly be lost.

Entering the drawing room, Driskell took his leave, allowing Fox to make a circle about the room, taking in its furnishings and artwork. Once again, it astounded him how wealthy he was and how this palatial townhouse was to be his home. He would ask his housekeeper to give him a tour of the place in order to familiarize himself with it, though he suspected he still might lose his way among the many corridors a time or two.

He sat, strumming his fingers against his thigh, a gesture of both impatience and unsureness. He forced his fingers to still, not recalling the last time he had experienced any type of anxiety. Perhaps it had been years ago when he had entered battle for the first time. That occurred so long ago that he could barely remember the occasion. He told himself that he was not confronting an enemy in the next few minutes. His nieces were family and young women, most likely sheltered since they had yet to step out into Polite Society. He had no reason to be nervous around them. *He* was in charge.

Yet Fox felt so very unsure of himself in this moment.

The door opened, and Driskell appeared again. "Lady Eliza and Lady Grace, Your Grace," the butler announced.

Fox rose, standing tall, his hands clasped behind his back as two nearly-identical young women came toward him. Both were exactly the same height, a couple of inches over five feet. Each was petite, with delicate features. Most likely, they shared a wardrobe since they were the same size. Even their faces looked remarkably similar. The only way they could be told apart was by their hair color. One was blond, and one had light brown hair.

He did not know whether he should embrace them or not and decided against exercising such familiarity with young ladies who, in effect, were strangers.

"Come closer," he urged, and the pair stopped a few feet in front of him, curtseying. Both looked at him with curious, dark brown eyes.

"I will not pretend this is not an awkward situation because it is," he began. "I have always been frank with the officers and men under my command. I will be the same with you. I won't embrace you today because we are not familiar with one another, but I am happy to make your acquaintance. Come and have a seat."

He returned to the chair in which he had been sitting. His nieces took seats together on a settee opposite him.

"I am Major-General Nigel Foxwell." He smiled wryly. "Or at least I was. I have now assumed your father's title of Duke of Abington. I was his younger, half-brother. After his mother passed, our father wed my mother. Twenty years separated us. When I was born, your father was away at university. When our father died, I was but two years of age."

He paused a moment, letting this sink in. Fox doubted Abington had ever mentioned him to his daughters, especially since his death had been an unexpected one.

Continuing, he said, "My mother and I moved out of the main house at Crosshaven and lived in the dower house on the estate. I never met your father in all these years. I knew he had wed and had two children by the time I went off to war, but there was never any contact between us."

The darker-haired girl said, "Papa never mentioned you to us, but Mama did. She tried desperately to provide an heir and kept losing babe after babe."

"Don't say that," the blond one chided. "He doesn't need to know that."

The other girl snorted. "Well, at least it tells him why he is the heir. Mama had no son. And Papa spent most of his time furious at Mama. Or us." She turned to Fox and boldly said, "I am Lady Eliza, the older of us. I am nine and ten and ready to make my come-out this Season."

The blond frowned. "I am Lady Grace, and I think it is a terrible idea. We should still be in mourning," she declared.

Fascinated, Fox studied them as they continued to argue.

"Why should we mourn any longer?" Eliza asked. "It has already been four months. By the time the Season starts, it will be five. It is not as though either of them would have mourned us if we turned up dead, Grace."

"You don't know that," Grace retorted. "Why, I am certain Mama would have missed us."

"Really?" Eliza shook her head. "Mama rarely saw us. When she did, she would fuss like mad over us and then return to not paying us a bit of attention. And Papa ignored us altogether. He never liked us." She glanced to Fox. "Because we were girls," she explained. "Papa had no use for females. Daughters couldn't be heirs, and Mama couldn't produce an heir. Therefore, we were worthless in his eyes. Well, I plan to get out of this house as soon as possible and find a husband. I will wed a man who is everything Papa wasn't. Kind. Thoughtful. Generous."

"Oh, hush, Eliza. What do you think Abington thinks of us, airing our personal lives in front of him? He is a stranger, after all."

"Hmm. He may be a stranger, but he *is* family," Eliza noted, staring at Fox. "You probably don't care about how we were treated by our parents. You will probably ignore us just as Papa did."

"On the contrary, I take my duties as your guardian quite seriously, Eliza."

"That's Lady Eliza," she snapped.

He frowned deeply at her until her angry expression turned meek. "I wish to be a good guardian to you girls. I do not want to be a parent to you, but I would hope to be an older friend.

Someone who might guide you into the next stage of your lives."

"So, you do *want* us to make our come-outs?" Grace asked, uncertainty in her voice.

"I want you to do as you wish," he stated. "If *Lady* Eliza believes she has mourned your parents long enough and wants to make her come-out this Season, I am happy to make that happen. If you, Lady Grace, choose to wait until next spring, you may do so. I will not force either of you into doing something you are uncomfortable with."

His older niece brightened. "I rather like that. You may call me Eliza, Abington."

"Perhaps you might call me Uncle Fox," he suggested, hating the thought of these two forevermore calling him by his title.

"Uncle Fox," Eliza mused. "I am not sure we can."

"Why not?" he asked.

"Well, Mama *always* called Papa Abington," she told him. "I never once heard her call him by his Christian name." She laughed. "I don't even know what it was. Even Papa's friends addressed him as Abington."

"We are family," he said. "Foxwell may be our surname, but I have always gone by Fox. And I am your uncle."

"You truly do not mind us calling you Uncle Fox?" Grace asked, looking unsure of herself.

"I would prefer it, truth be told," he confessed. "I never thought to be the duke. I assumed your parents had other children after I went away to war. Now that I am the Duke of Abington, it would be nice if my family could be a little more casual in their address."

Eliza flashed a triumphant smile. "I certainly will call you Uncle Fox. After all, you have told us to do so. A duke always gets his way in everything."

"He does?"

She shrugged. "That is what Papa always said." She paused. "So, Uncle Fox, may I be allowed to make my come-out this Season?"

"I will be delighted to help you do so, Eliza." He turned to Grace. "You do not have to make a decision today, Grace."

"Oh, but she does," Eliza proclaimed. "We must book a decent modiste at once. An entire wardrobe must be made up for the Season. If we do not start soon, it will be too late."

He frowned. "What goes into this wardrobe?"

"Oh, you must not worry about costs. You are quite wealthy now, Uncle Fox. Yes, it takes piles of money for a girl to make her come-out—but you are a duke, and we are daughters of a duke. All of Polite Society will look to us as the girls in our come-out class to set the pace. There will be balls and routs. Picnics and garden parties. Dinner parties and nights at the theatre and opera. We cannot repeat a single gown. We must wear something new to each social affair or be branded pariahs."

Fox thought it ridiculous to wear a gown only once, but he could recall his own mother saying something of the same nature when he was young.

Eliza went on to explain how there would be fifty or sixty balls held that Season and the time it would take to have a wardrobe made up for each of them.

"So, you can see why Grace must decide quickly, Uncle Fox." She turned to her sister. "Really, Grace. You are of age. Most girls make their come-outs at your age or even younger. I am the one who had to wait because Mama wanted us to be brought out together." She looked to Fox. "Mama had grand visions of a double wedding at St. George's for the two of us."

"Do you wish for a double wedding?" he wondered aloud.

"I want a wedding with all of Polite Society in attendance," Eliza said dramatically. "At St. George's, of course, because it is the only place a wedding should be held."

He looked to Grace. "What of you, Grace?"

"I would prefer something small. In the garden. With only a few in attendance. A wedding is an intimate affair."

Eliza laughed. "That's because you want to fall in love with your groom. No one in the *ton* falls in love. That is what lovers are for. You have your heir and spare, and then you take a lover."

"Eliza!" Grace chided. "You are talking out of turn."

Her sister sniffed. "I listen. I hear things. And I know that is the way of the *ton*. I do not care anything about love. I only want to wed a man who is extremely rich. An earl or a higher rank. He will buy me lovely clothes and treat me exquisitely."

Fox saw Eliza was going to be a handful. He would need to look for a strong man who could tame her and encourage a match between the pair. As for Grace, she seemed gentle and kind.

"What will it be, Grace?" he asked softly. "Do you wish to follow your sister into becoming a part of Polite Society? Or would you rather continue your mourning and make your debut next Season?"

She worried her lip and then said, "I do not wish to delay, Uncle Fox. I would rather have Eliza by my side as I make my debut. I only ask that you be patient with me." She hesitated. "I would like to find love if I could. It might take more than one Season to find the right man."

"Then do as you wish, Grace. Make your come-out next month and take your time. Committing a lifetime to another person in marriage is something you should not rush into. If you find the right man, marry him. If you do not, you can have a go at it the next year."

"We have large dowries, Uncle Fox," Eliza said matter-of-factly. "You will most likely need to get to know the men who court us. That means you must accompany us to the events this upcoming Season." She paused, looking at him from head to toe. "You will have to see a tailor. A duke cannot go about wearing an officer's uniform. Besides, you aren't an officer anymore. You are a duke."

He smiled. "I will not embarrass you, Eliza. I will see to having a wardrobe suited for a duke made up."

"You are very different from what I thought you would be," she told him. "You actually speak to us as if we are people."

"Well, you are," he agreed.

"Our parents ignored us, Uncle Fox," Eliza continued. "I have told you as much. Grace and I have been on our own a good deal of our lives. Yes, we had a governess who was with us and taught us to read and write. We take music and dance lessons. But we have not been around many others, especially adults. It is a bit refreshing to have you converse with us as you are."

"You really seem to listen," Grace added. "I do not think Mama or Papa ever heard a word we said."

Pity filled him. These girls had very different dispositions, but they had been sadly neglected by their parents, much as he had been by his own mother.

"I will do my best to always listen to what you have to say because you are family and important to me. Give me a day to get my bearings, and then we will see about finding a modiste for you."

"And a milliner," Eliza quickly added. "Hats are incredibly important to a lady's ensemble."

"We won't neglect a thing," Fox promised. "You will have your gowns and hats. Gloves and slippers. I will probably have to chase off the gentlemen that swarm about you because there will be so many of them."

His remarks brought a delighted burst of laughter from Eliza and a sweet smile from Grace.

"Shall we call for tea, Uncle Fox?" Grace asked. "We should get to know one another some."

"Tea sounds wonderful. Ring for it if you would, Grace."

Twenty minutes later, the teacart arrived with all kinds of sandwiches and sweets and plenty of strong, hot tea. Fox found himself revealing things about himself as a boy and talking about the army in generalities, all as he learned more about his nieces. He actually began to look forward to attending the Season as their escort and helping them decide upon their future mates.

Until Grace pointed something out which Fox hadn't given a thought to.

"You, too, will be looking for a marriage partner, Uncle Fox. After all, you will need a duchess who can provide you with an heir." She smiled apologetically. "You are rather old, so you should get started on this soon."

"I am only four and thirty and in the prime of my life, thank you very much."

Grace's words got him to thinking, though. He *would* need an heir—and that meant he needed a wife.

Oh, bloody hell.

CHAPTER THREE

D ELANEY WASN'T DESTITUTE. Far from it.

But she was dejected. And had been ever since her half-brother became the Earl of Kinnison. The new Lord Kinnison had quickly wed the daughter of a marquess in the middle of last Season. After the marriage, both the marquess and earl let the *ton* know in no uncertain terms that if they patronized Delaney's Designs, they would receive the cut direct.

Polite Society never crossed a marquess, much less his daughter and a powerful, wealthy earl. Immediately, her millinery shop saw no new customers come in. No old ones returned. No one sent a word or offered an apology for dropping her. She simply became dead to Polite Society. Clients who had commissioned hats to be made refused to pick them up and certainly didn't pay for them. Delaney spent the last two months of the Season without a single customer crossing her threshold.

With no work coming in, she had to let go of both milliners who fashioned hats from her designs and then the shop's clerk who worked alongside Delaney. Day after day, she came and sat in her shop, full of beautiful hats and bonnets, then she left at day's end without having spoken to a single soul. By Season's end, Delaney had closed up shop and retreated to the small estate her father had left her near High Wycombe in Buckinghamshire, knowing if she hadn't had the estate or the money Papa had left to her, she would now be out on the streets because of her spiteful half-brother and his father-in-law.

Chapwell Hall proved to be a godsend to Delaney. Only a little more than thirty miles from London, it was a house of twenty rooms and included a drawing room, a small dining room, a parlor and library, kitchen, and five bedchambers of varying size. There were a few other rooms for the servants, including a dining hall, laundry, office for the butler, and bedchambers for the staff.

Chapwell Hall became her refuge. Delaney took long walks through the countryside and planted an herb garden. She attended the local church and grew friendly with a few of the women congregants, even joining their sewing and altar circle. She read a great deal and despite having no clients, she filled a good two dozen notebooks with hat designs.

When the new year came, she decided to return to town, hoping the edict issued by Lord Kinnison and his father-in-law last year would be forgotten. She did not hire any new staff but brought her own creations to life, once more enjoying the feel of hats and going through the various stages to make them a finished product.

It was March now—and not a single person had entered Delaney's Designs. As more of the *ton* returned to town to prepare for the upcoming Season, she finally admitted to herself that her days as a London milliner had ended. She would need to sell the shop. With the proceeds, perhaps she could open a small shop in High Wycombe and cater to the middle class and gentry there. Her half-brother's country estate was far to the west in Devon, while his father-in-law's was in Cornwall. She doubted their influence would extend to High Wycombe. She longed to be selling her hats and bonnets again, if not directly to the *ton* in London, then to women of High Wycombe and the surrounding area.

She could live at Chapwell Hall and close off most of the bedchambers and several of the other rooms. She could get by with a handful of servants. If the estate became too much for her, she could sell it outright and live on the income from that sale, using the sale of her London shop to finance one in High Wycombe.

Delaney also toyed with the idea of hiring someone to run the former Delaney's Designs in London sometime in the future. She could change the name of the shop and hire a woman knowledgeable about fashion to be the face of the shop. This person could manage the millinery and talk to the clients while Delaney continued to design her hats in secret. She would hire new women to create the hats, not wanting to have anyone with her former establishment recognized.

Warming to the idea, Delaney decided it would be best to see her solicitor, Mr. Hodgkins, and have him sell the current shop. It was in a desirable area and would fetch an excellent price. She could retire to Buckinghamshire for several years, then buy a new place of business in London after time had passed. It would keep her busy to own her own shop outside of London in the meantime. She liked having work to do and no idle time on her hands.

She looked about her current shop, full of so many wonderful designs, and decided she would pack it all up and bring the goods with her to the new shop she would lease in High Wycombe. She would have to slash her prices, though. She doubted the citizens of High Wycombe would pay London prices for their hats. Thank goodness Papa had left her well-off financially, and she could continue to pursue what she loved without having to worry about money.

Her mind made up, she locked the store and took a hansom cab to Mr. Hodgkins' office. She did not have an appointment but still hoped the solicitor might be able to see her today. If not, she would schedule one for the near future and go ahead with her plans.

Delaney entered the solicitor's office and saw one client waited. Even seated, she could see he was tall and muscular, with hair as black as night and eyes a deep shade of brown. He had a scar on his chin and since he wore an officer's uniform, she imagined he had gotten the scar in battle. She nodded politely at him and made her way to the clerk's stand. No one sat there, and she supposed the clerk was seeing to something for Mr. Hodgkins.

"He should be back soon," the stranger said. "Mr. Hodgkins sent him on a brief errand."

"I see."

She decided to take a seat. "Have you recently returned from war?" she asked, making a bit of polite conversation.

"I have. I came from Spain and fought under Wellington's command. I am here to visit with Mr. Hodgkins about an inheritance."

"Will you return to the war afterward?"

He shook his head. "That will not be possible. I am learning that I have too many responsibilities to do so. I will admit I am a bit put out at how my life is changing. Things are out of my control." He paused. "What might you be seeing Mr. Hodgkins about?"

Even though Delaney usually wasn't so forward with a stranger, it had been a long time since she had really talked to anyone. "I am going to sell my millinery shop and need to speak with Mr. Hodgkins about that."

"Ah, you own your own shop? You must be quite the businesswoman."

She chuckled. "Apparently not. Members of the *ton* are returning to prepare for the upcoming Season. Unfortunately, none of them are frequenting my place." She shrugged. "I used to be quite successful until my half-brother blackballed me."

The stranger studied her a moment. "How did he do that?"

Hesitating a moment, she thought she was in for a penny in the conversation and might as well be in for a pound. After all, she would never see this army officer after today.

"I hope I will not shock your sensibilities when I tell you that I am illegitimate. My father was an earl. A lovely man who treated me with immense kindness. In fact, it was he who encouraged me when I began drawing designs of hats and clothes. Papa financed my millinery shop and it was quite successful for several years."

Delaney paused, blinking rapidly as tears misted her eyes. "Then Papa was gone. His heir always despised the time Papa spent with me. The new Lord Kinnison and his father-in-law, a marquess, let it be known throughout Polite Society that no one should patronize Delaney's Designs or else they would face the cut direct."

The man frowned. "I am afraid I am not aware of that term—but it doesn't sound good."

She shuddered. "It isn't. It means a deliberate public snub of the worst kind. Lord and Lady Kinnison would make eye contact with the other party and stare hard at them without a word before turning away. Whoever receives the cut direct is no longer invited to *ton* affairs. It is a type of social suicide, so to speak. Or rather, a living death, I suppose. You are alive but completely ignored by members of Polite Society, so you might as well be dead."

The officer shook his head in disbelief. "All because they bought a *hat* from you?"

"You now understand completely. No member of Polite Society has the nerve to go against both a marquess and an earl united against someone."

"And that someone is you," he noted.

"It is." Delaney sighed. "Papa didn't like his son much and now that son—my half-brother—has turned all his power against me."

"What will you do?"

"My shop is mine. Papa paid for the building it occupies years ago. I made a decent profit and had two women creating my designs and another helping me run the business. I had to let them go last Season when business instantly dried up. The space is in a prime location. I will have no trouble selling it. That is what I wish to see Mr. Hodgkins about. He was Papa's solicitor and now mine, even if I am a Colebourne on the wrong side of the blanket, so to speak."

Curiosity filled his face. "What will you do once you sell?"

"Papa left me an unentailed estate nearby in Buckinghamshire. I will move to it and open another millinery shop in High Wycombe, the nearest town to Chapwell Hall."

"You seem to have thought everything through."

She smiled. "Even my return to London. I will leave for a few years and then open another shop in town under a different name. I will continue to design my hats and let someone else run the place. I truly do not need credit for my designs. I merely enjoy doing something I love and giving ladies fresh hats for their wardrobes."

Mr. Hodgkins' clerk rushed in and spied her. "Ah, Miss Colebourne," he greeted, and then frowned slightly. "We were not expecting you."

"I do not have an appointment but was hoping Mr. Hodgkins might be able to see me sometime today."

The clerk went to his stand and consulted his scheduling book. "No, I doubt today will be possible." He turned a page and then another. "What about Friday morning at ten o'clock? Might that be convenient?"

"Yes, I can come back then. Thank you."

Delaney returned to stand next to the handsome army officer. "It was nice speaking with you, sir. I hope your inheritance woes work out well for you."

"You may have my appointment, Miss Colebourne," he responded.

"Oh! No, I could not take time you have scheduled with Mr. Hodgkins. My matter is not pressing in the least. I could put the building up for sale tomorrow. Next week. Even next month. Papa left me a comfortable amount, and I also have the proceeds from previously to see me through."

He stood and smiled at her. Her heart skipped a beat, thanks to the magic of that smile.

"I insist." He glanced to the clerk. "That won't be a problem, will it? Giving Miss Colebourne my appointment today? Actually, I have an hour scheduled with Mr. Hodgkins. I could use the first half of it and allow Miss Colebourne to have the remaining time. Yes, that will do nicely."

She listened as the stammering clerk said, "Well, y-y-yes, I s-suppose we could arrange it, Y—"

"See that you do." He turned to her. "I just need to have Mr. Hodgkins clarify a few things for me. It shouldn't take long. I will go see him now."

"If you insist," she said weakly as he strode down the hallway to where Mr. Hodgkins' office sat.

Delaney took a seat again, seeing the clerk's surreptitious glances at her. She hadn't meant to cause the man any trouble. She hoped the officer's time with Mr. Hodgkins wouldn't be cut too short. She hadn't wanted to infringe upon anyone's appointment, but the man had been so insistent. He had a magnetism about him, something which drew her in, and she decided he must have had a commanding presence in the field.

He returned to the waiting room and told her, "Mr. Hodgkins is happy to see you now, Miss Colebourne."

She rose and thanked the man, still not knowing his name. After this long a time, it almost seemed awkward to ask it. Perhaps Mr. Hodgkins might share it with her.

Entering the solicitor's office, he greeted her effusively. "Miss Colebourne! It is always a delight to see you. I hear that you are going to be selling your place of business."

"Why, yes, Mr. Hodgkins, that is my intention."

"Well, it is in a highly sought-after location. I won't have a bit of trouble finding a buyer for you. Do you still have wares within it?"

"I do. I will need a place to store them. My intention is to move to the property Lord Kinnison purchased for me in Buckinghamshire for a few years. I am thinking to buy or lease space in High Wycombe for a millinery shop there. I have not had a chance to peruse the area, however, so I am not certain what might be available."

"Let me take care of things at this end, Miss Colebourne. I can always arrange for the buyer to wait and take possession of the shop after you have found a new space and moved your goods to it."

"Oh, that would be ideal. Do whatever you must to list the property if you would. I will be going to High Wycombe in the next day or so to scout for a location for my new shop."

Sympathy filled the solicitor's face. "I am sorry it has come to this, Miss Colebourne. I have heard rumors of what the present Lord Kinnison has said about you. How your former clients are terrified to patronize your shop."

"He was a spiteful boy and has grown into an even more wicked man," she replied. "I am in no position to stand up to him. The best I can do is cut my losses and leave town."

"You won't have any losses, Miss Colebourne. It's a prime property you are selling. It will fetch a tidy sum, and I can easily negotiate your goods remaining within until you have a place to send them."

Delaney rose. "You are always so kind to me, Mr. Hodgkins. Thank you for handling this matter."

"Lord Kinnison thought the world of you. I promised him I would take care of you in whatever way I could. I will be in contact regarding the sale of your building."

She bid the solicitor farewell and returned to the waiting room, surprised to find the handsome army officer still seated there. Spying her, he rose.

"I hope you do not mind that I waited for you, Miss Colebourne. I will admit that I am most curious about your millinery shop. My inheritance allows me the flexibility to make certain investments. Since you mentioned your place was in a desirable area, might I be able to see it now?"

"You would be interested in buying it?" she asked, startled by the idea.

"It is certainly a possibility. I would also not mind seeing your hats. I have never known someone who designs them."

The prospect of selling so quickly led Delaney to say, "I would be delighted to show you both the property and a few hats." She paused. "Might I ask your name?"

He hesitated a moment and said, "I was Major-General Foxwell before I sold out. I am Abington now."

Shock rippled through her, hearing the name. Or rather, the title.

"Abington?" she echoed. "As in the Duke of Abington?"

Fear replaced shock as Delaney thought of how indiscreet she had been with this man. Telling him she was the bastard of an earl. Maligning her half-brother and his father-in-law.

A dark shadow crossed his face. "Yes. Does that make a difference?"

"I have certainly put my foot in my mouth, Your Grace," she said stiffly. "Denouncing Lord Kinnison. You must forgive me."

"Forgive you?" the duke questioned. "When you have been treated so poorly? I've a mind to confront Kinnison and—"

"No!" Delaney cried. "Please, Your Grace. Just drop the matter. I am sorry I took up your time."

She hurried from the waiting room and rushed from the building, tears blinding her as she raced across the street.

The shout of a coachman startled her, and she pivoted, seeing a carriage bearing down on her. Before she could react, suddenly she was yanked from harm's way and the vehicle raced past her. Her heart hammering at the violence that had just missed her, she turned to thank her rescuer.

And saw it was the Duke of Abington.

"Bloody hell," she spit out.

The duke roared with laughter.

CHAPTER FOUR

F OX WAS KNOWN for taking calculated risks on the battlefield. In Polite Society, though?

That was another matter.

Of course, Miss Colebourne wouldn't be considered a member of that so-called group. Being a bastard, she walked a fine line between two worlds, similar to his own, new path. For almost fourteen years, Fox had known his place and where he was headed. Since he no longer led men into battle, he seemed a lost soul.

Poor Miss Colebourne had most likely never fit in anywhere. He surmised the bastards of most gentlemen were never acknowledged. At least Miss Colebourne's father had claimed her and seemed to spend a good deal of time with her, even favoring her over his legitimate heir. He must have realized his daughter was talented and had set her up in business, catering to ladies of the *ton*, something she could never be. Yet he doubted this woman had been accepted by those in trade. They would have looked at her origins and been as suspicious of her as those born into the *ton*. The fact she had established a business and it thrived was remarkable. That it had not just been undercut—but sabotaged—by her half-brother, the new earl, was appalling. This Lord Kinnison hadn't cared that his own kin might not be able to take care of herself. No, the earl had gone out of his way to see that Miss Colebourne failed.

If anything, Fox had a strong sense of justice. Miss Colebourne had not received it.

And he had decided to do something about it.

Before Hodgkins could even open his mouth, Fox had told the solicitor that Miss Colebourne would be claiming part of the meeting time Fox had scheduled today. He then told the man that she would reveal she wished to sell the building her millinery was located in—and he would be the one who would buy it. He instructed Hodgkins not to tell Miss Colebourne who the eventual buyer would be. Now that Fox was wealthy, he wanted to invest in things and people. Buying Miss Colebourne's shop, located in a desirable part of town, would be an excellent way to start. It would give him a solid real estate investment, and at the same time, he could help someone who had been unjustly singled out.

And not just because she was extremely attractive.

He'd had his share of women over the years, both at home and abroad. He prided himself on being a courteous lover, attending to his partner's needs before his own. Miss Colebourne would make for an excellent lover. She was about four inches over five feet with a beautiful figure and perfect posture. He longed to run his fingers through her caramel-colored hair. Her warm, brown eyes didn't seem as if they would miss much. She had to be both creative and bright since she designed original hats and ran a business selling them.

It irked him that her half-brother had set about to ruin her, all because he was a spiteful, jealous man. Fox would help Miss Colebourne and then see what he could do about ruining this Lord Kinnison and the yet-unnamed father-in-law. After all, he was a duke now. He might as well put his title to good use.

In the meantime, Miss Colebourne stood before him, having cursed aloud, which delighted Fox. He enjoyed someone with spirit and this milliner had it in abundance.

Then an idea occurred to him, one which blossomed with

great speed.

What better revenge than elevating the delightful Miss Colebourne to the highest level of Polite Society?

In that moment, Fox decided to make her his duchess.

As Eliza had pointed out, he would need to wed and provide an heir. He was far from the *ton*'s idea of what a duke should be, and the same could be said of Miss Colebourne becoming a duchess. In fact, he thought it a great lark to team up with her and make her the social superior to her odious half-brother.

Of course, he couldn't share this with her now. She already was upset and out of sorts. Fox would bide his time, though. The attractive Miss Colebourne would bring new blood into the Foxwell family. Her views would be quite different from the usual woman who rose to become a duchess. Yet Fox couldn't help but think *his* duchess would become the greatest of them all.

"Forgive me for laughing, Miss Colebourne," he apologized.

She looked mortified, her cheeks now burning a bright red. "No, Your Grace, it is I who should be apologizing. I was indiscreet and never should have said the things I did to you. If I had known who you were, I would not even have begun a conversation with you."

He smiled at her, thinking how her blush suited her. "I understand that. I am learning all kinds of things with this title I never thought to inherit. You see, I was a second son, destined for war. I also had a half-brother who was twenty years my senior. A man I never met."

She frowned. "I can understand if you were a bastard as I am, why you might not have ever met. But you aren't."

"My half-brother was upset when my father wed again and shortly had me, another son. Unfortunately, the duke died unexpectedly, leaving Mama and me to move to the dower house on the estate. The new duke did not want anything to do with me. I did see him out and about on the estate a few times over the years. He was never long in the country, though, and I went away to school and university, followed by serving in His

Majesty's army. In fact, I had no idea how many children he had or whom he married until I received a letter from our Mr. Hodgkins, informing me the duke was dead and that I was the new duke."

Her mouth formed an O in surprise, making him want to touch his lips to hers. Miss Colebourne had extremely kissable lips. Fox chastised himself and told himself to focus on the matter at hand.

"I find myself returned from war to a society I was never a part of. I also am the guardian of two extremely interesting young ladies I will need to launch into society this Season." He paused. "I have no idea how to do something like that, Miss Colebourne. I believe you might be the solution to all my problems."

"I beg your pardon?"

"You may not have been a member of Polite Society, but you have dealt with them a good number of years, I imagine. You would know what my nieces would need to wear. How they should act. What my role in all this might be. I know you said you wished to sell your shop and leave London, but I am asking you to consider delaying your plans and help me and the girls."

She shook her head in disbelief. "I am not certain at all that I am the answer to anything regarding you and your nieces, Your Grace."

"You know clothing and hats, don't you?"

Slowly, she nodded. "I do. I grew up sewing clothes for my dolls. I have always had an interest in fashion."

"Then you could help give advice on what they should wear and how they should behave." He sighed. "Frankly, you would be doing me a great favor, Miss Colebourne. I know absolutely no one in London. I haven't the foggiest notion where to begin preparing Eliza and Grace for what lies ahead. I could use your guidance. You are an earl's daughter, after all. You act and sound like a lady."

"But I was in trade, Your Grace."

"You were. Emphasis on the past. You yourself said no one

was coming to patronize your shop anymore. You would be doing me—and my nieces—the greatest of favors. In return, I would do what I could to help you, as well."

Her brow furrowed. "How so?"

He sweetened the pot. "For one thing, I will buy your shop. That will give you financial security. I will even purchase another one for you in whatever town you mentioned you were moving to. As long as you delay doing so until after the Season ends." He paused. "Please, Miss Colebourne. My nieces are counting upon me. They wish to make good marriages." He chuckled. "Eliza wants a lofty title and someone who will spoil her. Grace has stars in her eyes and is looking for love. They had little direction from their mother and nothing but neglect from their father, merely because they were girls."

Fox cocked his head. "So, what do you say, Miss Colebourne? Are you willing to help out a stranger saddled with an unwanted title and the guardianship of two young ladies?"

Her cheeks continued to burn brightly, making her incredibly attractive to him. Fox thought Miss Colebourne would make for a delightful wife and duchess. His choice of a spouse would turn the *ton* on its ear, something he found immensely satisfying.

"I suppose I could help somewhat, Your Grace," she began. "I do know quite a bit about how a young lady should dress during her come-out."

"You said you design hats. What of gowns?" he asked.

She nodded to herself, and he saw the idea growing on her. "I could do that, as well. The design work, that is. You would have to hire a couple of seamstresses, good ones, and pay them what they are worth. Time is growing short."

"Do you know of someone who could make up my nieces' wardrobes? I suppose you will provide their hats."

"I believe I do. And I would be honored to design the necessary hats."

"Might you have time now to show me your shop, Miss Colebourne? If I am to purchase it, I would like to see what I am getting."

"Oh, it is a choice property, Your Grace. Papa made certain of that. He had faith in my talents and knew if I had the right location, I could make a go of things."

"You miss him," Fox said.

He saw tears flood her eyes. "I do. Dreadfully so. We spent a great deal of time together. He had two other daughters, one who died quite young. His other daughter and his son, as well, never showed much interest in anything. Papa called them dull and unintelligent."

"You were the child of his heart," he said softly.

"I was. We had much in common and could spend hours together. He wished he could have me make my come-out, but I told him what good would it do? No gentleman would be interested in wedding the bastard daughter of an earl."

This gentleman did.

"I am sorry you still mourn him," Fox said. "Time is a great healer, and your time will be taken up by Eliza and Grace. I only met them yesterday, and yet already I am quite fond of them."

"I look forward to meeting them, as well. As far as your question to me? Yes, I am happy to take you to Delaney's Designs now and show you the place."

"My carriage is over here," he told her, leading her to it and handing her up. "What is the address?"

She gave it to him, and he passed it along to his driver before climbing inside the vehicle. He sat opposite her, not wanting to crowd her. Fox could tell Miss Colebourne would be a tricky fish to reel in, and he would need to proceed with great care.

But something told him his patience would be rewarded.

"You, too, Your Grace, will need a new wardrobe," Miss Colebourne said.

"Yes, my valet mentioned that to me this morning."

"I can make a few recommendations to you as to tailors who do quality work. Are you a duke who is wealthy? I suppose you are since you have offered to buy my building."

"Aren't all dukes wealthy?" he asked.

"No. Some are gamblers. Or they have made poor investments. If you have money, you are lucky. It will allow you to wed whom you wish without having to consider the dowry your bride brings into the marriage."

"My nieces think I should look for a wife this Season," he tossed out, mostly to see her reaction.

"Then they have good heads on their shoulders. Any gentleman with a title who cares anything for it and his tenants must provide an heir. You mentioned when we first met that you have great responsibilities, Your Grace. Since you are new to this world of the *ton*, you will need to learn a great deal about your dukedom."

"What is your favorite thing about London?" he asked, deliberately veering from his new title.

Her cheeks pinkened. "Oh, I love everything about it. The hustle and bustle. The street vendors and food carts. The museums and architecture and most of all, the parks. You will need to take ladies driving in Hyde Park between five and six o'clock once the Season begins. It is the fashionable hour, and you will want to be seen. You must also attend as many social affairs as you can."

"I am not certain I will be able to since I know no one."

She laughed, a deep, throaty laugh that sent a dizzying chill through him. "You are a duke, Your Grace. You will be invited to every affair held, whether you know the hosts or not. It will be good for your nieces to go to as many events as possible. Hopefully, by Season's end, all three of you will have found a match."

"At least their father provided decent dowries for them." He named the amount, and she looked taken aback.

"Oh, dear. That kind of money will bring out the fortune hunters. You must do everything in your power to screen your nieces' suitors, Your Grace. They are young and most likely impressionable girls, and their heads may be turned by handsome looks and pretty compliments. You should learn everything you can about the suitors they grow partial to if you truly care for these girls."

"I will do my best. When do these suitors appear? At balls?"

Miss Colebourne laughed again. "Yes. At balls and every other social event scheduled. They also will come calling in the afternoons and stay for a quarter-hour or so. You must always be present to chaperone these visits."

"I am not certain what I should be looking for," he admitted. "Might you consider helping me in this endeavor?"

"Be at your morning calls?" she inquired.

"Whenever these gentlemen come calling."

"I could do so," she said thoughtfully.

"Perhaps you might come and live with us now and during the Season," he mused.

"No. That would be totally unsuitable, Your Grace. I am not of your social class, but it would still reflect poorly on you and your nieces to have me staying in your household. It is one thing to help chaperone when a few visitors come calling. Quite another thing to live with you and your family."

So much for that brilliant idea. Fox knew he would have to keep everything above board with this woman. No seduction. No long afternoons in bed. He would do things by the book. Whatever the book's rules were, that is. He would have to learn along the way.

They arrived at Delaney's Designs and left the carriage. Miss Colebourne unlocked the shop's door and led him inside. Immediately, he made one circle of the place, studying the hats on display.

Once he finished, he said to her, "I know nothing of fashion, having been on a battlefield my entire adult life, but what I see here is a plethora of beautiful hats. You designed all of these yourself?"

She looked pleased. "I did, Your Grace. I apprenticed with a top milliner for several years, learning my craft. When Papa bought the shop for me, I moved into strictly designing hat wear and had others create my visions. Papa had also schooled me in ledgers. From the time I was young, he opened his estate's ledgers to me and taught me what to record and how to keep my accounts."

"You are most talented, Miss Colebourne. Where does the name come from? Delaney's Designs?"

"Delaney is my Christian name, Your Grace. It was my grandmother's surname. Papa thought it different and special and so he asked my mother if he could name me Delaney."

Fox liked the name. It suited her. He liked everything about this woman. Even though he longed to take her in his arms and kiss her, he held back. He would be the picture of propriety until she had a ring on her finger. Being a bastard, he suspected Delaney Colebourne wouldn't begin to consider an affair with any man, be he duke or pauper.

"Do you think some of these hats would be suitable for my nieces?"

"Well, I would have to meet them first, Your Grace. Hats convey insights into a woman. I would never gift a hat to someone I had never met. I will need to meet your nieces and go from there."

"Will you dine with us tonight?" he asked. "You could meet Eliza and Grace and talk to them of gowns and whatnot."

She looked at him a long moment, as if on the brink of accepting or declining. Not just a dinner invitation but helping him for this Season.

"I would enjoy coming to dinner."

"I will send a carriage for you," he said. "Where do you live?"

"Above my shop. Have a footman come to the alley, though. There is a separate staircase leading to the private quarters."

"Then it will be here at a quarter till seven. We can spend time in the drawing room before dinner begins. You can learn something about the girls."

"All right."

ALEXA ASTON

Fox took her gloved hands in his, startled by the electricity that sparked between them. "I cannot thank you enough, Miss Colebourne, for doing me this favor. I will not only buy your shop but provide you with a salary for the task you are undertaking."

He named a figure, and she squeaked.

"Forgive me, Your Grace, but that is a little too generous."

"Not if it helps my nieces to find appropriate husbands."

She pulled her hands from his. He hadn't realized he still held on to them and felt bereft at having to let them go.

"I will see you tonight," she promised.

"Tonight," he agreed.

Fox left Delaney's Designs with a spring in his step. He had someone who would help guide his nieces through the Season, a woman of charm and intelligence who would see the girls properly clothed and chaperoned.

More importantly, he now knew who he wanted for his duchess.

CHAPTER FIVE

THE DOOR CLOSED behind the duke, and Delaney let out a stream of curses.

Why had she offered to help this man? A duke, of all people!

She chalked it up to several reasons. She was extremely bored, and this would certainly perk up her life. She hadn't really wanted to leave London, and now she could stay a bit. She always had liked being useful and if anyone needed someone useful about, it was this duke with no knowledge of the *ton* and two young women who needed launching into Polite Society.

What she would admit—only to herself and never even think about it again—was that she had felt a strong attraction to the Duke of Abington. It wasn't because he was a duke. In fact, that was a strike against him. She had been attracted to the rugged army officer, handsome and a bit world-weary with his sad eyes and prominent scar on his chin. Miss Delaney Colebourne might have considered a future with a man such as that.

But now that she had learned he was a duke, any kind of relationship would be impossible. As much as she had adored her mother and worshiped her father, she would not be one of those women sucked into an affair with a man of the nobility. And she certainly did not want a child to be a result of such a relationship. While her mother had told her to hold her head high whenever she went out, Delaney had suffered those slings and arrows of children in the village. Not simply children. A few of the so-called Christian matrons hurled insults at her, as well, as if she could have done anything about her heritage.

While Papa had taken her places in London, the thought of Delaney making her come-out to the *ton* had never entered his mind. He loved her—but he kept her separate from that part of his life. As a man, he had not suffered any kind of repercussions from his affair, while Delaney and her mother had been slandered far and wide by others. She would not do that to a child. If she ever wed—and she doubted she would—it would be to a man who was not a gentleman. She would consider anyone but a gentleman. A shop owner. A clerk. A farmer. Someone who would accept her and not judge her by the sins of her parents.

She would need to keep her head about her whenever the duke was near. She didn't believe that would be often and envisioned most of her time would be spent with his nieces, Lady Eliza and Lady Grace. Even if she did help chaperone the girls during morning calls, she could be at one end of the drawing room and Abington at the other. Delaney decided she would have as little as possible to do with the duke.

The better to protect her heart.

His generous offer to purchase her shop outright factored into her decision to help him, as did the obvious struggle he had trying to join a world he was unfamiliar with. He seemed genuinely fond of his nieces and would not want to let them down. That was where she could step in. She may not be a part of the *ton*, but she had experience with them and perhaps knew them better than they knew themselves.

The most important thing would be to find seamstresses to create the many gowns needed by these two young ladies. Delaney had the perfect workers—her former milliners. Dilly and Ruth had been with her ever since she had opened Delaney's Designs, and it was a bleak day when she had let them go. Dilly now worked as a seamstress, and Ruth was still a milliner. Neither woman was happy at her place of employment.

Though she knew she might be considered presumptuous in hiring these two, she doubted Abington would care. In fact, she thought it would take another seamstress and herself to help finish the number of gowns needed for the nieces' wardrobes. She would contact Fanny, her former clerk, who now worked at the same modiste Dilly did.

Mr. Farmington would also be someone to speak with. His tailoring shop was next door to her millinery. He was a hard worker and produced fine clothing but hadn't yet landed any prominent clients. Making up an entire wardrobe for a duke would certainly help him garner attention. Delaney decided to start first with Farmington. While she knew she was taking a risk setting up an appointment for the duke, as well as hiring women to provide his nieces' wardrobes, she knew it was the right thing to do and would stand up to Abington if he challenged her about it.

Going next door, she found Mr. Farmington polishing his counter.

"Ah, Miss Colebourne, what brings you to see me?"

"How would you like to completely outfit a duke?"

The tailor froze. "What did you say?"

"You heard me correctly, Mr. Farmington. What if I could arrange for a duke to come to your shop tomorrow? He needs simply everything. He has been an army officer his entire adult life and returned to England a handful of days ago with absolutely nothing to wear."

Farmington's eyes shone brightly. "He would need everything, now, wouldn't he?"

"He would indeed. I am willing to tell him about you and the wonderful clothing you make. Could you see him tomorrow morning?"

He rubbed his chin in thought. "It would take several hours. Besides measuring him, there would be fabrics to discuss and choose. We would need to arrive at the number of items he wanted commissioned."

Delaney thought a moment, somehow knowing the duke would not be happy spending his day selecting materials for coats and breeches.

"I will come with him and help in the process. That might help speed things along."

Farmington's broad smile was his reply. "I would be happy to devote the entire day to your duke, Miss Colebourne."

"Oh, he is not my duke," she said quickly, feeling her cheeks warm. "I am helping with his nieces' come-out and thought of you since he is in need of clothes now that he is a civilian."

"I am grateful to you, Miss Colebourne. This could be the difference between barely keeping my head above water and financial success."

"Then look for us tomorrow," she said. "Bright and early."

She walked two blocks to the modiste who employed Fanny and Dilly. Fanny met her as she entered the shop.

"It is so good to see you, Miss Colebourne, but what are you doing here? Madame is in the back, fitting a customer."

"Are you happy here, Fanny?"

The clerk's face fell. "No, Miss Colebourne. It is a job, however." Then hope filled her eyes. "Are you going to try and make a go of it again at Delaney's Designs? I would be happy to come work for you."

"No, but if you are willing to take a job for the Season as a seamstress, I will help you find another position after that. I am thinking of opening a shop in High Wycombe. You could work there if you chose."

Fanny's face was joyful. "I am a good seamstress, Miss Colebourne. I would be happy to work as one during the Season."

"What of Dilly?" she pressed.

"Dilly quit yesterday," Fanny confided. "She and Madame had a row that almost came to blows. Dilly stormed out and said she wouldn't be back."

The timing of Dilly's leaving could not have been better. Seeing as Dilly was one of the most timid creatures on the planet,

Delaney couldn't help but feel a bit of pride for her standing up to the modiste.

"Then have her come to my shop tomorrow morning at ten. You, as well. I am going to see Ruth now, and I hope she will join us."

"Oh, Ruth was let go last week," Fanny confided. "The owner of the millinery took a fancy to her and wanted to make her his mistress. When Ruth refused, he dismissed her on the spot. She is in need of work, Miss Colebourne. Oh, we could all be together again!"

"Then I will see the three of you at Delaney's Designs in the morning."

She left, thinking she would juggle her time tomorrow between assisting the girls and helping His Grace with their wardrobes. At least they would be next door to one another, which would make going back and forth easier to do.

What she needed to do now was get ready for her dinner with the duke and his nieces. Delaney returned to her shop and circled around to the alley, heading up the back stairs to her flat. She entered and heard Mary humming. The servant was the only one Delaney employed. Mary did all the cooking, cleaning, and laundry and helped Delaney to dress each day.

Following the sound, she found Mary in the kitchen peeling potatoes.

"Hello, Miss Colebourne," the servant greeted. "Have you had a nice day?"

"It has been . . . different from most. I am going out for dinner, Mary."

"Out? Why, that's wonderful, Miss Colebourne." Mary set down the potato and knife she held. "We must get you changed. What gown are you thinking you will wear?"

She had gone out often with her father and had suitable gowns to wear for tonight's dinner. At least she wouldn't be ashamed to see the duke again and meet his nieces. She did want to impress these young women, though. If she were being tasked to help them with their come-out wardrobes, she wanted to set the tone this evening.

"I am thinking of two gowns, Mary. Come and let us see which would be best."

They went to her bedchamber and looked at both gowns. One was a deep midnight blue, while the other was amber. She decided on the amber, hoping it would bring out the color of her brown eyes and the shade of her hair.

Mary heated water for Delaney to have a bath first and helped scrub her mistress from head to toe. She had also poured some of the vanilla scent into the bath and now Delaney smelled of it, which made her wonder if the duke liked vanilla.

"Bollocks!" she said aloud, causing Mary to give her a questioning glance.

She did *not* want to smell good for the duke. She did not want to even think about the duke. Focusing on Lady Eliza and Lady Grace was what was important.

Oh, why did he have to be blooming handsome?

"Shall I dress your hair for you, Miss Colebourne?" Mary asked.

"No, I can do that myself. Thank you for your help, Mary."

The servant left, and Delaney took her time brushing her long locks and twisting them up, pinning them into place. Then she removed a pair of amber earrings, a gift from her father when she turned eighteen, and screwed them into place. She studied her image, seeing the heightened color in her cheeks. Hopefully, she would calm some by the time she reached the duke's residence.

A knock sounded at her door, and she answered it.

"A carriage is here for you, Miss Colebourne. It's a ducal carriage!" Mary's excitement was obvious.

"Thank you," she said, collecting her reticule and a paisley shawl, wrapping it about her. "Do not wait up for me, Mary."

"I most certainly will," the servant said stubbornly. "You'll need help undressing—and I need to hear about your evening with a duke."

Knowing Mary would do as she wished, Delaney sighed. "All right. I will see you later this evening."

She opened the door and saw a footman on the landing. He greeted her by name and helped her descend the stairs to the alley.

"The carriage was too big to come around back," the footman told her. "It's waiting in front of your shop."

He escorted her to the vehicle and helped her up the stairs. The carriage then rolled into motion, and she took a deep breath.

"He's just a man," she said aloud. "A man like any other man. He may possess a title, but he is no different from a butcher or a chimney sweep. In fact, his manners may be rougher than most gentlemen because of his time away at war. It isn't as if he sat down to eight courses at his nightly meal. Most likely, he stood in a long line and had a bowl of stew dished out to him. Hard bread. No sweets of any type. Having a meal around a table will be something he must get used to. Remember, you are in charge here. If you do not like something he does or says, you can walk away. Find another buyer for the shop. Leave and head to High Wycombe immediately."

Then she thought of her three friends, women who had worked for her for years and how she had guaranteed them steady employment from now and running throughout the coming Season. Delaney couldn't walk away from the duke if only because of what she owed her former employees.

"Then you will be polite and firm. Do your job so these two girls can find matches. Ignore the duke as much as possible without causing a ruckus. Concentrate on the girls."

She had always talked aloud to herself, usually tossing in a few select curse words here and there, having picked them up from her father. He never corrected her for using them, and she soon realized he found it quite amusing to have a daughter who cursed as well as a man.

The carriage made a final turn and began to slow. Delaney's

heart began thumping wildly.

"You are the daughter of an earl," she reminded herself. "You know how to carry and comport yourself. You might not be the equal of those in this household—but you are awfully close. Get on with it. Make yourself proud."

The door swung open, and she moved to the opening, taking the hand offered her. As she descended the stairs, she experienced her first surprise of the night.

The Duke of Abington himself had come to greet her personally and handed her down to the pavement.

Raising her chin a notch, she said, "Good evening, Your Grace," proud her voice sounded even and calm.

"Good evening, Miss Colebourne," the duke greeted, slipping her hand through the crook of his arm.

Immediately, she was aware of the heat he radiated, something comforting and yet at the same time, it caused her pulse to leap. His bergamot scent also teased her senses.

Leaning down, he said softly, "I don't think this is usually done this way. A duke coming and greeting his guests personally. I wanted you to be comfortable upon entering my home. I know you are granting me an enormous favor by taking on the girls."

"I am certain to like them. You seem to."

He chuckled and led her toward the door. "I do. They are as different as night and day, and I find both endearing. I hope you will enjoy working with them. You will be able to tell them apart by their hair. Eliza's is darker than Grace's."

They entered the townhouse, the butler taking her shawl and reticule. She thanked him, knowing most members of the *ton* ignored servants and rarely showed their appreciation for even small tasks.

As the duke led her up the stairs, Delaney told herself that while she wanted to make a good impression upon these young women she would be charged with helping, she was no weakling. She would be polite but firm.

They entered the drawing room, and immediately she heard

the argument taking place.

"Why do we have to have someone to tell us what to do?" a brown-haired girl said. "I want to choose my own gowns. I have exquisite taste."

Her blond companion replied, "But you have never made your come-out, Eliza. This Miss Colebourne is older and wiser than we are."

"I don't see why—" Eliza halted, catching sight of Delaney and her uncle coming toward them.

Both girls turned and faced them. They were incredibly alike, favoring each other so much that she might have guessed they were twins. They were mirror images in size and shape, and their facial features were identical. The only discerning difference was in the shade of their hair. Lady Eliza's was a light brown. Lady Grace's was honey-colored.

"Good evening," she said, and immediately they curtseyed. Relief filled her. At least they had some manners.

"I would like to introduce you to Miss Colebourne. She will be guiding you in your come-out."

"Good evening, Miss Colebourne," Lady Grace said.

"You are younger than I thought you would be," Lady Eliza said.

Delaney bit back a smile. Eliza would definitely be the challenging one.

"It is impolite to mention a lady's age," she said. "A pleasant greeting when meeting someone new is what is expected, my lady."

Lady Eliza sniffed. "I do not always do what is expected."

"Eliza," her sister warned.

"If you wish to wed this lofty title you are interested in, you will do as I suggest."

"You know about that?" she squeaked, her accusatory gaze landing on her uncle.

"Most young women making their come-outs are interested in wedding the best title they can," she assured the girl. "It is nothing to be ashamed of. It is also not something to discuss. If you want to impress a gentleman, you must adhere to certain rules, Lady Eliza. One is acknowledging social niceties. It will endear you to the gentleman's mama. That is something which could weigh on your behalf."

"Bravo, Miss Colebourne," the duke said. "My elder niece has a bit of a bite. Hopefully, you can tame it."

Delaney accepted the glass of wine offered to her by the butler and then faced Lady Eliza. "Being spirited can work in your favor—as long as you do not step too far outside the rules of the *ton*. Not every man wishes for a meek, docile woman to be his wife. There is, however, a fine line to tread between showing spirit and crossing over that line. Do you understand, my lady?"

Grudgingly, Lady Eliza said, "I do, Miss Colebourne. But can you truly help me wed a gentleman with a high position in society?"

"I can give you advice. You may choose to take it if you wish. The first piece is that I believe you should ignore titles." When the girl frowned, Delaney added, "At least in the beginning. Get to know a good number of gentlemen. Those who express interest in you will call during the afternoons. You will get to know them better in that more relaxed setting. Only once you have a half-dozen you are interested in should you then begin considering what titles they might hold. Look for those who treat you and your family respectfully. Ones who volunteer to fetch something for you and look after you solicitously. That will say a lot about the person they are. You want to wed someone who will treat you courteously when you are his wife."

Lady Eliza nibbled on her lip. "I see. That does make sense. But I want him to be handsome."

Delaney laughed. "You will find many bachelors meet that description, my lady." She turned to Lady Grace. "Do you know what you are looking for in a husband?"

The girl turned starry-eyed. "I want to fall in love," she said breathily.

"Then my advice would be the same. Speak to as many gentlemen as you can. Dance every dance. Attend every event. Be pleasant and kind to all you meet. Love cannot be forced. It will grow over time. The men you are most interested in will quickly become apparent to you. Encourage their interest and speak with them of things which interest you."

Lady Grace nodded. "Yes, Miss Colebourne. I will do as you ask."

"Uncle Fox says you own a marvelous shop full of hats," Lady Eliza said. "Will we go there soon? I adore hats."

"We will go there tomorrow morning," she told them. "I have hired three excellent seamstresses to create your wardrobes. They will meet us at my millinery shop at ten o'clock. You will choose as many hats as you wish from my inventory, and then we will discuss your wardrobes."

"Yes!" Lady Eliza cried, clapping her hands, while her sister smiled sweetly.

Turning to the duke, she said, "As for you, Your Grace, you will spend most of tomorrow at the tailor who is next door. You cannot go about in your uniform forever, much less during the Season."

"I told him that very thing, Miss Colebourne," Lady Eliza declared. "While Uncle Fox does look handsome in his uniform, he needs to start looking like a duke. Can we help choose some of his wardrobe?"

Abington snorted. "Would you like me telling you what to wear?"

"No!" Lady Eliza proclaimed. "But I wager you will let Miss Colebourne help you decide. She seems most knowledgeable."

"I have always been interested in fashion," Delaney shared. "And yes, I can help His Grace make some selections, just as I will guide your choices. I do not plan to dictate to either of you girls but I, along with my seamstresses, can let you know what colors and styles look best on you. The same will be true with hats. While you may choose whatever you wish from my shop, I can make suggestions to help you always look your best."

She turned to the duke. "I do have one suggestion for the coming months, Your Grace, something that occurs in many households. I think it would be practical for my seamstresses to move here. It will save an enormous amount of time if they are working here and your nieces do not constantly have to go for fittings elsewhere."

"You think it best?" he asked.

"I do, Your Grace. We can set up a room for them to sew in and another for fittings to occur."

"I like that idea, Uncle Fox," Lady Grace said. "It would be convenient to have them here."

He nodded in agreement. "Then we can have them move in tomorrow after you have met with them."

"I know where we can have them work, Miss Colebourne," Lady Eliza said. "Would you like to see the room now?"

The duke shook his head. "I think Driskell was about to have us come in to dinner. Perhaps afterward you can show Miss Colebourne about." He offered his arm to her. "Shall we go to dinner?"

Delaney took the offered arm as the two girls hurried from the room. "You were right in saying that they are very different from one another," she noted, as the duke escorted her to the dining room.

"Eliza is a handful. Whatever man catches her attention had better watch out. Grace is pleasant and wants to please. She will be a good wife."

"They both will be good wives," she told him. "They will simply attract very different men. In the long run, that will be a good thing. We do not want it to be a competition between them."

"True," he agreed. "By Season's end, I hope they will both have found what they are looking for."

He smiled at her, and Delaney's heart nearly burst from her chest.

"Of course," the duke continued, "Grace is more interested in finding a love match. I have told her if she does not find it this Season, there is always the next one."

"That might prove difficult, Your Grace. Love matches are rare within the *ton*."

"She is a sensitive girl. Sweet and kind. I have explained to her that I do not expect her to rush into marriage with any gentleman. Marriage, after all, is the biggest commitment she will ever make. I wish for her to wed the right partner, be it this Season or five from now. She needs a husband who will care for her and treat her with respect."

If she thought his smile alone had melted her heart, Delaney practically swooned, hearing how protective and thoughtful he was of Grace. Giving his niece the option of not rushing into a marriage was the greatest gift he could give the young lady.

Abington himself seated her, breaking protocol, and she believed he would continue to do so. It wouldn't matter, though. He was now a duke and if anything, dukes abided by their own set of rules and not necessarily those dictated by the *ton*.

At least he hadn't protested when she suggested her seamstresses move to the ducal townhouse. He also seemed agreeable to going to Farmington's tomorrow. Things were off to a good start.

Then she glanced at him and saw he stared at her, a hunger in his eyes. Quickly, Delaney looked away, afraid he might see the same in her own eyes.

She told herself she must be very careful. One slip and it would be too late. She had always guarded her heart, never wishing to give it away. Only now, she realized she might not have control over it.

For the first time, Delaney understood it could be stolen from her.

CHAPTER SIX

F OX FORCED HIMSELF to look away from Delaney Colebourne.
It might have been the hardest thing he had ever done—
and that included going up against some of the fiercest troops he
had ever seen under Joseph Bonaparte.

The tempting Miss Colebourne had consumed his thoughts
ever since he had parted from her this afternoon. Now, hours
later, she sat at his table, sipping his wine, bantering with his
nieces. He had made a good choice in bringing her here. She had
an air of authority about her which Eliza seemed to respect.
Keeping his elder niece in line already had him worried. As for
dreamy Grace, Fox appreciated the advice Miss Colebourne had
given both girls about seeking a husband this Season.

Little did she know she had already landed one herself.

The more he was around her, the more Fox knew making
Delaney Colebourne his duchess would please him. He liked that
the girls had taken to her so quickly. Even if they were soon to be
gone from his household, he still intended to be in their lives.
After hearing how neglected they had been by their parents, Fox
was determined to be a surrogate father to them and a grandfather to their children.

He chuckled to himself, thinking of him and his duchess
being grandparents within the next few years.

"Something amusing, Your Grace?" Miss Colebourne asked.

Fox choked on the wine he was sipping, coughing and dabbing his mouth with a napkin. "No, Miss Colebourne. My wine simply went down the wrong way."

"It is excellent wine," she said.

"I had better in Spain," he revealed. "Army food is no better than slop for hogs but if you have to fight a war?" He smiled. "Spain is an excellent place to do so. The countryside is beautiful. The wine is rich and full-bodied. The Spanish people themselves were quite friendly."

He took another sip of wine.

"Did you have a mistress there, Uncle Fox?" asked Eliza.

Somehow, he got his napkin to his mouth in time to keep the mouthful of wine from spewing across the table.

"That is an impertinent kind of question, which is undesirable, Lady Eliza," Miss Colebourne said calmly. "If you think to be clever, you are only embarrassing yourself and your uncle."

"I was merely curious," the girl protested. "I read about men with mistresses in the gossip columns. Of course, they never name them. Polite Society spends half their day guessing at their identities. I simply wondered if army officers had them."

By now, he had recovered somewhat. "Miss Colebourne is correct, Eliza. It is a forward, unnecessary question. One which you shouldn't ask, and any gentleman in his right mind would refuse to answer."

"I am sorry," she apologized, not sounding contrite at all.

Oh, Fox liked his niece quite a bit—but she would certainly be a handful to any man who chose her as his wife. He would have to make certain any man wooing Eliza and asking for her hand would be up to the task.

"What did you do in Spain, Uncle Fox?" Grace asked. "I read more than the gossip columns in the newspapers. I know there simply isn't a battle every day in which you engage the enemy. What is life like in camp?"

"Boring," he replied succinctly and then decided he should elaborate. "Tedious, I would say. You are right in that we do not fight on a daily basis with Bonaparte's troops. Still, we must always be prepared to do so. That means countless drills. The men march. They take part in target practice with their rifles. Bayonet practice, as well. As a high-ranking officer, I also participated in a large number of meetings in which we strategized about what our enemy planned next. How we would act or react. We studied maps of the local areas and familiarized ourselves with them. Plotted maneuvers and talked the consequences of each."

"It sounds dull," Eliza said, biting into her roast beef with gusto. "I am glad I am female and never have to be in the army and go off to war."

"Did you ever have fun?" Grace asked. "The war has gone on forever. I cannot imagine being away from home for so long and fighting or thinking about fighting all the time."

"I rather liked the camaraderie with the men and my fellow officers," Fox said. "I didn't truly have a home to speak of. I grew up at the dower house at Crosshaven."

"We used to go there at Christmas," Grace said. "I do not recall you being there."

"That is because I had already left the estate by the time you were born. I went to university and then straight to war. My father—your grandfather—died when I was barely walking. I have no memory of him."

"That is when Papa became the duke," Eliza said.

"Yes, it is. My own mother died while I was fighting in Spain. She remarried after her husband's death. We were never truly close. I have spent much of my life in the army—almost fourteen years. To me, home has simply meant a tent and my men."

"Do you miss your parents, girls?" Miss Colebourne asked, easing the conversation along.

The heavy silence which resulted from her question permeated the room.

"No," Eliza finally said. "We did not see them all that much. Papa hardly ever and Mama only when she remembered she had children. They both contracted the pneumonia and died within a day of one another last year."

"I am sorry to hear that," Miss Colebourne said. "Even if you were not close, death in a family is never easy."

"What of you, Miss Colebourne. Do you like your parents?" Grace asked their guest.

"I did. Very much," she replied, her smile wistful, melting Fox's heart. "My mother was beautiful and determined. Some would call her stubborn. My father was quite witty and intelligent. They are both gone now. I miss them a great deal."

"Do you have siblings?" Eliza asked. "I have Grace to always count on. She cheers me up when I am blue."

A shadow crossed Miss Colebourne's face, fleeting, but he saw it, nonetheless. "Only half-siblings—and they have nothing to do with me."

"Like Papa and Uncle Fox," Grace said. She looked to her uncle. "I am sorry Papa ignored you as he did us, Uncle Fox."

He smiled indulgently. "It does not matter, Grace. We are all here together, now. We are family. I hope you will look upon me as a surrogate father and not merely your guardian."

Grace looked at him thoughtfully. "You really do seem to like us, Uncle Fox."

"I do." He grinned. "Even Eliza."

"Oh, pish-posh," his older niece said. "I am easy to like."

"You are," he agreed. "A bit opinionated. Perhaps stubborn, as Miss Colebourne's mother was. I find you quite amiable all the same."

"Are you stubborn as your mother was, Miss Colebourne?" Eliza asked their guest.

She grew thoughtful. "I believe some traits run in families, just as looks do. Take the two of you, for instance. You favor one another quite a bit. I would easily guess that you are sisters."

"We look like Mama," Grace volunteered. "She had blond hair like me. Eliza's got darker hair from Papa."

"Just as we inherit physical traits from our parents, I also

ALEXA ASTON

believe part of our identity is forged by them, as well. Our temperament. Our nature. I do believe, however, that a person forms his or her own character."

"But are you *like* her?" Eliza persisted.

"I would say I am more determined than stubborn. Stubborn signals someone who is obstinate and uncompromising. I like to think I am not so inflexible. I feel my determination shows I am steadfast and tenacious."

"Some would call a dog with a bone tenacious, Miss Colebourne," Fox pointed out, interested in her theory.

"True," she agreed. "But my dog would take after me and be—"

"Dogged!" cried Eliza.

The four of them laughed heartily at her pun.

"What kind of dog do you have, Miss Colebourne?" Grace wondered.

"I have no dog, my lady," she replied. "If I did have one, I would hope his temperament would be compatible with mine."

"Mama would not let us have a dog," Eliza complained. "She said they were only good for hunting. And cats were only needed to rid the barn of vermin. When I wed, my husband will let me keep dogs and cats. In the house!"

"I would like a cat," Grace mused. "One who would sit curled in my lap while I read."

"Where would you put your book?" her sister demanded.

"I would find a way," Grace persisted.

"You could have a servant hold it for you," Eliza offered.

"That is out of the question," Miss Colebourne said. "Servants should never be misused."

"But they are . . . servants," Eliza said, clearly puzzled.

"They are people, Lady Eliza," Miss Colebourne said. "Servants in your employ may work for their living, but you should always be considerate and thoughtful of them."

If Fox hadn't thought Delaney Colebourne was the one for him, that statement alone would have made up his mind. Far too many were thoughtless regarding their servants or even downright abusive.

"Miss Colebourne is correct. Servants are people, too, Eliza. They should be treated with respect."

His niece sniffed. "Papa would have had an apoplexy if he'd heard you say that, Uncle Fox."

"Well, he isn't here. I am—and I am now the Duke of Abington. I say servants should be treated with utmost respect. They work diligently on our behalf, and we should be kind to them."

"Well said, Your Grace," Miss Colebourne said, smiling at him. Her smile was genuine, traveling from her lips to her eyes, which glowed with approval.

Lust ran through him so quickly that he gripped the arms of his chair. If the girls had not been present, he would have leaped to her and ripped her from her chair, bending her against the table and having his wicked way with her. He felt his face flush from the thought of taking her on the slab of cherrywood and bowed his head, dabbing his lips with his napkin.

They finished their meal, and Grace thought she had a good room for the seamstresses to work in.

"It is the schoolroom upstairs. Eliza and I used to take our lessons there. The light is extremely good."

"We could use our old governess' room for the fittings," Eliza chimed in. "Let's go see it now."

Fox had Driskell light candles for them, and the four traipsed up the stairs to the top floor. The girls showed them the schoolroom and the former governess' room, looking to Miss Colebourne for her approval.

"Yes, these would be most suitable."

"If the seamstresses are to move in tomorrow, we should inform Mrs. Driskell," Grace said.

"Yes, both Driskells should be informed so rooms might be prepared for them," Fox said. "Why don't you and Eliza go tell Mrs. Driskell what we have planned? You can even help her determine where to put these three seamstresses."

"All right, Uncle Fox," cried Eliza. "Come on, Grace."

The two raced from the schoolroom, and Miss Colebourne said, "They are still childlike in so many ways. Very sweet and innocent."

"They will have some growing up to do," he agreed, glad they were now alone.

"That is true. I wonder if they are prepared to run a household. If their mother told them what is expected. Or . . ." Her voice trailed off a moment. "Or if she prepared them for other things."

"Such as?" he asked, uncertain why she was hesitating.

"Their wedding night."

Her words shocked him. "Do mothers even mention that to their daughters?"

"I suppose not many do," she said. "Especially those in the *ton.*"

He took a step toward her, so close he caught the scent of vanilla rising from her porcelain skin. "Did yours?"

She laughed softly. "You already know that my mother was not of the *ton* and certainly different from most women. She wanted me prepared for every aspect of life. She was a widow, in a way."

Confusion filled him. "How do you mean?"

Sighing, she said, "It is all part of what would be deemed my sordid past. Mama married a dairy farmer who, unbeknownst to her, was desperately in love with the local clergyman's daughter. Less than a year into their marriage, her husband ran off with this woman. They were never heard from again. Mama wound up running the entire dairy farm herself, growing it over time so that she was even able to hire workers for the most difficult tasks. She never knew what happened to the man she had married. If and when she became a widow."

"No wonder she had such determination. It would take a great deal of strength and ability to do what she did, managing a farm of that nature and making it a success."

"She was lonely, though. When my father came calling to check on her, having heard what happened, they took up with one another. Mama called me their love child because she said she did love the earl. Once his wife was gone, Papa begged Mama to marry him. She refused."

"She refused?" Surprise filled him. "She could have walked away from a hard life into one of luxury."

Miss Colebourne shook her head. "Mama did not see it that way. First, she had no idea if she were still wed herself and told me she would not consider marriage for that reason alone. More importantly, she knew the law would give her dairy farm and earnings over to Papa. Though she loved him dearly, she had already had one man take advantage of her and said she would be a fool to give up the financial control she had. They continued seeing one another until she died."

"How old were you?"

"Eight and ten. I had no desire to run the farm. I drew like mad upon every scrap I could find and more than anything, wished to open my own millinery shop. Papa helped me sell the dairy farm, and I apprenticed with a top milliner in London for several years. When I had learned all I could from her and felt confident enough, I began Delaney's Designs. Papa bought my shop outright as a gift to me, while I used the proceeds from the sale of the dairy farm to buy supplies and hire my staff."

"You have led an unusual life, Miss Colebourne," Fox said, moving closer, knowing he couldn't wait any longer.

He wouldn't say a thing about making her a duchess. After hearing the story of Delaney's independent mother—and suspecting that streak of independence had been passed along to the daughter—he feared she would take the lessons learned from her mother and wish to hold on to what she legally owned. While Fox would never want Delaney's Designs, he understood owning it gave her a certain freedom. Marriage, in her eyes, might rip that freedom from her.

No, he would bide his time and keep his plan of marrying her to himself. What he couldn't keep to himself were his hands and lips.

They belonged on Delaney Colebourne.

Yet even as he moved toward her, he knew she might reject him outright. If she did, he would have to completely begin anew in order to find someone to help his nieces. He doubted anyone would be as capable as Delaney.

Fox didn't care. The risk would be worth the reward—if she accepted him. Because it would change everything for the both of them.

He placed his palm on the nape of her neck, his thumb rubbing against the satin skin. Her eyes widened as he lowered his lips to her.

When they touched, Fox knew he was making the best choice of his life.

CHAPTER SEVEN

D ELANEY HAD FELT the current of electricity that simmered between her and the duke ever since she had arrived. She had deliberately ignored it, not wanting to fan the flames between them, concentrating instead on getting to know Lady Eliza and Lady Grace.

But those nieces were now gone—and only the two of them were here.

She liked that he listened to her. Most men didn't listen to a woman at all, but Abington was very much a good listener. In fact, he had drawn more from her than she had ever revealed to anyone. It was hard to understand why she was so relaxed in his company, and yet her senses heightened to a level of awareness she had never known before.

He was close, too close to her, and she thought she better move away before she regretted acting on the feelings stirring within her. Then he placed his large, warm palm against her nape, holding her in place. Her heart slammed against her ribs, and she began tingling all over. Anticipating what was about to happen.

A kiss.

Delaney had never been kissed before. She rarely was in the company of men. Her business revolved around women. True, the rare gentleman had come to her shop upon occasion, looking for a hat as a gift for his wife—or mistress. Those were quick business transactions, allowing Delaney to select a hat and then sending the gentleman on his way. Other than her father, she had spent no time around men, in general. She kept her own books, not needing a bookkeeper to do so. All her employees had been women. The only man she interacted with a few times a year had been Mr. Hodgkins, who had quickly learned that Delaney had a strong mind and even stronger will.

As the duke's lips touched hers, she prayed she would feel nothing. She didn't want to want him. She couldn't afford to be in the same position her mother had been. She refused to be a kept mistress to a gentleman of the *ton*. Actually, any man at all. She did not need one. She only needed herself.

But how quickly her body betrayed her. Resolve to keep this handsome, muscular man at arm's length crumbled in an instant as their mouths met. His lips were surprisingly soft, brushing back and forth against hers, teasing her. Something stirred within her, wanting to answer an unspoken call between them. Delaney's palms flattened against his chest, feeling the solidness of him. She sensed his fingers tightening slightly on her nape. Instead of feeling trapped, the touch brought her comfort, sensing she was secure in his presence.

His lips pressed against hers now, her head held in place by his hand. His other hand moved to her face, his fingers caressing her cheek. She sighed, her lips parting slightly. Somehow, that signaled something to the duke, a silent invitation she hadn't known she extended. One which took her by surprise as his tongue slipped into her mouth.

Gripping his waistcoat with her fingers to try and steady herself, she stilled as he stroked her tongue with his. He explored the inside of her mouth, his tongue slow and methodical, his actions causing her heartbeat to quicken. The place between her legs tightened and began pulsating. Her blood began to sing in her veins as it raced through her.

She answered his call and moved her tongue against his. He

groaned, his hand slipping from her nape and traveling down her back. It reached her waist, and he pulled her toward him, their bodies now flush against one another. Their tongues continued their sensual dance as heat spread throughout Delaney, a heat so tremendous that she thought she might go up in flames. His scent filled her, the mix of bergamot and something clean and masculine. She wanted to crawl inside him. Peel his clothes from him. Have his hot, bare flesh touch hers.

She didn't know how it happened, but her fingers were tangled in his hair, running through the dark waves of silk. It felt marvelous. Exhilarating.

Heat poured from her now, enveloping her. They were so close she didn't know where she ended and he began. Her breasts grew heavy and her limbs languid. His arms now encircled her, his kisses so hot and demanding that she believed she would burst into flames.

What was she doing?

She had let a handsome man's kiss turn her head. She was not going to make the same mistakes her mother had and have her world upended. She would hold on to her dignity. Her pride.

Her virginity.

Sliding her fingers from his hair, she moved her hands to his chest and pushed against it. Hard.

He didn't go anywhere.

She turned her head, breaking the kiss, but his lips merely caressed her cheek. They moved to her ear, his breath hot as his teeth found her earlobe and tugged. Hot lightning tore through her, sizzling, as he did so. Delaney shuddered and turned her head again to face him.

He took advantage of that, seizing her mouth once more, his kiss demanding. All-consuming. Branding her.

Her thoughts were scattered, and she forced herself to ignore the physical sensations. She must break free. If she didn't, she would wind up a puddle at Abington's feet.

And never want to let him go.

With every bit of resolve she could muster, she slammed her palms against his chest, knocking him back. The kiss broken, she scrambled to place the long school table between them. Panting, she fought to catch her breath as they gazed at one another, his smoldering, hers wary.

"Why did you do that?" she managed to get out, resting her hands on the table because she feared her legs might give out on her.

"Because I have wanted to ever since I met you."

His words, though truthful, rankled her. "I am not some object you might fancy yourself desiring, Your Grace."

"I do desire you, Delaney."

"You do not have leave to call me that," she spit back, hearing how ridiculous her words sounded. This man was a duke.

And he was dangerous.

Pushing away from the table, she was determined to stand on her own two feet and face him. "I did not ask for your kiss."

"You responded to it."

Irritation filled her, knowing he was right. "I did," she admitted. "I will blame curiosity."

Intrigue flickered in his eyes. "How so?"

"I have never kissed a man before. I merely thought I would see what it was like."

Astonishment filled his face. "You have never been kissed?"

Anger replaced irritation. "It is not as if I have had an opportunity to do so, Your Grace. I grew up in the country. Everyone knew I was the bastard daughter of the earl. I wasn't good enough for those in Polite Society, and the working class wouldn't have a thing to do with me. Boys my own age were warned away from me because no one wanted to draw the earl's wrath. I spent my early days being schooled by my mother before a governess took over. My later days, I drew like mad and shadowed my father. His own heir had no interest in the estate, but I did. Papa taught me everything about numbers and how to keep my ledgers for the day when I started my own business."

Delaney grew bolder, her hands now akimbo. "Then I apprenticed for years with a milliner, working long hours. When it came time to open my own place of business, I worked even longer. My customers are women. My employees are women. I am rarely in the presence of a man, certainly not long enough to get to know him or have him kiss me."

"Until we met."

"Yes," she hissed, angry now not at him for taking liberties with her, but angry at herself for allowing him to do so. She had never pictured herself with a man, especially one from the *ton*. Despite the fact that she had sold her wares to members of Polite Society, she despised them for thinking they were better than everyone else. Although this man's kiss had moved her in inexplicable ways, she would never become involved with him merely because he was a part of the *ton*.

"I am not my mother, Your Grace. I will not embark upon some impassioned love affair with you. I have lived between two worlds, never fitting in either, and I would never do that to my child. And that would be the result of us coupling."

"There are ways to prevent a child coming," he said quietly.

His words startled her. She had not known that. Of course, she should have guessed because her mother only had the one babe, and she had carried on with her lover for many years.

The thought intrigued her. What if she could explore what lay between a man and a woman without suffering the consequences of a child?

No, tempting as that might be, her heart told her it was wrong to do so with this man. He already stirred incredible physical things within her. If she became emotionally involved with him—if she fell in love with him—it would be a disaster.

"You are meant for some genteel lady bred in Polite Society, Your Grace," Delaney said stiffly. "If you choose to dally with someone, it will not be me. I have no interest in coupling with you."

"Did you enjoy our kisses, Delaney?" he asked, his voice

husky and low, sending shivers along her spine.

"They were . . . interesting."

He laughed. "Oh, come now. Admit it. They were more than interesting. They were earthshattering."

Confusion filled her. Had he felt it, too? The incredible pull between them? The yearning whose magnitude was a hundredfold from anything she had ever experienced?

"They were enjoyable," she amended. "But they will not be repeated, Your Grace. You have engaged me to help prepare your nieces for their come-outs. I will help them make their wardrobe choices. I am providing the seamstresses to sew their gowns alongside me. I am happy to spend time with your nieces and discuss topics they need to understand in order to be successful. I will even help chaperone them with their suitors if necessary.

"What is unnecessary is anything other than a business arrangement between us. You are paying me for my services. You have promised to purchase my building. We need not discuss anything personal between us. We are employer and employee for now, a limited time. In fact, I doubt I will see you much, as I will be spending most of my time in the company of Lady Eliza and Lady Grace."

Reaching for one of the candles on the table, she lifted it. "I will say goodnight to you, Your Grace."

Delaney left the schoolroom and had only gone a few paces when he caught her wrist.

"I am a gentleman," he said, his eyes glowing. "I may have spent years away from England, living a rough life. I will apologize for kissing you, Miss Colebourne." He paused. "What I will not apologize for is enjoying it."

She felt his fingers burn into her skin as those words washed over her.

"I told you I found your kisses enjoyable, Your Grace. It is not a performance I am interested in repeating, however. I hope this will end our evening on a better note."

"It does. I promise you this—I will never take advantage of

you."

"I appreciate you reassuring me of this." She cleared her throat, and his fingers fell away, leaving her feeling oddly bereft. "We are to meet with the seamstresses at my shop at ten, but you should be at the tailor's at nine. He is located next door to Delaney's Designs, and his name is Mr. Farmington. I hope I did not overstep when making arrangements for you to see him." She smiled. "Even your nieces realize it is time for you to attend to your own wardrobe."

The duke chuckled. "Well, I cannot go about embarrassing them, can I? Very well, Miss Colebourne. I will arrive at the tailor's at nine on my own and have my carriage bring Eliza and Grace to your shop at ten." He paused. "I don't wish to overstep, but I may need your help in this endeavor."

"I had already told Mr. Farmington I would accompany you, Your Grace. I can advise you in regard to the types of events you will be attending and what will be called for. I want to assure you that though Mr. Farmington runs a small establishment, he does extremely fine work. You will be good advertising for him," she declared. "I believe you will wear his clothes well and that others will want to know who your tailor is. As far as tomorrow goes, I can go back and forth between both places, but I did want to let you know that Mr. Farmington knows his trade."

"Very well, Miss Colebourne. I shall see you downstairs now."

He offered his arm, and she placed her fingers atop his forearm, feeling how solid it was. Delaney ignored the butterflies multiplying in her belly all because of this simple touch.

The butler offered her reticule and shawl to her and Abington walked her outside to the waiting carriage.

He took her hand and lifted it to his lips. "Until tomorrow, Miss Colebourne." He handed her up, and she sat alone, mulling over what had occurred this evening.

She had always thought herself intelligent. Capable. Flexible. Tonight, though, had proven that something lay beneath her surface. Something the Duke of Abington had stirred within her. An ember that smoldered, wishing for more oxygen so it could burn brightly.

If she were truly wise, she would cut all ties with him now. Then she pictured the sweet, unassuming Lady Grace and the feisty, entertaining Lady Eliza. No, she could not abandon those girls on the brink of their come-outs. She would stay the course and see that they were properly launched in Polite Society.

Delaney only hoped that she could do so without seeing too much of the duke over the next few months. She feared if she were around him much, she might succumb to temptation and want more than kisses from him.

She had always trusted her instincts, but now? This man seemed to challenge every notion she had ever possessed about herself.

No, she would see her task through and keep her virtue intact. Just because she'd had a taste of what physical pleasure was like did not mean she should explore it further.

Especially if it involved the Duke of Abington.

CHAPTER EIGHT

D ELANEY BREAKFASTED WITH Mary, as she did every morning, and decided to clue in the servant as to what lay ahead.

"Mary, I am going to sell Delaney's Designs. At least the building."

The servant nodded in agreement. "It's best to do so, Miss Colebourne. After that half-brother of yours ran off all your customers, I don't see how you would be able to make a living selling them hats. Will you go to Buckinghamshire?"

She saw a bit of doubt in Mary's eyes and knew her longtime servant worried whether she would be asked to go with Delaney or not.

"That is my plan. Of course, I would hope you might wish to come with me. It was different when I went and stayed there several months last year because I always intended to come back here. It is why I left you in London to look after things for me. But I would not leave you behind, Mary. We have been together a long time, haven't we?"

Tears filled the older woman's eyes. "We have, indeed, Miss Colebourne. I would be happy to go with you and serve in any way you wish."

"It won't be until the Season ends."

Mary gave her an odd look. "But . . . how will you sell any of your beautiful hats? I don't think those people who shunned you before will have changed their minds, Miss Colebourne."

"No, but I have been tasked with helping to bring out two young ladies of a newly minted duke."

Briefly, Delaney explained how she had met the duke and that he would be purchasing her building in exchange for her help in launching his two nieces into Polite Society.

"He has been away at war his entire adult life, Mary. He knows little to nothing about the *ton*. I can put my knowledge to good use and have already rehired Dilly, Ruth, and Fanny. Instead of making hats for me, they will be sewing the gowns for the two young ladies making their come-outs this year. Once the Season ends—and hopefully, both girls are betrothed—then you and I can head to Chapwell Hall. I have plans to open a millinery shop there."

"What would I being doing for you, Miss Colebourne?" Mary asked. "I know you already have servants there to look after you."

"I only have a handful of them at the estate. You may have your choice of what you wish to do there. If you are tired of cooking and cleaning, you could even become my clerk at the shop."

The servant shook her head. "No, Miss Colebourne, I am more comfortable in a household. We can work things out once we get to Chapwell Hall."

She rose from the table. "I am off to begin my new duties this morning, Mary. I recommended Mr. Farmington to create the Duke of Abington's wardrobe and will meet His Grace there shortly."

"My, that would certainly do Farmington's tailoring shop some good. Give it a real lift. To have clothed a duke for a Season?" Mary chuckled. "Mr. Farmington will be hard to get along with."

"I doubt it will go to his head. He is eager to please, and I know he does impeccable work. Later this morning, Lady Eliza and Lady Grace will come to the hat shop. We will meet with the others to talk about these ladies' wardrobes, as well as let them select a few hats."

"It sounds as if you will be quite busy, Miss Colebourne. I know you like it that way."

Delaney went downstairs and found Dilly and Ruth, along with Fanny, standing outside the shop's entrance.

She let them in and said, "My, all three of you are so early. The two young ladies will not be here for an hour and a half."

Ruth hugged her spontaneously. "We are just so happy to be back with you, Miss Colebourne. Tell us about these young girls."

"Well, as I am sure Dilly shared with you, they are making their come-outs this Season. They are identical in size by looking at them. Lady Eliza is very outgoing and perhaps a bit too outspoken. Lady Grace, on the other hand, is sweet-natured and seems to be a peacemaker. I am going to let them choose some hats from what remains on display, then we will need to talk with them about the events they will attend and what styles and colors will best flatter their figures."

"Thank you for thinking of us, Miss Colebourne," Fanny said. "I know we weren't seamstresses for you before."

"You may not have been, Fanny, but I knew all three of you possessed strong sewing skills. I am excited that you were all free and able to work with me as we launch these young women into Polite Society.

"I do have a question to pose to each of you, however," she continued. "There will be so many gowns to make up for the pair and we thought it might be wise if the three of you came to live at the duke's townhouse during the months of the Season. The schoolroom is at the top of the house and receives a great deal of natural light, which would be ideal for sewing. The governess' bedchamber, which stands next to it, could serve as a fitting room. Each of you would be given your own small room to sleep in. Would that appeal to you?"

"I like the idea," Dilly proclaimed. "It would save time traveling to and from the duke's townhouse each morning and evening."

"We could give up our room, Dilly," Ruth said excitedly. "Think of the money we would save, paying no rent for several months."

"I still live with my mother, but I would be more than happy to relocate to the duke's townhouse for the next several months, Miss Colebourne," Fanny said.

"Good. Then it is settled. Ruth and Dilly can give notice to their landlord and you, Fanny, can let your mother know she will have one less mouth to feed, at least until August."

The women discussed which fabric shops they might use and decided upon two which they believed to be reliable and carry an excellent quality and variety of fabrics.

"I will go with you today to take these two young ladies to choose materials. If we can get enough bolts of material for the gowns to be worn during April and May, we can return at a later date for more. I believe we will enjoy working with these two young ladies. For now, I am going next door to Mr. Farmington's. He is going to be making up the wardrobe for the girls' uncle. I said I would help advise His Grace on making some choices."

"This is an adventure, Miss Colebourne, and we are happy to be a part of it," Fanny said. "I suppose this means Delaney's Designs will not reopen for the Season."

Sadness flooded her. "No, Lord Kinnison has shut down all avenues of revenue. He and his father-in-law set out to see me ruined, and they succeeded. However, I will be selling this building by Season's end and would like to open a new millinery shop in Buckinghamshire."

"That is where your father left you property, isn't it?" Ruth asked.

"Yes. The place is called Chapwell Hall. It is near the town of High Wycombe. I am thinking about opening my shop there for at least a few years. Of course, I will not be catering to the same clientele I did in London. Most likely, my customers will be from the middle class and surrounding areas."

"If you do decide to open this shop, Miss Colebourne, I hope you will consider rehiring us to work for you," Dilly said. "We aren't wed to London, and we enjoy working for you."

"I agree," her sister said. "We would be willing to follow you anywhere, Miss Colebourne."

"Count me in, too," Fanny added enthusiastically.

Delaney was touched by the loyalty of her former employees. She doubted she would need all three of them because the venture would be small, but she would hire the entire trio, nonetheless. They could have steady employment until she decided if and when she would return to London and open a new shop under a different name. She could even leave Fanny and one of the sisters behind to run the High Wycombe shop and hire new staff for the London venture.

That was far down the line, however. For now, she would focus on the present.

"I will leave you then for an hour," she told the group. "Lady Grace and Lady Eliza are scheduled to arrive at ten o'clock, and I will return at that time. Talk among yourselves about various styles and materials. It will also be easier once you have met these two girls. You know how I like to tailor a hat to my client's personality. I believe we should do the same for the duke's nieces. I will be designing all their gowns for them, but I am open to your input on any and every gown we create."

Delaney left her shop and went next door, greeting Mr. Farmington, who looked jittery.

"There is no need to be anxious," she told him. "Your tailoring skills match those of the best tailors in London. This duke will be unlike any others you meet as your business flourishes over time."

"How so, Miss Colebourne?"

"I have told you he is new to his title, but he is also new to the *ton*. He is a career army officer and so has lived under tremendously harsh conditions ever since he left England years ago. I believe he will be easy to please."

A bell tinkled as the shop's door opened and in walked the

Duke of Abington, trailed by a man who Delaney guessed to be his valet. She had tried to prepare for this moment and knew she was failing miserably. Her breath came too swiftly. Her head swam. Her knees thought about buckling, and she willed herself to stay on her feet and remain calm.

But how could she when the duke looked so incredibly appealing? She could feel his mouth on hers, taking, tasting, delving deep as it sought all her secrets. She clasped her hands in front of her, her nails digging into her palms, trying to keep from leaping at him and devouring him whole.

Instead, she took a deep breath as he traveled across the shop to meet her. By the time he arrived, she thought she maintained a semblance of calm.

"Good morning, Your Grace," she greeted. "I see you have brought along your valet, which is an excellent idea." She turned to the tailor. "May I introduce Mr. Farmington to you, Your Grace? This is the Duke of Abington, Mr. Farmington."

The tailor bowed. "I am humbled to be able to clothe you this Season, Your Grace. You do me a great honor patronizing my shop."

The valet spoke up. "I would like to see samples of your work, Mr. Farmington, in order to see if it lives up to the standards of His Grace."

The duke's lips twitched in amusement. "This is Parchmann, by the way. He tells me daily how to be a duke. I assured him that Miss Colebourne would not have recommended a tailor to me unless he were suitable."

Parchmann wore a haughty look as he said, "I am aware of Miss Colebourne's reputation as a milliner. Still, it does not mean that her friend is the tailor for you, Your Grace. Come along, Farmington. Show me your work."

The tailor glanced to Delaney, and she nodded slightly.

"Right this way, Mr. Parchmann. I would be happy to show you samples of what I have sewn."

The two men left them and Abington said, "Parchmann

would make for an excellent duke. His nose is constantly in the air, and he thinks he knows everything."

Delaney couldn't help but laugh. "Yes, both valets and ladies' maids have the reputation of being quite protective of their employers and putting themselves above other servants."

"I thought my butler was snooty until I met Parchmann," the duke grumbled. "Driskell is a pussycat compared to Parchmann."

"I think it a good thing, Your Grace. I assume you inherited Parchmann from your half-brother."

"Yes, he served the previous Duke of Abington."

"Then Parchmann will be well-versed in what you need. It was a good thing you brought him along today. He will be quite helpful."

"He left me no choice. He assumed the moment I told him where I was going that he would be included in the outing."

She laughed again and this time, the duke joined in her laughter. "Then while they are checking over the quality of Mr. Farmington's work, you and I should discuss what you will require for this Season."

"Not only this Season," he said. "I hope the clothing Mr. Farmington creates will last a good while if it is as fine a quality as you have promised."

"Then let your schooling begin. You see, Your Grace, you will get a new wardrobe each year, just as ladies do."

"Each *year?*"

"Yes. I would suggest between two and half to three dozen coats, along with the same number of waistcoats and breeches. Shirts? You will need a good thirty to forty. We must see a separate shirtmaker for those. Mr. Farmington will have suggestions where to go."

"Good God, Woman! That is insane."

"Oh, and that does not even include your evening wear," she teased.

Delaney began outlining the various types of social affairs the duke would attend as he escorted his nieces throughout the

Season.

"That boggles my mind," the duke declared. "And you say this is to be repeated each year?"

"It does help employ a good number of people. It takes so many to put together wardrobes, including your cobbler and bootmaker. Hats, too."

"Could you make my hats for me? After all, it is your specialty."

"I have never designed men's hats, but I would certainly be up for that challenge. Yes, Your Grace, I believe I will handle your hats. It is good to flex my creativity every now and then. It will keep my skills sharp and fresh. After all, you must look your best."

"Because I am a duke?"

"Well, that goes without saying," she said. "Dukes always try to be the best-dressed gentlemen in Polite Society because they set the standard in all things. No, I am thinking you need to look your best for another reason. Surely, that puzzled look on your face will go away when I remind you that you must seek a bride of your own this Season. Just as you hope for your nieces to make excellent matches, you, too, must consider marriage in the near future if you want your ducal line to continue. Now, some men in Polite Society wait until they are past your age, which I would assume would be your mid-thirties."

"I am four and thirty," he told her indignantly. "I don't believe I am old at all. How old are you, Miss Colebourne?"

She batted her eyes coquettish at him. "Now, that is an impudent question, Your Grace. Perhaps Lady Eliza takes after her uncle."

His cheeks flushed with color. "I apologize, Miss Colebourne. I should not have asked such an indiscreet question of you."

She thought of the indiscreet manner he had behaved in last night in the schoolroom when those passionate kisses scorched her. Delaney pushed them from her thoughts.

"Only because we are frank with one another will I tell you. I am thirty years of age."

"You look much younger," he declared. "I would have guessed you to be in your mid-twenties."

She saw the teasing light in his eyes. "Flattery will get you somewhere with certain women. But if I were you, I would stick to complimenting ladies on their gowns."

"You truly believe I should seek a wife this Season?"

She chuckled. "Oh, they will be seeking you. You are an eligible duke, begging for an heir. Every time you look up, a flood of ladies will appear nearby."

"They do not even know me," he said earnestly.

Delaney smiled, thinking him almost as naive as his nieces when it came to life in the *ton*.

"Most marriages are made for political or financial considerations, Your Grace. Your title alone will make certain that women swarm about you. Not just single women—but married ones, as well."

"Married women will pursue me?"

She shrugged. "The *ton* is fickle. Marriages of convenience are the norm and oftentimes couples have little to nothing in common. Once a wife provides an heir for her husband's title— and hopefully, a spare—she usually is free to take a lover of her choice. As for a gentleman, a mistress is *de riguer*."

"That is scandalous behavior," the duke declared.

"It may be, Your Grace, but that is the way of the society you are now joining. You must fit in."

Irritation sparked in his eyes. "I don't have to do any such thing, Miss Colebourne."

Placing her hand on his forearm, she hoped to calm him. Instead, electricity crackled between them.

"Please try and do so for your nieces' sake," she quietly urged. "You want to help them make the best match possible."

He snorted. "You seem to tell me that most matches are not happy ones. Why should I wish for Grace and Eliza to shackle themselves to a fellow they will be unhappy with?"

Removing her hand, she told him, "It is true that most marriages are made out of convenience. There are happy ones, though, Your Grace. I would hope your nieces might make that kind of match. I will help you screen these candidates for their hands. Together, we will guide them to make the best choice possible and hope they will be happy. You, however, must do your part. Play the gallant duke. Be a protective uncle and look out for their interests."

"What of my own interests, Miss Colebourne?" he asked, his voice low, causing her mouth to grow dry.

"You seem to be a man who knows his own mind. If you were intelligent enough to strategize with Wellington, surely you will be able to navigate the waters of the *ton*."

One brow arched. "You lead me to believe these waters are quite deep, Miss Colebourne."

"They can be. Swirling and sometimes even vicious, truth be told." She smiled. "Something tells me you are a great swimmer, Your Grace. You will fight to keep your head above water. Rise above the crashing waves. You will do your duty as a guardian and find suitable husbands for Lady Grace and Lady Eliza. And a wife for yourself, of course."

He smiled at her, causing her to feel the pull of his magnetism. "I think you may be right, Miss Colebourne. I believe I will find the perfect duchess this Season."

CHAPTER NINE

DELANEY TAPPED A bolt of material and said, "This is one of my favorites."

Parchmann quickly agreed with her and set the bolt aside, determining they were done with it. She was happy the valet was present. As the Duke of Abington had said, his valet was most opinionated—but those opinions were thoughtful and precise ones. While the duke contributed little to nothing regarding their fashion discussion, she, Parchmann, and Farmington had decided upon all the elements for the duke's new wardrobe. Even though the weather was turning warm, the tailor had also suggested that he make up a greatcoat for the duke to use next winter. Abington had been agreeable to all their suggestions.

"I am going to leave the rest in the hands of you gentlemen," she said, rising and insisting they remain seated.

Still, the duke came to his feet. "You are leaving us to go to Eliza and Grace?"

"Yes. They should be arriving momentarily, and I want to introduce them to the three women who will be helping to create their wardrobes. I also want to go through my shop with Lady Eliza and Lady Grace as they pick out some hats for themselves."

"Will you return here afterward?" he asked solemnly, looking like a lost little boy.

"I will do so while the girls are being measured. That will be at least an hour or more from now. I will stop in to see how you are doing, and then we ladies will be heading to visit a couple of fabric shops so that we may make choices of some materials and start making up gowns as soon as possible. Is Mrs. Driskell ready for my seamstresses to move in? I told them of the plan. All three agreed it would be most convenient if they were on the premises for the next several months."

"I am sure my servants are prepared for them. Have them move in as soon as they wish to do so. Let me walk you back to your shop, Miss Colebourne."

"No, Your Grace, that is not necessary. It is right next door."

A steely glint entered his eyes. "I will escort you."

She looked at the other two. "Then I will see you later."

"We will stop and measure His Grace now," Mr. Farmington said. "Thank you for your assistance, Miss Colebourne. We accomplished a great deal."

"I was happy to help."

The duke opened the door of the shop and allowed Delaney to pass through. She saw the same magnificent carriage which had taken her to dinner last night now standing outside her own shop and assumed the girls had arrived.

They walked the few steps to Delaney's Designs, and the duke opened the door for her, seeing her safely inside. It surprised her when he followed her in.

She spied both his nieces trying on hats and moved toward them. "Good morning, Lady Eliza, Lady Grace."

They both turned, beaming. "Good morning, Miss Colebourne," they replied in unison.

"Dilly said it was all right for us to begin trying on hats," Lady Eliza added. "What do you think of this one, Uncle Fox?"

"I know little about fashion, but I do know you look good wearing it," he complimented, causing his older niece to glow.

"What do you think of this one, Uncle?" Lady Grace asked, holding out a hat and then placing it on her head.

The duke cocked his head and studied her a moment. "I like

it, Grace. It flatters you. It would be a fine hat to wear as you walk through the park."

"Or drive," Lady Grace promoted. "After tea is the fashionable hour in the park, Uncle Fox. We may have suitors who will ask us to drive through the park with them."

He looked to Delaney. "Do I allow this?"

"I am glad you are taking your role as guardian seriously but walking or driving through Hyde Park with a gentleman is one of the few times a young lady does not need to have a chaperone present. There are so many others who gather in the park from five to six o'clock, it is as if the entire *ton* acts as chaperones."

He looked to his nieces. "I may still want to come along with you on these outings."

Lady Grace frowned, but Lady Eliza shrugged and blithely said, "I do not care if you come or not, Uncle Fox, as long as I have worthy gentlemen ask to escort me through the park. It is simply the best place to be seen by others. Seeing that you are a duke, it will impress people to see me with you and know we are on good terms."

"Being seen by others is your objective, Eliza?" he asked.

"Of course, Uncle Fox. The more people who see me, the better chances I have of attracting more attention. Especially that of a—"

"Eliza, I know you wish to wed a titled gentleman, but there is more to a man than looks and his money."

"Oh, I am not worried about his looks, Uncle," she declared. "It would be nice if my husband had them, but I just want to be rich and be at least a countess. After all, I am the daughter of a duke. I have certain expectations to meet, both mine and those of the *ton*."

Abington glanced at Delaney, and she shook her head imperceptibly, letting him know now was not the time to address his concerns.

Instead, she said, "Well, we will want you to look your best as you make your come-outs. Your uncle needs to go be measured now by his tailor. We ladies will conduct business of our own." She looked to the duke. "I will be certain to stop in before we leave for our visits to the fabric stores, Your Grace."

Knowing he had been dismissed, the duke gave her a curt nod and left the shop.

"Do you always have to think about money?" Grace demanded. "There are more things in life, Eliza."

Her sister crossed her arms. "You and I both know that most married couples in society go their own ways, Grace. I want to be comfortable in the marriage I make and have the freedom to do what I want. You might be looking for love—but I have no interest in it. I want to look my best, attract a wealthy lord, and live my life the way I see fit."

Grace shook her head. Delaney knew there would be no changing Eliza's mind.

Unless the girl did fall in love.

"All right," she said brightly. "Let us pick out a few more hats you like and set them aside. Then we will get down to the true business of today."

A quarter-hour later, Eliza had chosen seven hats and Grace five. Fanny offered to place them in labeled boxes and set them aside as the others went and sat at a table in the corner of the shop.

"You both look to be of a similar size, but what we must discuss now is your specific tastes," Delaney began. "Are there any colors you are partial to or styles you believe best suit you?"

As expected, Eliza spoke up at once, reeling off colors she preferred and cuts of gowns which she admired. Delaney took notes as the girl spoke and then said, "Let me hear from you now, Lady Grace."

Lady Grace seemed much less confident than her sister in this area. "I do like shades of pink. I am not certain what other colors might look good on me. As for the style of gowns, I will leave that up to you, Miss Colebourne, and your seamstresses. You know more about these matters than I do."

"I think you would also look good in more shades than pink although with your skin tone and hair color, blush will definitely be one of your colors to play up this Season. I can see a satin ballgown in blush now, off the shoulders."

"What about with an underskirt slightly darker?" Ruth suggested.

Soon, ideas flew fast and furious, and Delaney struggled to get everything down. She talked to the girls about the different social events since they only seemed to know the Season involved balls.

"Yes, usually between fifty to sixty balls are held each Season. You will have a new gown for each," Delaney promised. "There are many other social events you will be attending with your uncle."

She detailed those and then explained how the girls would also need numerous day dresses.

"You must have gowns in which to receive your callers. Ones to wear when you go and take tea with people who invite you to do so. You will also need to have gowns for walks and drives in the park."

"My, this is certainly a lot of gowns," Lady Grace said. "Will you have time to make up all of these for us?"

"We can and will," Dilly assured the pair. "Residing in your household will help. We will start immediately and have almost a month before the Season begins. Naturally, not all gowns will be finished by then. We will complete as many as possible but Ruth, Fanny, and I will be sewing night and day until the Season's end."

"I wish we would have known how much went into this," Lady Grace said apologetically.

"Mama would have prepared us," Lady Eliza said breezily. "She would have made certain all happened in good time."

Delaney saw doubt fill Lady Grace's eyes and moved to reassure her. "It is as Dilly has said, my lady. We will complete as many gowns as possible, but everyone will be sewing the bulk of every day on your wardrobes throughout the next several months. I will join the others in between designing your gowns." She paused. "I had not thought to ask, but do you know how to dance?"

"Yes," Lady Eliza told her. "Mama loved to dance, and we have been taking lessons from a dance master for a good three years now. He still comes to the house once a week to work with us."

She scribbled a note to ask the duke if he knew how to dance. Something told her with all the time he had spent on the battlefield, learning how to dance had not been a priority for him.

The bell jingled above the door, and Delaney realized she had not posted any kind of sign that she was permanently closed. No client had walked through her doors since last spring, when her half-brother had issued his edict to Polite Society, cutting her off at the knees.

"Excuse me," she said to the others and went to see who might have stepped into her millinery. She came upon a tall woman, so tall she must be just a couple inches shy of six feet. The statuesque beauty had abundant, fiery hair and moss green, twinkling eyes.

"I am sorry, my lady, but my establishment is no longer open for business. I can suggest two or three other milliners who are quite good, however."

The woman's eyes skimmed the shop. "But you have an abundance of beautiful hats. Are they for show and not for sale?"

"Perhaps you do not realize who I am, my lady, and I would not want to get you and your husband into trouble."

"Why would say such a thing? How would I get into trouble looking at—or buying—a new hat for myself?"

She sighed. "My name is Delaney Colebourne, my lady. I do not wish to air the sordid problems from last Season, but I must warn you that Lord and Lady Kinnison have threatened the cut direct to anyone who patronizes my shop. I would not want to see you suffer merely by making an innocent mistake and purchasing a hat from me."

A determined look filled the woman's eyes. "Ah, yes, I do believe I heard some rumor of this going around last spring. I dismissed it as idle gossip." She paused. "I am sorry I did so, Miss Colebourne—for I would have come directly to your shop, along with my friends. We would have bought every hat available from you."

Delaney gasped. "Oh, my lady. You would not wish to cross Lord Kinnison. He is one of the wealthiest members of the *ton* and one of their most influential."

"Why would the earl have singled you out, Miss Colebourne? For Lord Kinnison to take notice of a milliner and try to destroy her business is most unusual."

She needed to nip this woman's unneeded charity in the bud. "Since I will never see you again, my lady, I will be brutally frank. Lord Kinnison and I share a father. Lord Kinnison is a result of Papa's *ton* marriage. I am a product of his longtime affair with my mother. Lord Kinnison hated me from the moment he learned of me. Once Papa passed last February, my half-brother set out to destroy me by having others blackball my business. The hats you see here were all created for last Season. With no warning or apologies, my clients simply stopped coming to my millinery shop. Lord Kinnison and his father-in-law had warned others if they patronized my establishment, they would receive the cut direct."

Anger now sparked in this beautiful redhead's eyes. "What right does Kinnison have to dictate to Polite Society?"

"I am not a part of Polite Society, my lady, but I do understand its workings. I know my father was a most wealthy man, and he left my half-brother with most of that wealth. And money is power."

Sympathy filled the woman's eyes. "Did your father acknowledge you, Miss Colebourne?"

Delaney smiled wistfully. "He most certainly did. Papa even tried to convince my mother to marry him, but Mama always refused. After her death, Papa brought me to London, and I apprenticed at a milliner's. He then helped me set up this business and was most proud of me. It is mere jealousy on Lord Kinnison's part since he was never close to our father."

"I cannot see an injustice such as this," the woman declared. "I plan to do something about it."

"No, my lady, I beg you to stay out of this affair. It is all right. For this Season, I have been commissioned to help launch the two nieces of the new Duke of Abington, who are in my shop as we speak. I am supervising their wardrobes and will help chaperone their afternoon callers. My former milliners are the very ones who will sew their wardrobes for their come-outs. Then I will leave town and open another millinery shop in Buckinghamshire. Papa left me a small estate there. I am not destitute, my lady. I would not have you sacrifice your social reputation for a stranger."

The woman smiled. "I do not think we are going to remain strangers for long, Miss Colebourne." She paused. "I am the Duchess of Westfield. I dare Lord Kinnison to try to ostracize my duke and me from the *ton*."

Fear rippled through Delaney, hearing this woman was a duchess. Of course, she knew who the Duchess of Westfield was. Everyone in Polite Society did. The duchess, the former Lady Margaret Townsend, had wed the Duke of Westfield, and her husband encouraged his beloved wife to continue painting the portraits she had done before their marriage. The gossip columns had named the duchess their new darling, and she continued accepting commissions for portraits even though she now had given birth to a child.

"I can see from your expression that you know exactly who I am."

"Yes, Your Grace. I do. You have conquered Polite Society and are the envy of every woman because of the great love between you and your husband. But once again, I implore you not to take up this battle on my behalf. I have accepted things and will take the high road. After helping Lady Grace and Lady Eliza make their come-outs, I will retreat from London, bloody but unbowed."

"I hope you will give that matter some more thought, Miss Colebourne. Why don't we discuss it over tea tomorrow afternoon?"

To think that a duchess had invited her to tea thrilled Delaney, but she knew she could not accept such a generous invitation.

The door to her shop opened once again and a handsome gentleman, tall and broad of shoulders, with coal black hair and gray eyes approached them. She assumed this was the Duke of Westfield.

"Darling, I want you to come next door and meet someone."

"The Duke of Abington?" the duchess asked, smiling.

Her husband chuckled. "How you know these things, I will never guess."

"I know them through Miss Colebourne here." She introduced Delaney to the duke and then said, "Miss Colebourne is assisting Abington and launching his nieces into society this year."

"Abington did mention the girls and that he was their guardian," the duke said. "I would like to ask him to tea. He is new to town, back from the war, and could use a friend."

"Then we will have him come for tea tomorrow. When Miss Colebourne does." The duchess turned and smiled at Delaney. "You will come, Miss Colebourne, won't you? And you already know His Grace. It will be a most enjoyable teatime, I believe."

Papa had always told her there were some women you simply could not say no to. Delaney believed the Duchess of Westfield to be one of those women.

"I would be delighted to come to tea, Your Grace. Thank you for your kind invitation."

"I am glad that is settled. Go back and visit with Abington for a few more minutes, my love. I see a hat or two I wish to purchase. Miss Colebourne is also going to introduce me to Lady Eliza and Lady Grace."

The duke brushed his lips against his wife's cheeks, an extraordinary show of affection in public. Instead of being shocked by the display, Delaney liked him all the more for doing so.

"Don't be too long, my love."

The duke exited the shop, and the duchess said, "Let me meet these two young ladies, Miss Colebourne, and then I insist that you help me select a few hats."

Delaney couldn't tell a duchess what she could or couldn't do. She only hoped Her Grace would not regret stepping into Delaney's Designs and offering its owner her friendship.

CHAPTER TEN

FOX HAD ALLOWED Farmington to measure him from head to toe. Parchmann assisted the tailor, insisting he would do a better job than the tailor's own assistant. The valet was thorough and seemed determined to turn Fox into a duke. He idly wondered what the servant's relationship had been with the previous duke and decided he did not want to know about it. The past should remain in the past. Either Parchmann would whip Fox into ducal shape or he could bloody well seek employment elsewhere.

"You may step down, Your Grace," Farmington said.

Fox stepped off the raised box he stood upon. "Is that it?"

"We could still discuss things, Your Grace," the tailor said hopefully.

He frowned. "I believe we have discussed my new wardrobe to death. Am I truly needed here for much longer?"

"Are you tired of wearing your uniform?" Farmington asked. "If so, I have a few things already made up close to your size. They are good quality. You could try them on and allow me and my assistants to make a few adjustments. It would give you something to wear over the next few days, at least until we can finish some items up for you. You must also go to the shirtmaker's."

"And the bootmaker's. Also, a cobbler. Yes, I know. Miss

Colebourne made me aware of that." Sighing, he said, "Bring me what you have, Mr. Farmington. I am certain it will not be up to Parchmann's standards, but I do need something new for the interval." He glanced to the valet. "Would that be acceptable, Parchmann?"

"Yes, Your Grace," the servant said begrudgingly.

Farmington's assistant rounded up a few pieces, and Fox tried them on, actually pleased with how well they fit.

"Just a few adjustments will need to be made to some of them, Your Grace," the tailor assured him. "Actually, what you wear now suits you well. We could use it as a guide. As for the others? You could even wait while we do those and then try them on again."

"Must I?" He was already weary of being there and everything being about a duke. He had not had so much attention paid to him since . . . well, never.

"No, you can leave if you choose," Farmington said.

"I will stay behind, Your Grace, and see that things are done properly," his valet said.

"Very well, I will go next door and see how my nieces fare as soon as I change."

Once he had done so, he left the dressing room and headed toward the door just as it opened and another gentleman came in, one even taller than Fox, with dark hair and gray eyes and an air of authority about him.

"Hello," he greeted. "My horse threw a shoe and my coachman has gone off in search of a blacksmith. My wife spied a millinery and ducked inside the shop. Ladies' hats are the last thing I wished to look at. Might I browse in here instead?"

"I am just leaving," Fox told the stranger. "Mr. Farmington is all yours."

"Westfield," the man said, offering his hand. "The Duke of Westfield, that is."

Fox took it, interested to be meeting a fellow duke. "I am the Duke of Abington," he told the man.

"Ah, yes. I read of Abington's death in the newspapers a few months ago. The pneumonia, wasn't it?"

"Yes, Your Grace. I did not know I was my half-brother's heir. We had never met in person."

"It is obvious you have come from the Continent. Where did you serve?"

"Under Wellington in Spain. I was a major-general."

"You had climbed the ladder quite a ways," the duke said, nodding to himself. "I suppose that was hard to walk away from. The life you had created for one you did not know would consume you."

"And all the more difficult when I discovered I was guardian to two nieces," he confided.

The duke smiled. "I am the father of a daughter. She recently turned a year old and is my heart."

Fox thought how differently his half-brother had felt toward the two girls he had fathered. "I wish I had advice for you for the coming years, but I only have arrived a handful of days ago. My nieces are much older and will make their come-outs this spring."

"I assume you will be escorting them."

He shrugged. "Do I have a choice?"

Both men chuckled and Westfield said, "Most men are partial to boys, but I find I quite like having a daughter. I hope you, too, will come to enjoy your nieces as much as I do my Norrie." He glanced about. "What brought you to this establishment today?"

"I am having Mr. Farmington create an entire new wardrobe for me. My valet has looked over his work and assures me that Farmington is up to snuff."

Parchmann approached them. "Your Grace, forgive the interruption. Since you are still here, you have two more items to try on. And a sample of a greatcoat."

Westfield nodded knowingly. "You are getting everything, I see."

"Except for shirts, Your Grace. I must find a shirtmaker."

"And boots, Your Grace," Parchmann added. "Perhaps His

Grace might have a recommendation?"

"Forgive my cheeky valet, Westfield," Fox said.

"Not at all. He must be taking lessons from Johnson, my valet," quipped the duke. "Why don't you finish up with Mr. Farmington? I will check on my wife and her hat spree and then recommend my shirtmaker to you."

"That would be kind of you, Your Grace."

The duke grinned. "Well, we cannot have a former major-general looking like a slob in Polite Society."

Fox laughed aloud. "I shouldn't be long."

"Neither will I."

Westfield was as good as his word and returned a few minutes later, chatting with Fox as he finished with the tailor.

As Parchmann helped Fox into his officer's red coat, he told Fox in a hushed tone that Westfield was one of the most respected noblemen in England and advised that Fox become chummy with him.

"Would you care to do that for me, Parchmann? Or shall I have you stay here and continue your consultation with Farmington regarding my wardrobe?"

The valet gave him a sour look. "I will remain behind, Your Grace. While Miss Colebourne had impeccable taste and her selections were acceptable, I am needed here to finish with Mr. Farmington."

"Then I will see you at home, Parchmann," Fox said airily, accompanying the duke next door.

"Did your wife find a few hats? The owner of the millinery shop is helping to dress my nieces for their come-outs this Season."

"Miss Colebourne?" Westfield asked. "I did meet her. She seemed quite lovely."

"Yes, Miss Colebourne," he said as they entered the shop.

Immediately, Fox's eyes were drawn to the beautiful redhead talking with Delaney Colebourne. They were laughing, and he thought if no one had known, they might think the two of them had been friends for many years.

"Ah, there you are, Daniel," the duchess said. "And you must be Abington. Your nieces are delightful young women."

He took her hand. "It is good to meet you, Your Grace. Thank you for the compliment, but I had nothing to do with the girls. I am only reaping the benefits of becoming an uncle to them since my recent return to England."

"Yes, they told me you had been at war. A major-general?"

"You have a good eye, Your Grace."

"I am a painter and enjoy observing others and all aspects of life."

"You paint?"

"Yes. I am a portrait painter."

His nieces joined them. "Oh, you should have Her Grace paint you, Uncle Fox," Eliza declared. "Mama and Papa had their portraits done, both separately and together." She sniffed. "Probably the longest they ever spent together in a room."

"My lady," Miss Colebourne said, her tone ominous.

"I am sorry, Miss Colebourne. It was an indiscreet remark. I will think before I speak in the future."

"How did everything go?" he asked Miss Colebourne.

"The girls have given us their preferences, and we have shared with them what we believe would look best on them. They have had their measurements taken, and we are about to head off to the two fabric stores I mentioned." She turned. "Fanny, would you bring Her Grace's boxes, please?"

"You sold hats to Her Grace?" Fox asked. "Good for you, Miss Colebourne." He looked back to the duchess. "Did Miss Colebourne try to warn you away from purchasing anything from her?"

"She did, Your Grace. I, for one, do not care what the loathsome Lord Kinnison has demanded. I plan to make that known."

"Hmm, this sounds like a story I should hear," Westfield said. "I know of the new Lord Kinnison and have seen him at my club, but we have not been introduced."

The duchess slipped her hand through her husband's arm. "I will tell you all about it. Or we can talk about it at tea tomorrow. Did you ask His Grace?"

"Balderdash! I forgot. Would you care to come to tea tomorrow, Abingdon?"

"I would like that very much."

"Good. I know my duchess is itching to paint. Our carriage is ready. The coachman notified me that he found a blacksmith and a quick repair was made to the horse's shoe. Shall I take you home, my love? Then His Grace and I could go to White's." Looking back to Fox, Westfield said, "I doubt you have had time to go to your club."

"No, I have barely arrived," he admitted. "I am happy to accompany you to White's. Miss Colebourne, I will see you and the girls back at my townhouse then?"

"Yes, Your Grace. I can give you a full report of our day when you return. My seamstresses will also be moving in this afternoon after we have chosen bolts of fabric to get them started."

The duchess turned to Miss Colebourne. "I am so happy we were forced to stop because it led to our meeting, Miss Colebourne. I look forward to taking tea with you and His Grace tomorrow afternoon."

Now, that was interesting. Fox hadn't known Miss Colebourne would be coming.

"Perhaps we could go together to the Westfields' residence, Miss Colebourne."

"It is something we can work out tomorrow, Your Grace," she said.

Everyone left Delaney's Designs, and she locked the door.

"I will be with you in a moment, Your Graces," Fox said, heading to his own carriage to help his nieces and Miss Colebourne into it.

"Oh, no. I will walk with the others," she told him. "It is but a few blocks."

"You will not," he insisted. "I will find them a hansom cab."

He took her hand, that pleasant tingling moving through him as he did so and handed her into the carriage.

"We can walk, Your Grace," one of the seamstresses said. "It's only a couple of blocks."

"All right. But I will send my carriage for you and a wagon to help move your things. Tell Miss Colebourne I said so, and she can instruct my butler if I am not home in time to tell him so."

"Thank you, Your Grace," the trio chimed in unison.

"What are your names?" he asked. "I should know them if you are going to live under my roof."

"I'm Ruth. This is my sister, Dilly, and our friend, Fanny."

He nodded to them. "Thank you for taking care of my nieces. I appreciate the time and effort you will put into their come-outs."

Fox returned to the duke's carriage. Westfield stood outside the vehicle, waiting for him.

"That was quite decent of you, Abington," he said. "You must have been an excellent officer who truly cared for his men."

"I did, Your Grace. And I miss them every day."

The two men climbed into the carriage, the duke sitting beside his wife and Fox opposite them.

"I quite like Miss Colebourne," the duchess said as the carriage began to move. "As I browsed through her shop, I was amazed at her talent. She told me she had designed every hat in the shop. It is a pity what Lord Kinnison did to her."

He found his ire toward the earl bubbling up again. "I could not agree more, Your Grace. Miss Colebourne is most talented. I am lucky that she agreed to help with my nieces' wardrobes. I hadn't the foggiest notion what to do to launch the girls into Polite Society. Apparently, their mother hadn't told them much of anything and their father ignored them."

"But you like your nieces, don't you, Your Grace?" the duchess said, her gaze intense.

"I find I do. Even though I have no experience with children, Grace and Eliza are interesting individuals."

"Do you find Miss Colebourne interesting?" the duchess pressed.

Fox felt himself grow hot. "I admire Miss Colebourne quite a bit."

"What her half-brother did to her was appalling."

"I agree. And I plan to make it up to her," he said fervently.

Mirth filled the duchess' eyes. "I thought I caught a spark between the two of you."

He tamped down his surprise at her remark. "I realize that I will need to wed. I must provide an heir. I believe Miss Colebourne would make a far better duchess than some simpering young miss the age of my nieces. Miss Colebourne is the daughter of an earl—even if on the wrong side of the blanket—and she has a grace and maturity about her that cannot be taught."

"Does she know how you feel?" the duchess asked.

He shook his head. "She knows I am attracted to her, but she has no idea I have decided to offer for her. She thinks I will attend the Season with Eliza and Grace and find some perfect young woman to become my duchess. I don't want young. I don't like perfection. I need Miss Colebourne."

The duke finally chimed in. "Then follow your heart, Abington. I did—and I have never regretted it for a moment." He lifted his wife's hand and kissed her fingers, their heated gazes locked on one another.

The intimate gesture shocked Fox. Then he found he wanted the same with Delaney Colebourne.

"You are new to the *ton*, Abington," the duke continued. "We freely offer our help to you in navigating its ways." His eyes lit with amusement. "And with helping you win Miss Colebourne's heart."

"I am touched by your offer of friendship," he said frankly, thinking this couple unique. "I do believe I will need all the help I can get in convincing Miss Colebourne to become my duchess."

The Duchess of Westfield rubbed her hands together in glee. "Oh, I do love a project such as this. Bringing two people who love one another together."

Fox stiffened at her words. "I said nothing about love, Your Grace."

The duchess looked at him knowingly. "You didn't have to, Abington. It was obvious."

CHAPTER ELEVEN

T HEY DROPPED THE Duchess of Westfield at home, and then the coachman took them to White's. On the way, the Duke of Westfield told Fox a little about the establishment.

"It is a good place to go and see friends," the duke said. "You can sit and read your newspaper and depending upon the time of day, have a cup of tea or coffee—or something stronger. I enjoy going there with three of my friends, the Dukes of Linberry, Stoneham, and Bradford."

Fox wondered if dukes had a tendency to only associate with other dukes. "Will these dukes be there this afternoon?"

"None of them are in town at all for this Season. The Duchess of Linberry gave birth to their first child, a son, last month. The Duchesses of Stoneham and Bradford will both deliver their first child sometime in April."

"Then I am sorry I will not be able to meet them," Fox said.

"They—like me and Margaret—value family. I mentioned to you our daughter, Lady Lenora, who was a year-old last month. Norrie is a joy to me each and every day."

He frowned, not quite understanding this man once again discussing his infant. Of course, Fox had never truly been around children, growing up alone with no siblings close to his own age.

Westfield quickly picked up on his ambivalence. "You seem puzzled by the fact that I take such pride in a daughter. True,

Norrie cannot be my heir, but I hope my duchess and I will have many more children. If all of them turn out to be girls, it won't bother me in the least. Most of those in the *ton* have children and then promptly forget about them. I—and my friends—have a much different philosophy."

Fox shared, "My father died when I was but two years of age. I do not know what our relationship would have been like. As for my mother, I rarely saw her. She lived in London a good part of the year and left me behind at the dower house at Crosshaven after she remarried. The housekeeper and my tutor were more parents to me than she was. Then I went away to school. There were entire years I did not lay eyes upon Mama."

Westfield looked knowingly at him. "And you want more for yourself and your children, don't you?"

"I actually do. I had never thought to have children, being a career army officer. With this new chapter in my life, I find my priorities changing." He hesitated and then said, "I hope I wasn't too bold sharing with you my interest in Miss Colebourne."

"Not at all," the duke assured him. "In fact, I am happy to keep your confidence and will not share it with anyone else. Miss Colebourne seems delightful. I can see why you were drawn to her."

"But I do not love her," Fox insisted.

Westfield studied him a moment. "There is a line in one of Shakespeare's plays, *Hamlet*, I believe. 'The lady doth protest too much, methinks.' It is quite all right to fall in love, Abington. I would highly recommend it. I, too, did not think love was for me, but Margaret and I are a love match. Our love makes my life richer and me stronger every day. There is no shame in loving a woman. In fact, it takes a great deal of strength and patience, sometimes. Yes, Polite Society will think you have gone mad if you are seen showing you love your wife. I say bugger them all. In the end, it is your happiness—and hers—that counts."

"Although I have not been exposed to the *ton*," Fox said, "I fear they would not accept Miss Colebourne because of her background. I believe they would be judgmental, not only because she is illegitimate, but because of her being in trade. It does not matter to me because I see spending a great deal of time in the country at Crosshaven. I have yet to visit my country seat since I have returned, though, or any of my other properties. As I mentioned, I grew up at the dower house and never met my half-brother when he assumed the dukedom. I have never even set foot in the main house. It hurt me back then, but I suppose he felt hurt, as well, with his father remarrying after his mother's death and producing me."

"And you bore the brunt of his hatred," Westfield said.

"Most likely. But I plan to be the best duke I can be and look after his girls to the best of my ability. They, too, were ignored by their parents, mostly because they were girls."

"Polite Society does not know what they are missing," Westfield declared. "I rather enjoy being the father of a daughter and look forward to watching her mature over the years. As far as the *ton* accepting Miss Colebourne? I know she runs her own business with her millinery shop."

"She does design all her hats, but she no longer sells them," Fox told him.

Quickly, he explained what had been left unsaid during their carriage ride. How close Delaney had been to her father, causing the jealous outburst from her half-brother when he became the new earl.

"Kinnison threatened others in Polite Society with the cut direct if they patronized her shop. Overnight, her business dried up last spring. She is ready to sell the building and move elsewhere to try and start a new life. I would rather her start one with me. I only worry about the *ton* accepting her and our children."

Westfield chuckled. "I—and the three friends I mentioned who are dukes—seem to be experts at marrying unsuitable women. Margaret painted portraits before our marriage, and I have encouraged her to keep at it. My friend Linberry's wife plays several instruments and composes music. He, too, has insisted that Fia continues following her passion despite her status. A new friend I made only last Season, the Duke of Stoneham, wed Miss Nalyssa Shelbourne, who was known for taking men who had inherited titles—second sons to distant cousins—and turning them into gentlemen. Most likely, she will continue along that avenue, as well. As for the Duke of Bradford's wife, she designs and sells furniture. I cannot see her stopping that anytime soon.

"So you see, Abington, you would be in good company in marrying Miss Colebourne and encouraging her to continue with her designs and her millinery shop. After all, you are a duke and could give the cut direct to Lord and Lady Kinnison if you wish to. Polite Society will always follow a duke and his duchess over anyone else."

"I had not even thought of her continuing her work, but I know it is important to her. You can just look at her creations and see how talented she is." He paused. "Are we truly this powerful? Being a duke?"

Westfield shrugged matter-of-factly. "It is so. You simply must choose to use the power you hold for good. Make no bones about it, Abington. If you decide to wed Miss Colebourne, society will fall into line and fawn over her the same as they will you. I encourage you to follow your heart, Your Grace. If Miss Colebourne is your choice, persuade her of that."

The carriage slowed, and they went inside White's, exploring the various rooms on different levels. It was not as crowded as Fox would have thought, but then again, it was still early yet, being only March. He assumed by the time the Season was in full swing next month that White's would be buzzing as a beehive every day.

As they went through the place, the duke introduced him to a few gentlemen. After leaving their company, he would tell Fox about each of them. He noticed there were some Westfield skipped altogether, and Fox supposed that was for a reason. Then he heard his name.

"Fox? Nigel Foxwell?"

Turning, he saw a man sitting in a chair, holding a newspaper. Happiness filled him at the sight.

"Morton!" he declared.

His old friend tossed aside the newspaper and leaped from his chair, throwing his arms about Fox, clapping him on the back enthusiastically.

"What the devil are you doing in London?"

"You are looking at the new Duke of Abington, my friend."

"What? Abington is dead?"

"Yes, he and his wife both contracted the pneumonia and went within a day of one another November last."

Then remembering his manners, he turned. "Your Grace, may I introduce Lord Morton, my closest friend at university?"

The two men shook hands, and Morton said, "It is good to finally meet you, Your Grace. And you already know Fox? I mean, Abington. Sorry. It will take me time to adjust to referring to you the correct way."

"I hope I am always Fox to you," he said to his friend.

"Then I would be honored to call you Fox in private. For now, though, you remain Abington in public."

Fox watched Morton studying him. "I simply must introduce you to Lady Morton. I have told her stories of our hijinks over the years." Then he smiled. "She has a sister, Abington. A quiet, pretty one about six years younger than the two of us. Her husband was a captain who lost his life at the Battle of Ciudad Rodrigo."

"That was a violent conflict," he agreed. "I am sorry to hear of your sister-in-law's loss."

"Her loss could be *your* gain, my old friend. You are going to need a wife. Of course, being a duke, you will have your pick of the litter, but I can vouch for Mrs. Damson's good character. Why don't you come for dinner tomorrow night? I would ask you for tonight, but we only arrived in town a few hours ago. Lady Morton would have my head on a platter if I wanted a guest on our first night in town. She likes to get settled in. We have three children, and it takes time to get everyone back into a routine when we return to town each year. But Mrs. Damson has been living with us, and so she will be in attendance at dinner. It would be good for the two of you to meet."

Fox had no desire to meet up with another woman, considering he had decided to make Delaney Colebourne his wife. Yet Morton was a dear friend from the past, and so he said, "I would be happy to come and sup with you and your family."

"Splendid. Let me give you my card. I will jot my address upon it."

Morton did so, handing over the card to Fox. "Come at seven tomorrow evening. We can have drinks and get to know one another all over again before dinner." Morton placed a hand on Fox's shoulder and squeezed it. "It is very good to see you again, Fox. It was also nice meeting you, Your Grace," he told the duke.

Fox and Westfield returned to their tour and finally found a corner with two chairs. Taking them, Westfield smiled.

"I told you it would start quickly, but I didn't think you believed me. It is good that you connected with your friend and that he is thoughtful enough to seek a new husband for his sister-in-law."

"I accepted his invitation out of selfishness," he admitted. "I do want to visit more with him and meet his wife. As far as his sister-in-law goes? I am sorry she lost her husband, but I have made up my mind."

"You said you do not love Miss Colebourne," Westfield pointed out. "I highly recommend a marriage rooted in love, Abington. Perhaps you should meet this pretty widow and other eligible women during the Season. You may find someone who appeals to you even more than Miss Colebourne does, a woman you will come to love."

"I promise to give it time," he told his new friend, not sharing that he would never change his mind.

Delaney Colebourne was the one for him. Despite what

Westfield preached to him, a marriage did not have to involve love. Fox believed as long as he and his wife shared a mutual respect and they enjoyed one another's company, that would be more than enough to be successful in their marriage. He wanted more than a marriage of convenience, where he would go a separate way from his wife. He wanted a companion and friend, as well as a lover.

Over cups of delicious coffee, he passed an enjoyable hour with Westfield, who clued him in to some of the odd, unwritten rules of Polite Society, and then they left White's. The coachman dropped Fox at his townhouse.

Westfield said, "I look forward to having tea with you and Miss Colebourne tomorrow afternoon." The duke offered Fox his hand and he clasped it. "I hope we will become firm friends, Abington."

"I hope for the same, Your Grace. Why don't we start with you calling me Fox?"

CHAPTER TWELVE

D ELANEY BREAKFASTED WITH Mary and then took a hansom
cab to the Duke of Abington's residence. She knew she
should have gone around to the back for admission but boldly
walked to the front door and knocked.

The footman who answered actually greeted her by name.
"Good morning, Miss Colebourne. Please, come in."

She did so and replied, "Good morning," in return before
making her way up the grand staircase. She came across Lady
Grace, who was descending.

"Good morning, my lady," she said cheerfully.

"Hello, Miss Colebourne. I was just going to breakfast.
Would you care to join us?"

"Thank you, but no. I already ate before I arrived, my usual
tea and toast with a poached egg. I am a creature of habit. I have
much to do today, however."

"Uncle Fox told us that the two of you are going to tea at the
Duke and Duchess of Westfield's this afternoon. I was thrilled to
meet her yesterday. She really is as beautiful as the newspapers
say."

"Her Grace does have an incandescent beauty," Delaney
agreed. "More importantly, she is most kind. As for your uncle
and me attending tea together, we are merely two invited guests.
Her Grace may have asked others, as well."

"Uncle Fox said he liked both of them very much. That they were down to earth." Lady Grace frowned. "I thought that a most unusual description for a duke and his duchess."

"You will meet many during your come-out Season who are a bit snobbish. Hopefully, though, you will come across more people who are as charming and friendly as the Westfields."

Delaney's dislike for the ton in general did not keep her from liking individual members of it. Yes, she had had a great number of haughty clients who seemed to barely tolerate her as little more than a servant when they came to her establishment, looking for the perfect hat. Still, on the other hand, a handful of titled women had been gracious to her and her staff.

Looking to this young woman, she added, "Although you may be the daughter of a duke, my lady, it is always good to be polite to all you encounter, be they duke or charwoman."

"I try to do that very thing, Miss Colebourne." Her nose wrinkled. "My sister is too caught up in titles, though."

"You cannot control others and their actions, Lady Grace. Do not worry about your sister. Focus on yourself and your experiences. I bid you a good day."

Delaney climbed to the top floor of the townhouse and continued on to the schoolroom. Entering it, she saw Fanny, Ruth, and Dilly already hard at work.

The three women greeted her, and she checked with each to see what they were working on. She opened the satchel she had brought and laid out several pages for both Lady Eliza and Lady Grace, telling the others to stop a moment and come look at them.

"Here is where we will keep a record of each gown and its progress," she told the three. "There will be a page for each gown, and we will check off every step until it is completed. At the top, I have listed what type of event the gown shall be worn to and which young lady will wear it. Once invitations begin coming in, it will be easier to designate a specific gown for an event. I had an idea which I wanted to speak to you about. Since both our clients are exactly the same size, their gowns are interchangeable."

Ruth frowned. "But Miss Colebourne, we all know a lady never wears the same gown during a Season."

"True, but once a gown is seen in public, I do not wish for us to retire it. One way to change it is to dye the fabric. Another would be to trim it in a different fashion. We could do that with several of the gowns we spoke of and let the other sister wear the gown with its new adjustments."

"That is an excellent idea," Fanny proclaimed. "Dyeing the gown alone will help in changing its appearance but embellishing it with different trims or adjusting the sleeves could make a huge difference."

Ruth nodded. "Especially if is worn by a different sister. It will be unexpected."

"It would save us time in sewing," Dilly observed. "I quite like the idea, Miss Colebourne." She hesitated. "Are you going to tell the young ladies of your plan?"

"I haven't quite decided," she admitted. "They will have so many gowns they will be trying on, they might not even notice."

Dilly snorted. "Lady Grace might not—but that Lady Eliza? Nothing gets past that one."

"Then I will share this idea with them. For now, get back to your sewing. I will be working on more designs and patterns."

Delaney sat at the long table, where countless numbers of Foxwell pupils must have sat over the years, and opened her sketchbook. While sketching hats had been her life for a good many years, she had forgotten how she loved drawing designs and sewing gowns for her dolls years ago. She truly wanted both Foxwell girls to make decent matches and was eager to design for them.

Hours passed and both Lady Grace and Lady Eliza stopped by the schoolroom to see what was going on. Delaney showed them the designs she had been working on for both of them, and they discussed which ones they liked best. Lady Eliza had Delaney make a few changes in some of the sketches, and she praised the girl's eye for detail.

"If you were not insistent upon wedding a titled nobleman, my lady, you could have had a future as a dress designer. I do have something I want to discuss with you, though."

Delaney explained her idea of remaking gowns already worn and having the other sister wear the new version.

Lady Grace said with enthusiasm, "This would certainly help speed things along. I think it a lovely idea, Miss Colebourne." She turned to her sister. "What do you think, Eliza?"

The girl crinkled her nose. "I am not certain I like this. I have never worn hand-me-downs. If I am going to catch a marquess or a duke, I cannot be seen in an old, tired gown."

Delaney said sharply, "Wearing a gown your sister has worn for a few hours is not a hand-me-down, my lady. I can assure you that the gown would look so different each time that you would not recognize it."

Mollified somewhat, Lady Eliza said, "I would need to see the gown before I agreed to wear it."

"I can accept that," she said, knowing she and her three seamstresses would do more than enough to please this headstrong young woman.

Lady Grace smiled timidly at Delaney. "I am happy with whatever you and the others make up for me, Miss Colebourne. I trust your judgment and sense of fashion."

"Thank you for the vote of confidence, my lady."

The daughters of the household left, and the seamstresses returned to their work. Delaney, however, left her sketches on the table and rose, telling the others that she had an engagement to attend.

She left the duke's townhouse and walked from the square, hailing a hansom cab back to Delaney's Designs. She wanted to change her gown before she went to tea with the Duke and Duchess of Westfield. She thought about the kindness the duchess had already shown her and knew she needed to tamp down any desire on the woman's part to try and publicly defend her.

Mary helped in changing Delaney's gown, and she slipped into a spencer and bonnet since the day was still cool and the March wind brisk. She bid Mary farewell and went downstairs. A carriage stood in front of her shop.

And the Duke of Abington was on the pavement beside it.

Despite everything, her heart began to race at catching sight of him and butterflies exploded in her belly.

The duke stepped forward. "I thought I would escort you to tea this afternoon, Miss Colebourne."

"That was thoughtful of you, Your Grace," she said quietly, trying to get a grip on her emotions.

She wanted to do everything she could to push this man away. She couldn't be in close proximity with him. The fact they were already attending tea together today was difficult enough. Every time she looked at this man, she yearned for his touch.

"Then shall we?" he asked, taking her hand and helping her into his elaborate, ducal carriage.

Sitting on the plush cushion, she thought of how she had never known such luxury and was now becoming spoiled by riding in Abington's carriage. Instead of sitting across from her, however, the duke took the seat beside her, his side nestled against hers, causing heat to ripple through her. And longing. A deep yearning for something she had yet to put a name to.

"I spent a pleasant afternoon with His Grace yesterday," Abington told her. "He introduced me to several members at White's. Something tells me that Their Graces are quite different from most people in Polite Society."

"I could not agree more," Delaney said. "The duchess was most friendly to me during our encounter yesterday. Having dealt with members of the *ton* for several years, I can see she has a friendliness and forthrightness about her which few of her rank display."

"The duke seemed quite the same to me. His offer of friendship was unexpected but most welcome."

They sat in silence the remainder of the way, Delaney constantly aware of the duke's heat and scent.

Arriving at the Westfield townhouse, they were taken upstairs to the drawing room, where the duke and duchess greeted them warmly.

"I am delighted that you could both come to tea today," the duchess said. "I hope you will enjoy what Cook has prepared for us."

The teacart was rolled in by two maids, and the duchess poured out for the four of them. Delaney bit into a raspberry scone and thought it was the best she had ever tasted. She told the duchess that.

Looking at the tea tray piled high with sandwiches and sweets, she added, "I am used to a much simpler tea each afternoon. This is both elaborate and delicious."

"I like tea better than any other meal," Westfield confided. "I do not know if it is the type of food or the more relaxed atmosphere, but teatime is one of my favorite times of day." He caught his wife's hand and brought it to his lips for a kiss.

Delaney had read in the gossip columns about the duke and duchess' courtship and the duke's daring marriage proposal, where Westfield had dropped to one knee in the midst of dancing the waltz and proposed in front of the entire *ton*. The newspapers had proclaimed the couple madly in love, and Delaney could see for herself it was true. For a moment, she gazed at them wistfully as they looked at one another, yearning for something she could never have.

Then she sensed Abington's gaze upon her and turned. The heat in his deep brown eyes almost caused her to drop her cup and saucer. All she could think of was his mouth on hers, his tongue deep inside her mouth. She knew they had a physical attraction and was determined not to pursue it under any circumstances. She needed to learn from the past and her own parents' relationship. They had been from much different classes of society and while they brought one another happiness, her mother had recognized she would never be accepted in the earl's world and maintained her independence.

Delaney could not let things progress between her and the Duke of Abington. Unlike her mother, she did not believe she wanted or needed a man. Yet the way the duke had made her feel, even now, caused her breath to hitch slightly. She sipped from her teacup and then set down the saucer, afraid her shaking hands would betray her thoughts.

"Daniel and I have discussed what Lord Kinnison has done to sabotage Delaney's Designs," the duchess said.

"I was appalled at a gentleman acting in such a manner," the duke said. "Kinnison might be a lord of the realm—but he is no gentleman. Please let my wife and me do what we can to help you, Miss Colebourne."

"I am grateful for your interest, Your Graces, but there is simply nothing to be done. My business dried up instantly last Season. No one will ever again buy my hats in London. That is why I am thinking of relocating my millinery shop to Buckinghamshire. My clientele will be different, but that is not what is important to me. I thrive on staying busy, and I enjoy exercising my creativity. The citizens of High Wycombe and beyond will hopefully take to my designs."

"I still think Lord Kinnison should be brought to heel for his outrageous behavior toward you," Abington interjected.

"No," she said firmly. "There is no need for any of you to become involved in this sordid business. As far as I am concerned, it is in the past. Delaney's Designs has no more patrons. My focus now is on seeing Lady Grace and Lady Eliza dressed appropriately for the Season and helping them make good matches. After that, I will leave London. I appreciate your concern, but the battle is already over. A wise soldier knows when a defeat cannot be turned around."

"It is wrong for Kinnison to chase you from London," Abington insisted.

"I do not look at it that way at all, Your Grace. Instead, I view it as a new opportunity for myself. I can always say that some of the most influential women in Polite Society wore my creations. That gives me great satisfaction. Every woman, however, should have a quality hat or two in her possession. If I can help others of lesser means look and feel their best when they dress, it will make me as happy as providing hats for members of the *ton*. I would ask that the three of you respect my feelings in this matter and hopefully agree to change the subject now."

"We will respect your wishes, Miss Colebourne," the Duke of Westfield said. "I do hope, however, that you would be willing to come to the ball which we plan to host. It will open the Season this year."

The thought of attending a ball hosted by a duke and duchess overwhelmed Delaney. While she would love to attend, simply to see all the fashions on display and the way in which the ballroom had been decorated, as well as see her charges dance, she would be completely out of place.

"While it is a gracious invitation you extend to me, Your Grace, I must decline. I am not a member of Polite Society and not only would I be uncomfortable, I would most likely make others uncomfortable with my presence."

"You are a friend to me now, Miss Colebourne," the duchess insisted. "I invite whomever I wish to our home."

Delaney shook her head. "Once again, Your Grace, I will respectfully decline. I thank you all the same for thinking of me."

The topic shifted to Norrie, their daughter who was walking now and getting into everything.

"I would take you up to the nursery to see her, but she has a cold," the duchess said. "She has slept a good deal today. You must return another time, Miss Colebourne, so that you can meet Norrie."

Although she hated to encourage a friendship with this caring woman, knowing no good could come of it, she said, "I would enjoy meeting Lady Norrie, Your Grace."

The duchess asked about Abington's nieces, and he told a few stories which demonstrated their very different temperaments.

"I enjoyed meeting them yesterday, Abington," the duchess said. "Perhaps we can have you to dinner, and you could bring them along. Miss Colebourne, you should come as well to help round out our numbers."

To discourage further all such topics as this, Delaney said, "I am afraid it would be in poor taste for me to attend a social affair with my employer. Tea today was an exception. Perhaps another time, Your Grace."

Abington cleared his throat. "We should be going, Miss Colebourne. I know you have things to do."

They thanked the couple for a lovely teatime, and Abington led her back to his carriage. Once inside, his temper flared.

"Are you always so prickly?" he demanded. "They were merely asking you to dinner. My nieces already think highly of you and would mimic you in such a social situation. They have had no guidance from their mother. The least you could do is help them regarding etiquette."

Blindsided by this, she quickly apologized. "I am sorry, Your Grace. I did not know the circumstances. I can go over manners with the girls and how to respond in various social situations." She paused. "It is not as if they are heathens."

"But they have hardly been with anyone other than themselves," he said, bitterness tingeing his words. "You could make the difference. I thought that is what I was paying you for."

She bristled at his words. "I am happy to accommodate you in this matter, Your Grace. Thank you for making me aware of it. I will work with Lady Eliza and Lady Grace on this very thing, beginning tomorrow."

"See that you do," he spat out.

Then he turned to her, his eyes stormy. "And you probably could help me with things, as well, Miss Colebourne. I have led a rough life on the battlefield for many years now. Every moment, I fear I am going to do or say something unacceptable and hurt my nieces' chances."

"You were perfectly fine at tea, Your Grace," she said evenly, her own anger bubbling under the surface. "Follow your instincts. I am sure you learned good manners from your housekeeper and tutor. Use your common sense, Man."

He turned to face her, his hands capturing her shoulders. "Common sense tells me to take advantage of our time alone, Miss Colebourne."

Suddenly, his mouth crashed against hers.

CHAPTER THIRTEEN

FOX KNEW HE shouldn't kiss Delaney Colebourne again. He had fully intended to keep his hands—and lips—to himself. He had even promised her that he would not take advantage of her again. He told himself his best move was to continue to get to know her and then bit by bit break down the tall walls that surrounded her.

But desire flared within him, and it seemed he lost all control where this woman was concerned. It was madness. Yet he needed her now as much as he did the very air he breathed.

There was no gentleness to the kiss. No soft, subtle touches. Instead, the kiss was born of fire and need, which rippled through him and pierced his very soul. He thought she might protest and kept enough of his head to release her if she did.

She didn't.

Instead, her fingers pushed into his hair and fastened tightly to it, holding him in place. Fox kissed her with everything he had, and she responded in kind, heat and desire fanning the flames between them. It was as if they were atop a funeral pyre, fire burning all around them, consuming them. In lieu of turning to ash, though, he felt his body burning brighter, stronger. He slipped his hands from her shoulders and lifted her into his lap so that she straddled him.

Ah, better. Her rounded bottom wriggled against him as she

kissed him hard, her breasts pressing into his chest. Fox had never kissed a woman this way, for this long. Yet if all he did for the rest of his days was to kiss Delaney like this, he would do so gladly. Even for all time.

He wanted more. He wanted to worship her body with his mouth and hands and fought that feeling. If he were to have any chance at a future with her, he couldn't make a misstep now. Much as he hated to, he broke the kiss, resting his forehead against hers, their breaths coming harshly.

"Delaney," he said, his voice rough, "we—"

"Don't talk," she snapped, her hands framing his face. "Just kiss me."

Her lips collided with his, and the kiss began all over again. Fox wrapped an arm about her to anchor her to him, but his left hand went to her breast. He began massaging it, hearing her groan into his mouth, the noise whipping him into a frenzy. He broke the kiss again, his lips gliding down her throat and to the swell of her breast. His hand dipped inside her gown and lifted the breast, freeing it.

Then he greedily feasted upon it, licking, laving, kissing, sucking. Delaney moved restlessly against him, causing his cock to balloon. Her fingers twisted in his hair again, almost painfully, and yet he welcomed them. He sucked hard, causing her to whimper, but she held his head tightly against her. Fox let his teeth graze her nipple, and she gasped, "Blimey!"

He chuckled, repeating the action and got a "Crikey!" for his effort.

He had never been with a woman who cursed.

And found he rather liked it.

As he continued his assault on her breast, she let her fingers drift from his scalp to his shoulders. Her nails dug in hard as he kept stroking her nipple with his tongue. She whimpered and then stiffened in his arms.

"What . . . what . . . I don't understand," she gasped as her body began to shudder.

Fox knew what was happening to her. He had never brought a woman to orgasm this way and was delighted to have done so. He kept teasing her nipple while his hand kneaded her other breast.

"Oh, bloody fucking dickens!" she cried, her body now quivering uncontrollably against him, rocking as she found her release.

He stopped what he was doing just so he could gaze upon her. Her face was filled with rapture, her lips plump and tempting. He cradled her nape and brought her mouth to his, his tongue plunging inside her mouth as she continued moving against him.

Fox sensed when the orgasm played out because she went limp against him. He gentled the kiss and then broke it, pressing her head against his chest, stroking her back.

"What *was* that?" she asked, wonder in her voice. "I have never felt so marvelous and so befogged."

He chuckled. "The French call it *la petite mort*. The little death. It is a release of the greatest magnitude."

Delaney raised her head, their gazes meeting. "It certainly was moving. Tell me what it was."

"It is called an orgasm. It is experienced at the height of arousal as your feminine core experiences pleasure."

She grew thoughtful. "We did not have . . . that is . . . we . . ." Her voice trailed off, and her face flamed a bright red.

Fox cradled her face, feeling the heat of her cheeks. "No, we did not engage in sexual intercourse, Delaney. For that to occur, we would—"

"Bloody bollocks!" she cried, scurrying off him and falling onto the cushion opposite him, pulling her gown up to cover her breast.

He grinned. "You have quite the vocabulary."

She fanned her face with her hands. "Papa was the most gentle man, yet he cursed like a sailor." She shrugged. "I picked up on whatever he said. No matter how many times Mama punished me, I would let a curse slip every now and then." She smiled wistfully. "Papa thought it quite humorous."

Fox didn't tell her that he thought it more than humorous.

It aroused him.

He made certain that his hands remained in his lap, covering that very arousal.

"We cannot do that again," she said stubbornly, her bottom lip thrusting out in a seductive pout.

"I did try to stop," he reminded her.

She sighed. "I know. I told you we could not kiss again but . . . it felt so good I did not want you to stop. I know you tried to do so, and I forced you to continue."

Chuckling, he said, "No one forced me. If I did not want to kiss you, I would have kept my lips to myself." He paused. "But I found I very much did want to kiss you, Delaney."

She blew out a long, frustrated breath. "You confuse me, Your Grace."

"You could call me Fox," he offered.

"No. I cannot. You are my employer. We are in business together. No good can come of our . . . kissing. Or these . . . what did you call it?"

"Orgasms."

"Yes. Those. We shouldn't be doing anything that causes it."

He smiled at her. "Usually, it takes more than what we were doing to cause one."

She frowned, clearly clueless. "Such as?"

He shrugged. "It is a little hard to put into words." Looking at her hopefully, he added, "It would be easier to show you."

"No!" she cried. "Enough of these orgasms. I swear you have bloody bewitched me, Fox. I am thoroughly addlepated."

He liked that she had called him Fox.

And he especially liked that she was utterly confused.

"Perhaps another time."

Delaney shook her head. "There can *be* no other time." She crossed her arms protectively, not realizing it merely emphasized and lifted her breasts. "We cannot be alone again. We must always have one of your nieces about or my seamstresses or your servants. I should never have even gotten into this carriage with you," she proclaimed.

"I'm glad you did," he told her, giving her a wolfish smile.

Instead of being angry, she burst out laughing. He loved the joy in that laugh. He loved being with her and being challenged by her.

Hell's bells . . .

He loved *her*.

Fox went utterly still, his thoughts swirling. Yes, Delaney Colebourne was attractive. Intelligent. Charming. Talented. He enjoyed being with her, kissing or not kissing. But it was as if someone had swatted him with a plank, knocking sense into him.

He loved her. He truly, utterly loved her.

"Will you marry me?" he blurted out.

Her eyes grew large. "*What* did you say?"

He couldn't take it back. He didn't want to take it back. "You heard me. I was speaking clearly. Will. You. Marry. Me?"

She let out a string of curses, her cheeks flushed, which only made her that much more appealing to him. Fox let her continue her tirade even as he sensed the carriage slowing and knew they had returned to Delaney's Designs.

"Are you quite finished?" he asked. "Because I would like an answer to my question."

"Absolutely not," she told him. "I do not wish to marry anyone. Ever. Least of all some nob of the *ton*. A bloody duke! No, no, in no uncertain terms. No!" she cried.

He leaned toward her, gripping her knees. "Would you wed me if I weren't a duke?"

Her mouth fell open. She was speechless.

"You cannot hold it against me, being a duke. I wasn't a bloody duke my entire life. The news reached me and turned my world upside down. I once knew my place in the world, Delaney. I was known for my daring and confidence. I was fearless as I led men into battle. Then one letter, one page of writing—*one sentence*—changed my life forever. All of a sudden, I found myself selling my commission and returning to England, the holder of a title I never knew I would possess."

Fox paused. "If I am not leading men into battle, I am lost—and I will never have that opportunity again. I need help becoming the Duke of Abington. I need *you*."

She stared at him a full minute, and he realized the carriage had come to a halt. Any moment now, his footman would open the door.

She must have realized the same for she grabbed his wrists and threw his hands off her.

"I cannot wed you, Your Grace. You have no choice. You now belong to the *ton* and will never escape it, but I *do* have a choice. I never want to be a part of Polite Society. My father understood that. That is why he did not try and bribe some lowly baron with an enormous dowry to take me on. He knew I would be uncomfortable in a society of hypocrites and sycophants."

Delaney wet her lips. "Thank you for your kind offer, but I must decline."

The last word had just left her lush lips when his footman opened the door. Fox bounded from the carriage, finding it suddenly restricting.

He had asked. She had turned him down. As was her right.

Reaching up, he handed her down and escorted her to the door of Delaney's Designs.

"I am not a man who will accept no," he told her.

Her brows arched. "You once told me you were a gentleman. I have given you my answer, Your Grace. Take it like a man. Go find yourself some empty-headed chit and get her with child. It will not be me. It will never be me."

Turning, she reached into her reticule and brought out a key, inserting it in the lock and opening the door.

Looking over her shoulder, she said, "Good day, Your Grace."

Fox watched her close the door and hurry through the shop. He stood, watching her figure recede. Grim determination filled him.

He would do whatever it took—but Delaney Colebourne would be his.

CHAPTER FOURTEEN

"**I** REALLY WISH you had spoken to me about this engagement, Your Grace."

Fox eyed his haughty valet and replied, "I did not realize I would have to allow you full access to my social schedule, Parchmann."

"It is just that you do not have anything appropriate to wear for dinner with Lord and Lady Morton," the valet complained. "While the clothes Mr. Farmington provided you with to get by for a few days are adequate, they are truly not fitting of a duke, much less dinner with an earl and his countess."

"It was good of Farmington to even give me a few extra clothes," he pointed out. "I know he and his staff are working tirelessly to provide for my wardrobe needs. I am not going to let the cut or color of my coat prevent me from dining with my old friend and his wife."

Fox left out the part about Mrs. Damson being in attendance at the dinner. He didn't want to give his valet any further ammunition to fire back at him or add to gossip in his household.

"Perhaps you would prefer to wear your officer's uniform," Parchmann suggested. "After all, you were a major-general, Your Grace. The insignia on your uniform is quite impressive. It would be more than appropriate to wear it this evening."

"Why didn't you say so, Parchmann? Yes, ready my uniform

at once, and I will wear it to dinner with Lord and Lady Morton."

An hour later, he was exiting his carriage and knocking on the door at Morton's townhouse. The butler greeted him and took Fox upstairs to a drawing room. This was the first house in London he had been in besides his own. Then he remembered tea at the Westfields' townhome. However, he saw how his was far more lavish than that of the earl's.

The butler announced him, and Fox entered the drawing room, immediately spying his friend standing next to a dark-haired, attractive woman. Nearby stood another younger, dark-haired woman who resembled the other, whom he assumed had to be the widowed sister-in-law. He moved across the room, pasting a smile on his face. He told himself he was happy to be here and meet his old friend's wife, but he would have to maintain a social distance as far as the widow was concerned. He did not want to give her the false impression that he was here to court her.

Especially since he had already offered for Delaney Cole-bourne.

"Ah, Your Grace, come meet my countess," Morton said. "Darling, this is His Grace, the Duke of Abington."

Lady Morton welcomed him. "It is so good to meet you in the flesh, Your Grace. I have heard quite a number of outlandish stories of your days at university with my husband. It surprises me that either of you got an education, let alone your degrees, with all the horseplay you participated in."

He chuckled. "Those days are long behind me, Lady Morton. The army certainly made a man of me. When one goes to war, one must grow up quickly and set aside foolish pranks."

Turning, he faced the countess' sister and saw the woman's face drained of color. Only then did Fox realize that wearing his uniform to dinner this evening had not been a wise move. Most likely, his bright red coat reminded Mrs. Damson of her late husband.

"And this is Mrs. Damson, Lady Morton's sister," his friend

ALEXA ASTON

continued. "His Grace."

Fox took the widow's hand and said, "My condolences to you, Mrs. Damson. Morton told me of your husband's loss at Ciudad Rodrigo. I am certain he fought valiantly and represented England well."

Tears welled in her eyes as she said, "Thank you, Your Grace. It was quite a blow to learn of my husband's death a year ago. I had wanted to go war with him, but Captain Damson refused to allow me to accompany him to Spain."

Fox knew of a good number of officers who brought their wives to war with them and had never understood the practice. He thought it selfish and that these wives lived hard lives.

"Your husband was merely being protective of you, Mrs. Damson. Camp life can be harsh and is truly not for women."

"It was difficult being separated from him," she continued. "We had been playmates since childhood and always knew we would wed. I have nothing to remember Captain Damson now since our only child died of crib death shortly after his father left for the war."

Pity filled him. "You have suffered a double tragedy, Mrs. Damson. My sympathies go to you. They say time heals all. I hope when your healing is complete that you remember only the good things about your husband and child and do not focus on the sadness you feel now."

"Thank you, Your Grace. You have gotten to the crux of the matter in but a few words."

"Shall we have a drink?" Morton asked, and the butler distributed glasses of wine to the four.

"Come, let us sit," Lady Morton invited.

They moved to a setting of chairs near the fire, and Fox took a seat on a settee beside Mrs. Damson. They spent an hour in conversation, with Fox learning what his old friend had been up to since their graduation from Oxford.

"I mentioned that we have three children," Morton said. "Two girls, who are eight and ten years of age, and our son, who is six years old."

"I would enjoy meeting them sometime soon," he said.

Morton laughed. "You? Meeting children? The Fox I knew wouldn't have cared a whit for a child. Pardon me. Your Grace, I mean."

"No, I have asked you to call me Fox in private. As far as children go, I did not see the value of them in my youth. If you recall, I was my mother's only child and had no other siblings."

"Except Abington," Morton reminded him.

"I never met my half-brother." He turned to Lady Morton. "My mother was the duke's second wife, and my half-siblings were quite a bit older than I was. My father died when I was two years of age, and my half-brother assumed the dukedom. We never came face-to-face, and I knew little about him before I left to join the army."

"It must have been quite a surprise to you then to learn that you were his heir," Mrs. Damson remarked.

"It truly was," he admitted. "I had intended to spend my entire adult life in the military and hopefully retire to a small cottage in the country one day once my service to my country ended. The letter from Abington's solicitor came out of the blue. Not only did I learn I was now a duke, but I also became guardian to my two nieces, Eliza and Grace."

"How old are these girls?" Lady Morton asked. "Perhaps they would enjoy playing with our daughters."

"They are old enough to be making their come-outs this Season," he revealed. "My household is upside down now, with three seamstresses having moved in to sew new wardrobes for the girls' debut into Polite Society."

"It must be exciting for them, despite the fact they lost their father. What of their mother?" Mrs. Damson inquired.

"Both the duke and duchess contracted the pneumonia and passed away within twenty-four hours of one another. I am all the girls have now."

"Surely, you must need help in getting them ready for their

come-outs," Lady Morton declared.

"Actually, I have engaged the services of someone to help me with that very thing. Are you familiar with Miss Delaney Colebourne of Delaney's Designs?"

Lord and Lady Morton exchanged a quick look and then returned their gazes to him.

"You have been gone a long time, Fox," Morton said. "You will not know the ins and outs of the *ton*. My advice is to drop any association you have with this Miss Colebourne immediately."

"I could help with your girls," Lady Morton quickly offered. "But any connection with Miss Colebourne is not wise, Your Grace."

Anger stirred within him. "Why not? Do you even know Miss Colebourne?"

Lady Morton flushed. "Well, I did purchase hats at her millinery shop. They were some of the best in London, but I cannot shop there anymore."

"All because of Lord Kinnison's declaration, I assume," Fox said.

Lady Morton gasped. "You know of this, Your Grace? If you do, then you know why you must disassociate yourself from Miss Colebourne. While it is true that she is an earl's daughter and has excellent taste, you do not wish for Lord and Lady Kinnison to—"

"To what, my lady? Give me the cut direct? I am a duke," he said firmly. "No one—especially Lord and Lady Kinnison, whom I do not know—will order me about and tell me who I may or may not associate with. Miss Colebourne's taste in fashion is excellent. I find her manners beyond reproach. She is designing gowns and supervising my nieces' wardrobes. I think it appalling that her half-brother sabotaged her business out of vanity or pride. From what I gather, Miss Colebourne and her father were quite close, and he was very proud of her."

"Now, Fox, calm down," Morton told him. "You have to think of your nieces and how they will be viewed by society."

"What I know is that they will be two of the best-dressed

young ladies making their come-outs this Season, Morton. And they are daughters of a duke, as well. Lord and Lady Kinnison may have ruined Miss Colebourne's reputation and warned others away from her business, but they could not take away her keen sense of fashion. Eliza and Grace will wear Miss Colebourne's creations and be proud to do so. I tell you, no one—no one—will dare say a word because I outrank Lord Kinnison and his father-in-law. I am not the only one who supports Miss Colebourne," he added. "The Duke and Duchess of Westfield also are in her corner."

"Westfield!" Lady Morton said. "Why, he is one of the leaders of Polite Society. True, he and his wife are a bit unconventional, but if the Westfields support Miss Colebourne, the *ton* will follow their lead. And yours, as well, Your Grace."

Mrs. Damson had been quiet throughout the discussion, but she now spoke up. "I think it was wrong of this earl to try and marginalize his half-sister out of jealousy. I admire you, Your Grace, for giving this woman a second chance. It is something everyone deserves."

Fox liked this woman. Under different circumstances, he might have decided to pursue a relationship with her. He didn't want to give her false hope, though.

"You are both sensitive and kind, Mrs. Damson. I know your period of mourning is ending and hope that you will attend the Season with your sister and brother-in-law. When I make friends, I will be certain to introduce them to you."

He watched her reaction to his words and saw understanding glimmer in her eyes. Mrs. Damson knew they were not meant for one another, and as she smiled at him, he knew she accepted that fact.

The butler entered and called them to dinner, and Fox offered Mrs. Damson his arm.

"Thank you for being forthright with me, Your Grace. I know Morton most likely pushed me upon you this evening. I do not wish to be a burden to him and my sister and do hope I will make a match this Season. I am looking forward to meeting your nieces and Miss Colebourne, too."

"She would also enjoy making your acquaintance, Mrs. Damson. I will see if I can arrange a meeting between the two of you."

The dinner was enjoyable, Fox happy to be in his friend's company once more. Afterward, they retired to the drawing room again, and Lady Morton played the pianoforte for them for a quarter-hour.

Fox rose and told them, "Thank you for having me this evening. I enjoyed meeting my good friend's wife and was delighted to make Mrs. Damson's acquaintance, as well." Looking to Morton, he added, "Perhaps we will see one another at White's tomorrow."

"I will be there, Your Grace," his friend said, turning to formality once more.

He returned to his waiting carriage and almost gave his coachman directions to take him to Delaney's Designs. Instead, he climbed into the vehicle and was driven home. On the way, he mulled over the best way to convince Delaney to become his duchess. By the time he arrived home, he had yet to come up with a convincing argument.

As he entered the foyer, Driskell rushed to him. "You have a visitor, Your Grace."

"This late? Who on earth would be calling upon me?"

The butler steered Fox away from the footman at the door and down the corridor toward Fox's study.

"It is a very delicate matter, Your Grace," Driskell said, his voice low. "You will want to discuss it in your study."

A mixture of curiosity and dread filled him as he entered the room. A man of average height and build leaped to his feet, worry clear on his face.

"This is Marsh," Driskell said. "Your butler at Crosshaven."

"Good evening, Your Grace," the butler said.

"Both of you sit," he commanded, taking a seat behind the desk as his two butlers perched on the chairs before him. "Spit it out."

"Your steward—Mr. Fulghum—has quit, Your Grace," Marsh revealed. "He left without giving notice, taking one of the parlor maids with him. The maid's sister works in the kitchens as a scullery maid. She came to Mrs. Marsh, who is my wife and your housekeeper, and shared that Fulghum had told her sister they would be wealthy. Fulghum bragged about skimming from various estate funds."

Fox gripped the arms of his chair. "The steward was stealing from the estate."

"That is what the scullery maid said, Your Grace. Fulghum is the only one who ever looked at the estate's books. Mrs. Marsh and I keep separate ledgers for the household accounts." The butler shook his head sadly. "If the scullery maid told the truth, Crosshaven's steward may have been embezzling money for some time."

"Did this scullery maid have any idea where he and the sister ran off to?"

"No, Your Grace. I came straightaway to London once this came out, however. I knew you would wish to be notified as soon as possible."

He sighed. "I was due to visit my country estate before the Season began. I will leave for Hertfordshire first thing in the morning. You will accompany me in my carriage, Marsh, and catch me up on the workings of the household and estate."

"Of course, Your Grace."

"I will see that Parchmann packs your things, Your Grace," Driskell said. "And notify your coachman of the journey."

"How long will it take to get there?" he inquired.

"Crosshaven is ten miles south of Hertford, Your Grace," Marsh said. "The journey should be twenty miles or so. It is actually quite convenient to London. We will be there in an hour and a quarter, possibly sooner."

"Very well. We will depart tomorrow morning at eight o'clock."

Though he would have liked to have a private word with Delaney before he left, this business was too pressing. Hopefully, by the time he returned to London, he would also have an argument to persuade her to marry him.

"I will be ready, Your Grace," promised Marsh.

"Thank you for coming directly to London and telling me of this, Marsh," Fox praised. "It is good to meet you."

He dismissed both butlers and sat at his desk for several minutes, worried about the shape he would find Crosshaven in and determined to see nothing untoward occurred on his other estates. In fact, he decided a quick tour of his properties would be in order. It would give him time to familiarize himself with what he owned and give Delaney time to think over his offer.

And hopefully, miss him dreadfully.

CHAPTER FIFTEEN

D ELANEY FINALLY ROSE from the bed, having gotten very little
sleep. She had left Abington after his unexpected proposal
and spent hours crying a river of tears and cursing the duke.

Why had he turned her life upside down?

She wished she had never met him. That she had gone to Mr.
Hodgkins' office and put up her building for sale without ever
laying eyes upon the attractive army officer.

Instead, she had let her head be turned by his good looks and
demeanor. She despised the *ton* and everything about it and had
thought him to be different because he was not of it. True, he had
been born into it, the son of a duke, but from what she knew of
his upbringing, he had never walked in that world. He did so
now, though, and did not know what he was getting into. He
would be a flat-out failure if he tried to bring her into Polite
Society by making her his duchess.

Delaney snorted. Her, a duchess? That was rich. Papa would
have had a good laugh at that.

But it was Mama's words that always stayed with Delaney.
Her mother had cautioned her only daughter about men in
general and those of the *ton*, in particular. She told Delaney those
born into Polite Society thought themselves far better than others
and treated those outside their limited class with disdain. That
with Delaney being illegitimate, men of the *ton* would consider

her a woman of loose morals. She was never, ever to become involved with one of them because it would be the end of her.

Once, when Delaney had overheard her father asking for her mother's hand in marriage, she had talked over the offer with her mother after Papa had left. Mama admitted that the earl had asked her numerous times to become his countess. Delaney was excited by the idea, knowing how hard Mama worked on the dairy farm, knowing as a countess she would live a life of leisure.

When her mother told Delaney that she had no intention of ever wedding the earl, Delaney was perplexed. Mama said no matter how much she and Kinnison loved one another, love would never be enough to help her transition into Polite Society. Mama had known the *ton* would look at her with disdain and never accept her as one of them, much less their love child. Mama told Delaney she would be miserable as a countess, not wanting servants to wait upon her and not wanting to feel she was above others. She preferred remaining a dairy farmer who happened to have a handsome lover on the side. She warned her daughter about involvement with men and said in the long run, Delaney should only count upon herself.

Delaney had grown up with a foot in both worlds and yet had never been accepted in either. Yes, Papa hired a governess for her and claimed her as his daughter, but he never took her to any society events. Those who worked on the dairy farm and in the surrounding area always watched her with suspicion.

The first time she truly felt accepted had been when she went to work as an apprentice milliner. She was of the same social status as the other apprentices and through ingenuity and hard work proved her worth.

Once she was ready to open her own shop, she did allow Papa to buy the building, but Delaney used the proceeds from the sale of her mother's dairy farm to pay her employees and buy supplies, which would create her merchandise. She interacted with the *ton* on a regular basis at her shop before her half-brother's edict and found most of them not to her liking. The women, for the most part, were self-centered and treated her in a subservient fashion. Oh, she knew there were exceptions in Polite Society. She had even met two of them in the Duke and Duchess of Westfield. Those exceptions, she gathered, were few and far between. While someone such as the Duchess of Westfield would welcome Delaney with open arms if she wed the Duke of Abington, she knew the majority of Polite Society would look at her as an oddity and speak ill of her behind her back. Why put herself in such an uncomfortable situation?

Children were also a consideration. If she wed the duke, they would naturally have children. Delaney would not see her own flesh and blood ostracized and belittled because their mother had been a common milliner.

No, she had been right to turn down the duke's offer of marriage. Just because they had shared a few intense, passionate kisses, it did not mean they must spend their lives together. It wasn't as if someone had caught them kissing and a forced marriage must occur. Abington would find his duchess soon enough—but it would not be Delaney Colebourne.

She washed her face, pressing a cold compress to her swollen eyes. She would shed no more tears over this duke. In fact, she would tell him today that they no longer needed to interact with one another. She would simply be there for his nieces. As far as helping chaperone them during morning calls from suitors, Delaney thought that inappropriate now. Eventually, someone would mention to Lord and Lady Kinnison that she did so and that might ruin Lady Eliza and Lady Grace's chances of making a favorable match. She would speak to Abington today and explain how he would always need to be present when the girls received their daily callers. Her role would be to stay upstairs designing their gowns and helping to sew when she was needed.

She rang for Mary, and the servant helped her to dress before they breakfasted together.

"You haven't touched your eggs, Miss Colebourne. Is there something wrong?"

She pushed the plate back and picked up her teacup, taking a sip before replying. "No, Mary, I am just simply not hungry this morning. I didn't sleep well. I suppose I am a bit out of sorts this morning. I think I will leave for His Grace's now."

She hailed a hansom cab, the traffic a little heavier than usual. When she arrived at Abington's townhouse, she asked his butler if she might have a word with the duke.

"I am sorry, Miss Colebourne, but His Grace was called away to Crosshaven and left just a few minutes ago."

She shouldn't feel the sadness billowing through her at this news. She shouldn't feel anything for this man.

"Thank you for letting me know, Driskell," she said crisply. "I will speak to His Grace upon his return."

Delaney went upstairs, where the three seamstresses were hard at work. She found Lady Eliza sitting at the schoolroom table, however, a pencil in her hand.

Joining the young woman, she asked, "What are you working on, my lady?"

"Just a few ideas for a new gown." The girl hesitated and then turned her sketch around, pushing it toward Delaney. "What do you think, Miss Colebourne?"

She studied Lady Eliza's drawing. "I think you have quite a talent, my lady. What fabric were you considering using for your design?"

They chatted amiably for several minutes and decided to make a trip to the fabric store to see if new bolts of material might have come in, especially one which would be suited for this design. By now, Lady Grace had also appeared and was eager to accompany them on this errand. Knowing Fanny had a good eye for fabrics, Delaney asked her to join them, as well.

They spent a good two hours going through various bolts of material, selecting another dozen to bring home with them. As they pulled up to Abington's townhouse and went inside, Delaney relaxed, knowing she would not be seeing the duke anytime soon.

FOUR DAYS LATER, Delaney arrived at the duke's townhouse, a dozen new sketches in her satchel. She'd had a moment of inspiration last night and not only drew several sketches of new dresses to be made up, but she had also designed three hats each for both young ladies, along with a few for the duke. She decided she would start working on these hats today and pass along the sketches to the seamstresses if Lady Grace and Lady Eliza approved the designs.

When she entered the townhouse, the footman greeted her and said that Mr. Driskell needed to see her.

"He is in his office, Miss Colebourne. I can take you there."

"Thank you. I have never been there and do not know its location."

The footman led her to the kitchens and beyond, pausing at an open door and knocking on the frame.

"Miss Colebourne is here, Mr. Driskell."

The butler motioned for Delaney to enter and asked her to sit. Then he handed her a letter, saying, "His Grace has written to the both of us. Please read your letter at once, Miss Colebourne, because we must make plans."

She was ambivalent as she broke the seal and opened the letter.

My dear Miss Colebourne —

I am writing to you from Crosshaven, my ducal seat in Hertfordshire. I left abruptly because of a crisis which had occurred and needed my immediate attention. The estate's steward was embezzling funds from the previous duke and absconded with what I believe is a good deal of money, leaving with one of the parlor maids. I have no experience in estate management and cannot make heads nor tails of the ledgers he left behind.

I recalled you mentioned that Lord Kinnison had worked with you, teaching you about financial matters using his own estate's ledgers. You also have said that you manage the books for Delaney's Designs, as well.

I know this is a most unusual request and one which is inconvenient, since you are working with my nieces on their wardrobes now, but I could use someone with your skills and experience to explain these matters to me. Someone I can trust. I do not have many choices available to me, Miss Colebourne. In fact, you are my only choice to help me figure out these matters.

I know it is a great deal to ask but if you could find it in your heart to come and tutor me in estate matters, for a few days, I would be most grateful. I would also seek your advice on hiring a new steward, as well as combing through the ledgers to see if you can spot the falsehoods buried within them.

If you agree to come, please let Driskell know. I have written to him of the possibility of you coming to Crosshaven. He will make all of your travel arrangements.

I remain your faithful servant.

Abington

Delaney continued to stare at the page as if reading it, buying time to think on what she had just read. Going to Crosshaven would most likely be a huge mistake on her part. Yet she understood how Abington was struggling in his new role. Thanks to Papa, she did have the experience to help this man. She had lied to herself until this moment—but she finally acknowledged that she had feelings for the Duke of Abington. Strong feelings. Being in close proximity with him would be extremely unwise. If she were in her right mind, she would refuse to help him.

But she had changed from the moment she had met him. She might not wish to be his duchess, but she did want to explore what was between them. Being in the country would make that much easier, away from his nieces and her seamstresses. He had told her there were ways to prevent a babe from forming. She decided not only would she help the duke clean up his estate's ledgers, but she would give herself the freedom to experience one night of passion with him. One night when they could remove all barriers between them and come together.

Would she regret doing so?

Delaney decided she wouldn't. She might not wish to wed him—but she was willing to suffer the heartbreak that would occur for one night with this man. A man she would only admit to herself that she loved.

Glancing up from the letter, she told Driskell, "Please make the arrangements for me to go to Crosshaven," knowing there would be no turning back.

CHAPTER SIXTEEN

F OX RAKED HIS fingers through his hair in frustration, leaning
back in his chair. The estate's records littered his desk, and he
hadn't the background to understand any of it, especially how his
former steward might have taken advantage of the previous Duke
of Abington.

It had been a risk to ask Delaney to come and help him, but
he was at his wit's end. He had tried for two days to figure things
out on his own and in frustration had spent the third day riding
about the estate, meeting various tenants. That was what he
enjoyed, contact with others. He learned a great deal just from
speaking with those farmers and now eagerly looked forward to
the time when he could leave London and spend months in the
countryside. It was also good to be back at his boyhood home. He
had wandered the grounds of this estate as a child and had
enjoyed being out in nature. He only hoped Delaney would come
and rescue him.

Once he had returned from his rounds about the land yesterday afternoon, he had written to Delaney, pleading with her to
come and assist him. He sent a rider immediately to London with
the letter so that she would receive it first thing this morning. He
had been open and honest with her and believed, despite the way
they had parted, she would come because he was in desperate
straits.

When the knock sounded on his study's door, hope filled him as he said, "Come."

Marsh entered and gave Fox a letter, saying, "The messenger you sent to London just returned with this reply."

"Stay," he told the butler as he opened the note. Relief swept through him as he read that Delaney would be arriving today, hopefully by noon, according to Driskell.

Looking to Marsh, he said, "Have Mrs. Marsh prepare our best guest bedchamber for a Miss Colebourne. She has agreed to come and help me with the ledgers. She should be arriving by noon."

"Very good, Your Grace." The butler left Fox to his thoughts.

A giddiness swept through him, knowing he would soon see Delaney again. Fox examined that feeling, the happiness which bubbled up from him in knowing she would be at Crosshaven soon.

Was that love?

Having had no experience with love, he was unsure. He had impulsively thought he loved Delaney, which had led him to offer for her on the spot. What he did know was that he had missed her incredibly during these past four days. He missed her wittiness. Her laugh. That warm vanilla scent that emanated from her. He felt encouraged by the fact that she had agreed to come. Once again, he told himself not to rush things between them. He wasn't very good at listening to himself when it came to her, though. He had decided after kissing her to back away and give her time to get used to the idea of them being together. Instead, he had gone and blurted out that he wished to wed her. No wonder she had rejected his clumsy effort.

He was a former army officer and would show restraint. Even patience. He didn't see these new, fragile feelings for her going away anytime soon. Instead, he would see if they grew during her time with him at Crosshaven. And if they did, he would pray that her own feelings might blossom for him.

Fox did his best to straighten his desk and then paced the

room as a caged tiger, watching out the window for her arrival. He had instructed Driskell to hire a post chaise to bring her to Crosshaven. If she came, they could return in his carriage.

When he spied the bright yellow vehicle coming down the lane, his heart thumped rapidly. He was glad his study overlooked the front lawn and tried to calm himself as the vehicle drew near.

Rising from the chair, he strode from his study and out of the house, wanting to greet her personally. He waved off the footman and opened the carriage door himself, holding up a hand to Delaney. Their gazes met as she accepted it and that ever-present spark flashed between them as it always did whenever they touched.

Helping her down, he said, "Thank you for coming, Miss Colebourne. I already feel relief, knowing that I am in your capable hands."

"I anticipate that I will be able to help you, Your Grace. I believe I can. Papa was an excellent tutor to me and discussed every aspect of estate management with me. His heir apparent had no interest, and so I was the one who soaked up my father's lessons. Hopefully, I will be able to transfer some of that knowledge I gained to you."

He tucked her hand into the crook of his arm and led her inside, where the Marshes awaited.

"This is Marsh and Mrs. Marsh," he told her. "My butler and housekeeper. They will see to your needs during your stay."

"Would you care to go to your room and freshen up, Miss Colebourne?" asked Mrs. Marsh.

"Yes, I would like to do so."

"Mrs. Marsh, if you will wait on Miss Colebourne, you can bring her to the drawing room after she has settled in. Have tea sent if you would and a slice of Cook's spice cake. I am sure Miss Colebourne is famished after her journey."

He looked back to Delaney. "I will see you in a few minutes."

Making his way to the drawing room, Fox circled it a good dozen times, nervousness filling him. Then Delaney appeared, and all his anxiety melted away.

"Come, Miss Colebourne, and have a seat. Our tea should be here soon."

Two maids rolled in the teacart under Marsh's supervision, and Fox asked Delaney to pour out for them.

"Thank you again for coming so promptly," he began. "I know you are extremely busy taking care of my nieces."

She laughed and warmth rushed through him. "Lady Eliza will make certain that everything runs smoothly in my absence. She has even started designing gowns on her own. We went and chose new fabric for one of her designs, and Ruth is currently making it up. Your niece has quite a talent for the work."

"And a strong will?" he said teasingly, taking a sip from the tea she had given him.

"Lady Eliza will always be opinionated, Your Grace, but she is a delightful young lady."

"It is just us, Delaney," he said. "Would you please consider calling me Fox? At least while we are here?"

She worried her bottom lip, causing desire to flare within him, and then nodded. "Just for now. While we are at Cross-haven. I suppose we can be a bit less formal since it is merely the two of us."

He smiled, thinking they were off to a good start.

"When I could not figure out anything in the ledgers, I tossed them aside in frustration and headed out on the estate," he admitted. "It did help clear my head, and I enjoyed meeting several of my tenants."

"I suppose it is different now with you returning as the duke."

"The land is still the same. I wandered it freely as a boy. Being in this house is quite different, however, from the dower house."

"It is a very beautiful house," she complimented.

"I always liked the looks of the outside of it and wondered what it looked like inside. Mrs. Marsh gave me a tour of the place, and it is even larger than my townhouse in London. I think of how much my life has changed since I received the letter informing me that I was the Duke of Abington. Already, my life as a soldier seems far behind me."

"Soldiering is all about meeting challenges," Delaney declared. "Being a duke and taking on ducal responsibilities is simply a new challenge. You will meet it and find success, Fox. I know you will."

He liked hearing his name come from her lips. He wanted his lips on hers and gripped his knees, reminding himself to take things slowly. She was here. She was calling him Fox. He would gladly accept these small victories. They would build upon one another.

At least he hoped so.

"Tell me of my nieces. I have only been gone from them for four days, and yet it seems like much longer."

"Lady Grace was saying just yesterday how much she missed you. You have made quite an impression upon both of them, Fox. Those two were starved for affection. You came in and accepted them for exactly who they are. You listen to them. You tease with them. You are a good role model to them. They will have a better idea what they wish for in a husband because of your treatment of them."

"It is odd to think how quickly I took to them, having never been around children before. Oh, I know they are more young ladies than children, but I still see where they need my guidance. I dread—and yet look forward to—meeting the men who plan to woo them. Something tells me that I will think none of them deserving of my nieces."

She laughed, that rich, vibrant laugh. Fox wanted to hear that laugh until his dying moment.

"This spice cake is quite good. Do you like your staff here as well as you do yours in town?"

"I would say my predecessor—or his duchess—did an excellent job in hiring competent staffs in both places. Things in both households seem to run like clockwork." He frowned. "Except for this situation with my steward."

"Tell me about it," she encouraged.

Briefly, he outlined what he had been told by Marsh, who had learned of the supposed discrepancies from the scullery maid.

"And this maid had no idea where her sister and the steward ran off to?"

"No, she didn't. I interviewed her myself. She's a timid thing, worried about losing her own position in the kitchens because of her sister's rash actions. I assured her that would not be the case. I did learn that my steward was in his early forties and had always had a roving eye since his arrival. Marsh told me that after his departure, several other female servants stepped forward and spoke of the unwanted attention they had received from him."

"If they thought to marry, they might have headed for Gretna Green," Delaney mused. "We need to see the extent of what was stolen from you. You might want to hire a Bow Street Runner to find the pair."

"I am unfamiliar with that, Delaney. Tell me more."

"Bow Street runners do all kinds of things. They began as a small force trying to rid the London streets of thieves. Nowadays, they investigate everything from missing persons to robberies to murder cases."

"That does sound like a good option once we return to London."

"Town," she prompted. "Although I have been working with your nieces on all manner of things, especially how to run a household, I have neglected your own education. No one in the *ton* refers to London as London. They always call it town."

"Ah, another of those unwritten rules. Westfield and I had a conversation about several of those."

"I would encourage a friendship between the two of you, Fox. The Duke of Westfield has a sterling reputation. He would be a good man to associate with."

"I agree. He has three other close friends he mentioned to me, all dukes." Fox chuckled. "I thought at first that dukes only associated with other dukes when he told me about them, but he clarified that. I also ran into Lord Morton, my good friend from university days, at White's. I had dinner with him and Lady Morton before I left for Crosshaven."

"It is good that you have connected with your friend." She set down her empty teacup. "Enough talk. You have delayed the inevitable." She smiled at him. "Let us go examine your ledgers."

As she rose, she picked up two ledgers from a table. He had not even noticed she'd come in with them.

"What are those?" he asked.

"I brought two ledgers for us to study before we look at those from your estate. One is from my own shop and demonstrates how I handle my clients' accounts. It contains records of ordering supplies to create my hats and lists my inventory. Those sorts of things.

"The other is a ledger from Papa's estate, one I learned from. It was decades old but had all the information I needed to become proficient. It became my bible of sorts, as Papa taught me about his own affairs. I will use it to teach you and then leave it in your care."

"No, I could not keep something so valuable."

"I learned my lessons from it and am more than happy to pass it along to you, Fox."

Her eyes gleamed at him, and he wondered exactly what that might mean.

They retreated to his study, and Delaney spent half an hour going through the ledger from Delaney's Designs with him. He saw how organized she was and how neatly everything was noted.

Setting the book aside, she took up the other one she had brought and started from its first page, walking him through it for the next two hours. By the time she finished, Fox had a much clearer understanding of estate management and felt confident he could look through his own books and comprehend most of what was there.

"We have been at it for some time," he told her. "Would you

like to take a break? Stretch our legs?"

"That is a good idea. I find looking at figures can be tiring. It is always good to clear your mind. In fact, we may want to wait and tackle your ledgers first thing tomorrow morning when we are fresh."

"Then why don't we start by taking a walk through my gardens?" he suggested. "They are beginning to bloom, and I have yet to visit them since my arrival."

"I do love flowers. Let me retrieve my spencer. I will meet you in the foyer."

Fox waited for her and watched as she descended the staircase, her posture perfect, her beauty unsurpassed. He met her at the bottom of the stairs, offering his arm to her. They left the house through the front door and walked alongside the length of the house, turning to go around the structure.

When they reached the gardens, she gripped his arm more tightly, and he placed his free hand atop hers. She did not try to throw it off, and it encouraged him. He reminded himself that small steps added up.

Entering the gardens, they strolled slowly. He talked of the estate and some of the improvements he would like to make to it after having spoken to several of his tenants.

In turn, she recommended a way for him to find a new steward for Crosshaven.

"You might consider having one of your other stewards come to Crosshaven. I am certain you receive periodic reports from those men who manage your other estates."

"Yes, Hodgkins mentioned something of this. That these reports came to him because the previous duke showed no interest. I can ask him for those copies and play a more active role than my half-brother."

"If you really like one of those employees, it might be better to bring him to Crosshaven and simply replace him at the smaller estate. Mr. Hodgkins could help guide your decision since he will be more familiar with these estate managers."

"I like that better than hiring someone unknown to me to run Crosshaven. You are full of good ideas, Delaney."

She gazed up at him, a smile playing about her lips. "I have another idea, Fox," she said huskily. "One I hope you will like."

Her hands moved to his waistcoat and gripped the fabric. Delaney yanked him down and he found his mouth on hers.

CHAPTER SEVENTEEN

D ELANEY HAD DECIDED to give her body free rein over her head. She still wasn't interested in wedding the Duke of Abington.

But she certainly wanted to experience more of what might lay between them.

His kisses made her head spin. His touch had brought her to orgasm. And her body craved his. She would selfishly take what she could of him during her short time at Crosshaven and soak up the experience. She doubted she would ever have another lover after this man. He had slowly become her entire world. If she didn't experience everything he could offer now, she knew there would never be another time they could come together.

As she kissed him, Delaney held nothing back. She wanted to be open and feel every single bit she could. His mouth bruised hers. His arms banded tightly about her, crushing her to him. He kissed her as a man dying of thirst, draining her of everything, including her will.

Fox broke the kiss, looking down at her, a bit dazed. She smiled up at him, feeling a bit of feminine pride, knowing he was as affected by their kisses as she was.

What she didn't want was him speaking to her about marriage. Delaney danced a fine line now, knowing she would be asking him to commit his body to her—but only for a short period. If Fox knew she had no intention of marrying him, he would be gentleman enough to turn her down. She couldn't bear that. She needed to experience the act of physical love with this man.

"I would like you to make love to me, Fox," she said breathlessly, seeing his eyes widen. "No talk of tomorrows. Just savor what is between us. Here. Now. Can you do that?"

"I will do anything you ask of me, Delaney," he said, his voice harsh and low. "And I want you to know how much I do want you."

He seized her mouth again, his kiss deep and long, making her toes curl and causing shivers of delight to run through her. Her thumbs caressed his cheeks as she inhaled his marvelous, masculine scent.

The kiss went on until she almost collapsed, her knees buckling. Fox swept her into his arms and moved along the garden's path until they reached a gazebo. He mounted its steps and sat on the bench, cradling her in his lap.

"I used to come here," he said softly. "When I was a boy. I explored these gardens and loved the scent of roses most of all. Abington only came to the property for two weeks around the Christmas holidays. I had this place to myself the rest of the time. I thought these gardens were magical." He paused, gazing deeply into her eyes. "They are. Because I am here in them with you."

His lips returned to hers, his kisses soft and sweet now. Delaney wound her arms about his neck, and they kissed for a long time, her body tingling all over. When Fox broke the kiss, she cursed.

He laughed. "Ah, that's the Delaney I know and love."

She stiffened.

Love?

Surely, he was merely using an expression. He couldn't possibly love her. She closed her eyes and buried her face against his chest, not trusting herself to meet his eyes.

He stroked her hair, murmuring to her, his words so soft she couldn't understand them. Gradually, she relaxed.

Lifting her head, she asked, "When might we couple?"

Looking about, he said, "I would say here and now, but it is too cool and would be far too uncomfortable." Then he grinned wickedly. "I want you in my bed tonight, Delaney. And don't count on getting any sleep." He kissed her softly. "If we do this tonight, you understand things will change between us, don't you?"

She put him off, saying, "We can talk about that later, Fox. Kiss me again."

He grinned. "With pleasure."

She gave over to his kiss, thinking she could keep kissing him through eternity. Delaney pushed aside the guilt that rose within her, knowing she was being dishonest with him.

When they finally stopped kissing, he said, "It grows dark. We must return to the house. You have loose strands of hair to repair."

"I can do so. I have done my own hair all my life."

Quickly, she slipped the pins from it and finger-combed her long, caramel locks, twisting and repinning them. She stood, smoothing her skirts. "Do I look presentable?"

"Only if no one looks at your mouth," he told her. "It is swollen from our kisses."

"Hopefully, no servants will focus on it then. Perhaps I could take a tray in my room for dinner. You could tell Mrs. Marsh that I am tired from my journey and our long afternoon studying numbers. I think it best."

"I can do so." He took her hands in his. "I will come to you tonight when the house quietens. Country hours are observed here, and everyone goes to bed early."

She placed her palm against his cheek. "I will be waiting for you, Fox."

He lifted her palm and pressed a fervent kiss into its center. "Until tonight."

They left the gazebo, walking more briskly than before, returning to the house. Delaney went straight to the bedchamber she had been taken to earlier and sat at the dressing table. Gazing into the mirror, she saw how brightly her eyes sparkled and how swollen her lips were. She touched them reverently with her fingertips, thinking of Fox's mouth on hers—and how she longed for his lips to be other places on her.

Tonight she would learn about the mysteries of lovemaking. She would give her body to Fox. He already possessed her heart and soul. She would savor their time together, knowing it would be short and sweet. Then they would return to very different lives, ones which were not compatible. He would wed a worthy woman and settle into his marriage. She would move to Chapwell Hall and begin a new business. But she would always cherish the memories they made here at Crosshaven.

Dinner arrived a short while later, brought by a maid. Delaney thanked the servant, who said she would return for the tray in an hour.

She picked at the food, her hunger for what was to come consuming her. When the maid came back, she offered to help Delaney undress and get ready for bed. After the servant left, she sat at the dressing table, pulling her brush through her hair, her heart quickening as each second passed. She decided to leave her hair down tonight and went to draw back the bedclothes.

Retreating to a chair, Delaney sat and waited, on edge, finally hearing the light tap on her door. She rose, swallowing hard, knowing there would be no going back from what would happen in the next few hours.

She opened the door and saw Fox in a dark blue banyan, looking so handsome it caused tears to spring to her eyes. Quickly, she stepped aside, and he moved into the room. She closed the door, and he caught her shoulders, turning her so she faced him.

"Thank you," he said.

"For what?"

"For trusting me. I promise to take care of you, Delaney. I

always will," he said, his voice tender.

Guilt swept through her, knowing she was deceiving this good man. She opened her mouth to tell him she couldn't go through with this—but his mouth took hers in a slow, bone-melting kiss. Her good intentions fled, replaced by throbbing need. Desperate for him, she wrapped her arms about his waist, pulling him to her.

He moved her back a step, her body against the door, his crowding hers. Capturing her wrists, he brought them above her head, pressing his body to hers as he kissed her deeply. Delaney groaned, her body shuddering, his masculine scent invading her senses. Fox pinned her wrists together with one hand. His other cradled her cheek and then slid slowly down her body, finding where she had belted the sash to her dressing gown. With nimble fingers, he loosened the knot and parted the dressing gown, his hand cupping her breast.

"Fox!" she cried before his mouth covered hers again, his tongue mating with hers as his fingers toyed with her nipple, tweaking it, dragging his nail across it, causing her to tremble.

Breaking the kiss, he moved his lips to her ear, his teeth tugging on the lobe.

"Do you know how much I want you?" he whispered into her ear.

She shook her head, words beyond her at this point.

"Then let me show you."

Delaney writhed against him as his lips nipped at her throat, his hand moving down her body, cupping her core, which pulsed in an ancient rhythm.

"Do you want me to touch you here?" he asked, rubbing his palm back and forth across the mound.

"Yes," she said, her breathing already ragged.

He moved his hand back to cup her cheek, his lips caressing hers. Then they slid down to her throat again, his teeth grazing it, chills rushing through her. She struggled to free her hands, and he laughed softly.

"No, your hands will only get in the way. Distract me from my mission."

She couldn't help but laugh. "You sound like the major-general you once were. It is not a battle between us, you know."

"No. But I not only want to conquer your whole body, Delaney, I want to win your heart and soul."

He kissed her hard, his free hand bunching her night rail and dragging it up before it disappeared beneath the material. She felt his hand, rough and callused, skimming her thigh and then moving to where her core throbbed almost painfully.

Gazing at her steadily, he said, "I am going to push my finger inside you. You will like it there. You will beg for more."

She swallowed, knowing her eyes went large.

"Blimey," she whispered.

Ever so slowly, Fox began running his finger along the seam of her sex, causing her heart to beat erratically. She held her breath, their gazes locked, wondering when he would do as he promised.

Then he did, pushing his finger inside her and then stroking her deeply.

"Fuck me!" she cried.

"That's exactly what I plan to do," he promised.

She had used the curse word on occasion but really had no idea of the meaning behind it.

His finger teased her, moving slowly, driving her mad. Then it moved faster. Another joined it, stretching her, causing the drumbeat to strengthen. Her entire body now pulsated with some ancient rhythm.

"Blazing tarnation!" she managed to get out as his hand moved faster and faster, the motion heightening her awareness of everything about him. She met each stroke of his hand, pushing against it, craving his touch.

And the pressure began building, building with such an intensity and force that she was about to scream. Fox must have sensed it because he covered her mouth with his, his tongue plunging deep inside, moving in rhythm with his fingers.

Then stars exploded, a pleasurable feeling so intense rocking her that her body spasmed. Delaney shuddered violently as something rippled through her like lightning.

Fox broke the kiss. "That's it, love. Ride the wave."

She did as he instructed, reaching a peak and then crashing down, her body going limp. As it did, he released her wrists and scooped her up, carrying her to the bed and placing her upon it. She watched as he untied the sash to his banyan and slipped from it. He was naked beneath, and all she could do was stare.

His cock had swollen to an enormous size and jutted from a dark thatch of hair. He also had a matting of dark hair on his muscular chest. A line of it trailed down his belly. His limbs looked rock hard, his belly flat.

And his eyes glowed with an intensity that should have frightened her, but she knew it was his desire for her.

She sat up, pushing away from the bed, and wrapped her arms about him, pulling his mouth to hers. As they kissed, he slid her dressing gown off her shoulders, and it puddled on the floor. Fox broke the kiss and captured the hem of her night rail, pulling it over her head and tossing it aside. He wrapped his arms about her again, kissing her hard and long as his cock pressed against her bare belly.

He stepped away from her, placing his banyan on the bed and spreading it out. She had no idea why he did so and didn't have the time to ask. Instead, he swept her off her feet again and placed her atop it, joining her on the bed. His mouth fused with hers as his body hovered over hers. Once more, his fingers teased the seam of her sex.

Then she felt his cock pressing against her. It slid inside her. For a brief moment, a sharp pain erupted, and Delaney gasped. Fox's kiss reassured her, though, as he savaged her mouth. When he began to move, her body joined his, a dance of fire and passion like nothing she could ever have imagined. They moved as one, their sweat-slickened bodies part of some ancient ritual.

The sensation began in her again, building as before. His kiss intensified as he moved deeper and faster. A kaleidoscope of colors erupted around her as her body was awash in pleasure. He abruptly pulled out of her and something warm puddled on her belly. She realized it was his seed. No babe would be made this night. A touch of disappointment filled her as she floated back to earth.

Fox kissed her again and then reached into his banyan's pocket, withdrawing a handkerchief. He used it to wipe her belly clean and then pushed off the bed. Idly, she watched him go to the basin, and he poured water from the jug into it. He rinsed the handkerchief and then returned with it, wiping it against her now-sensitive core.

"There's a bit of blood," he told her. "Not much. You will be sore in the morning, though."

Delaney realized that was why he had placed his banyan across the bed, protecting the bedclothes—and her reputation.

He rinsed the handkerchief again and returned to the bed, slipping the banyan from beneath her and then climbing into the bed, enfolding her in his arms. Her head nestled against his beating heart and its rhythm lulled her to sleep.

When she awoke, she realized he was untangling their limbs and leaving her. She reached up and captured his hand, bringing it to her cheek.

"Don't go," she said.

"I must. If I stay, I will want you again. Your body needs to rest." He bent and kissed her brow. Smiling, he added, "It would not do to be discovered here with you. At least now."

She knew he still intended for them to wed and knew she should tell him that would never happen. It would ruin this moment, though, and so she kept silent.

"Sleep, love," he urged. "You will need your wits about you tomorrow as we tackle my ledgers."

Fox tucked the bedclothes about her and then slipped into his banyan. Delaney watched him leave, knowing he was much too good for her.

But she would have the memory of this night to sustain her for a lifetime.

CHAPTER EIGHTEEN

T HOUGH FOX ONLY had gotten a few hours of sleep, he awoke invigorated. He could not wait for the time when he would awake each morning and find Delaney beside him.

His duchess . . .

He had known they would be more than compatible in bed, based upon the chemistry between them. It went beyond the physical, however. He sensed the emotional bond between them and knew without a doubt that he loved her. He pictured the Duke of Westfield kissing his wife's fingers and Fox smiled, knowing he would show Delaney in little ways each day just how much he loved her.

They would have much to discuss about their future, starting with when their marriage should take place. He was of a mind to purchase a special license the moment they returned to London. No, town. He grinned, thinking of all the small things Delaney was teaching him. He looked forward to teaching her things, too. Already, she had proven a delight in bed, and he looked forward to the growing intimacy between them.

He bounded from bed and rang for Parchmann, who commented on Fox's good mood as he shaved him.

"Miss Colebourne is responsible for it," he told the valet. "She has a head for numbers and the experience I was looking for to help me discover the discrepancies in my ledgers. I believe we will be able to return to town today. Pack my things so they are ready in case I wish for us to leave promptly."

"Very well, Your Grace," Parchmann said.

After dressing, Fox went down to the breakfast room, surprised to find Delaney already there. He drank in the woman who would be his duchess, one who would sit at breakfast with him every morning.

"Good morning, Miss Colebourne," he said brightly, taking a seat near her.

"Good morning, Your Grace. I have already spent a few hours looking over your ledgers this morning and have found the beginnings of when your steward's dishonesty began."

Her words surprised him. "You have already been examining the ledgers?"

A blush tinged her cheeks as she said, "Yes, Your Grace, I found myself awake early this morning and could not go back to sleep. I decided to put the time to good use."

He bit back a smile. "I see. Yes, Miss Colebourne, we will move to my study once we have breakfasted. You can show me what you have found."

Half an hour later, they were seated in Fox's study, several ledgers opened on his desk.

"I went back to the time six years ago when Mr. Fulghum was hired by the previous duke. Fulghum began diverting funds almost immediately. Two months into his tenure here. The amounts were small at first, as if he tested the waters. He grew bolder as more time passed."

"He must have learned how infrequently Abington came to Crosshaven. My nieces confirmed their father kept to his pattern of only returning to the estate once a year during the Christmas season. He preferred town over the country. The duke also showed little interest in any of his country estates. His disinterest gave Fulghum the ability to continue stealing."

Delaney walked Fox through Fulghum's tenure, pointing out small adjustments the steward had made that didn't ring true when regarding other reports from the estate.

"You can see last summer and autumn is when he grew bolder as he doctored the books. The last six months he was employed, he stole quite a large amount. This continued up until he most likely learned you had arrived in England, and so he up and vanished with the parlor maid. It is a substantial amount of money, Fox. Nothing, of course, which would bankrupt you. You are worth a thousand times more than what Fulghum stole. Still, he should not be allowed to get away with such thievery."

"We should return to town at once. Take these ledgers and show them at Bow Street. I want Fulghum found and prosecuted to the fullest extent of the law."

"What of the maid?" Delaney asked. "She most likely is not complicit in any of this."

"We shall see. If the investigation proves she merely had stars in her eyes and was dazzled by this criminal, I will see she goes unpunished. I will have Marsh pack up these ledgers, and we can return to town at once."

"Then I will go and pack my things," she said, rising. "It won't take me long because I did not bring very much."

He caught her wrist. "How are you today? I did not want to ask in front of the footmen at breakfast."

She smiled wryly. "A little sore, but you told me that was to be expected. I am fine, Fox. Truly. I will meet you downstairs in half an hour."

He brought her hand to his lips and kissed her knuckles and then let her leave. Fox summoned Marsh, instructing the butler to have the carriage readied and their luggage placed atop it.

Good to her word, Delaney met him downstairs ten minutes later. Parchmann climbed up next to the driver, and Fox assisted Delaney into the carriage. He wanted to make love to her on the way home, but decided the jostling of the carriage would be too rough on her, especially because she was still tender from the lovemaking the previous night. It didn't mean he wouldn't do so in the future, though. Something told him he would never get enough of his duchess.

"Remember, after going to Bow Street, you must visit with Mr. Hodgkins," she reminded him. "You need to have all estate reports sent to you and not him. He can best advise you on which of your other estates' stewards would be most suited to take up the reins at Crosshaven. If any of your stewards have assistants, one of them might fill the open position vacated by the promoted employee."

He linked their fingers together. "You think of everything. It will be good to have you as my partner in life."

He kissed her and felt her hesitation for a moment. Then she responded to the kiss.

After a few minutes, she pulled away. "I do not need to appear at Bow Street with a bruised mouth," she told him.

Fox knew she was right and slipped his arm around her shoulders, needing to have her close. She rested her head on his shoulder. He thought they should speak of their wedding but decided to wait, content in the blissful silence.

They arrived at Bow Street and went in, taking the ledgers with them. Fox explained to the clerk that he did not have an appointment, but when he gave his name as the Duke of Abington, they were quickly shown to see a Mr. Franklin.

"What might I do for you, Your Grace?" the man asked.

"I am new to my title and was recently made aware of the fact that the steward at my ducal country seat abruptly quit the estate, taking a parlor maid with him and leaving no forwarding address. Miss Colebourne here was able to comb through my ledgers and found glaring discrepancies."

"You say this steward was stealing from you, Your Grace?"

"He was. I want him found and brought to justice." He indicated the satchel they had brought in. "The ledgers within here are evidence of his crimes."

"We will not need those at this point, Your Grace," Mr. Franklin said. "Our first action will be to locate Mr. Fulghum and the maid and take them into custody. I will put two of my best agents on your case. Would you care to meet with them before they go out on assignment?"

"No," Fox said. "It will not be necessary. Speed is what is important. Send this team of men to find the pair, and we will go from there. I will not require any kind of official report until Fulghum is taken into custody."

Mr. Franklin chuckled. "Oh, you will get a most thorough report. One of my agents that I will assign to this case is meticulous in the reports she writes."

"She?" he questioned.

"Yes, Miss Slade is her name. She is the only female Bow Street runner and one of my top agents. Miss Slade's specialty is locating missing people. I will send another agent with her. He, too, is excellent at running down leads and finding those who do not wish to be found. This pair will be on your case initially, and then I have others with more financial expertise who can help build the case against Fulghum before we bring it to the authorities."

Delaney spoke up. "Why don't we leave these ledgers with you now, Mr. Franklin? That way your agents could become familiar with what lies within them and have already built their case. It would be ready for prosecution by the time Mr. Fulghum is found."

"An excellent point, Miss Colebourne," Franklin said. Turning to Fox, he added, "Then leave the satchel with me, Your Grace."

"Might I remain behind and go over the ledgers with your agents, Mr. Franklin?" Delaney suggested. "I have already marked certain pages and would like to apprise them of why I did so." She turned to Fox. "That way, you could go and handle your business with Mr. Hodgkins, Your Grace."

"Thank you, Miss Colebourne," he said formally. "It will be a good use of both our time. I will see you back at my townhouse. I assume you will want to go and check on the progress your seamstresses have made during your absence."

"Yes, I will, Your Grace. We also have things to discuss beyond that, as well."

Fox hoped she referred to their upcoming nuptials. He took his leave and headed straight to Hodgkins' office, where the clerk escorted him to see the solicitor.

"I have found Fulghum, my steward at Crosshaven, to be an embezzler," he announced, getting straight to the point.

Fox took a quarter-hour to elaborate on the events of the past several days, from the time Marsh arrived in town until Delaney examined the books and found where the funds had gone missing.

"This occurred over a long period, almost the entire six years Fulghum was employed by the former duke. I know my predecessor had all estate reports forwarded to you, but I want these to come to me from now on. I intend to have my hand in the running of all my estates."

He gazed pointedly at the solicitor, who squirmed under the scrutiny, and then added, "I find it most troublesome, Hodgkins."

"What, Your Grace?" asked the man as he fidgeted like a small boy who knew he was about to be reprimanded.

"That all estate reports came to you—and you did nothing about this." He narrowed his eyes as he studied the solicitor. "Any professional worth his salt would have picked up on the questionable nature of these reports."

Hodgkins looked as if he wished the ground would swallow him whole. "I should have discovered that funds were missing, Your Grace. For that, I profusely apologize. My only excuse is that the previous duke instructed me never to look at the ledgers. He was a very private man. I was merely the conduit, forwarding them to His Grace."

The solicitor swallowed visibly. "I am never careless, Your Grace. I can assure you of that. I hope that you will see it in your heart to give me a chance to prove it to you. I would appreciate being able to serve you in any capacity you see fit." He hesitated. "Then again, if you wish to sever our connection, I would not blame you."

He could start from scratch, trying to replace this man, or he could trust his instincts, which told him Hodgkins would never be negligent again. After all, no one wished to lose the business of a duke.

"Very well. I will retain your services—but I do expect you to be vigilant and attentive in regard to my affairs from this point on."

The solicitor thanked him, and then Fox told Hodgkins how he wished to replace Fulghum with the most reliable of his other stewards.

"That would be Mr. Craft," the solicitor said. "He runs your estate in Surrey. It is only three hours from London."

"How much experience does Craft have?"

"He has only been in charge of the estate for two years, Your Grace. I know that seems a short amount of time, but his father was the previous steward for twenty-five years or more. Craft worked closely under him for a good dozen years before he took up the reins. He is in his early thirties now and would be able to serve at Crosshaven for many years."

"Summon him to London. I wish to meet him before making my final decision. If I do decide to send him on to Crosshaven, do you have any idea who might replace Craft?"

They talked for several minutes of potential replacements and decided on the best candidate, based upon Hodgkins' experience in dealing with the various estates. The solicitor promised to send word immediately for Craft to come to London to meet with Fox, assuring that Craft could be in town sometime tomorrow.

"I have one other matter to discuss with you, Hodgkins. I am going to marry soon and will need you to draw up the marriage settlements."

"Congratulations, Your Grace. If you will give me the name of your betrothed's solicitor, I shall contact him. I will also need to know what you have in mind regarding the contracts."

"Actually, you are solicitor to both of us," he revealed. "I hope that will not be a conflict of interest. My bride will be Miss Colebourne."

Hodgkins' brows shot up and then a slow smile spread across his face. "Ah, Lord Kinnison would be most pleased at this news. The earl adored his daughter. Since you are to be Miss Colebourne's husband, I do not feel as if I speak out of turn. Miss Colebourne is quite well off, financially speaking. Not only does she own the building in which Delaney's Designs is located, but Lord Kinnison left her a decent-sized estate in Buckinghamshire, as well as ten thousand pounds. She has no dowry, obviously, but she would bring quite a bit into the marriage."

"I want her to keep everything she has now. Nothing is to become mine. She retains ownership of Chapwell Hall and whatever monies she has in the bank. She continues as the owner of Delaney's Designs and keeps possession of the building it occupies. I know I had told you I would purchase the building from her, but Miss Colebourne may decide to keep the shop open. I want not a penny from her, Hodgkins, and I need that spelled out in the marriage contracts."

The solicitor steepled his fingers. "I see. Well, Your Grace, usually money brought into a marriage from the dowry is designated as the dowry for any future daughters resulting from the marriage. Are you certain you wouldn't wish to use her ten thousand pounds for that purpose?"

"When the time comes, I will see that all my daughters have an appropriate dowry. Go ahead and draw up the contracts then, Hodgkins. I will let you know when we will sign them."

Both men rose, and Hodgkins offered his hand. "You are making a wise decision in taking Miss Colebourne as your bride, Your Grace. She is a remarkable woman."

"Thank you. I think so, too."

Fox asked the solicitor how to go about purchasing a special license and headed straight for Doctors' Commons to do so. Being a duke seemed to cut through any bureaucracy, and he accomplished the errand quickly. Arriving back at his townhouse with the special license in his breast pocket, he entered and was greeted by Driskell.

"Where are my nieces?"

"They are about to take tea in the drawing room, Your Grace."

"And what of Miss Colebourne?"

"She is upstairs in the schoolroom."

"Summon her to tea, as well."

Fox proceeded to the drawing room. Eliza raced to him, throwing her arms about him.

"Uncle Fox! You are finally home."

He kissed her cheek and then turned, finding Grace nearby. "Come here, you," he said, enfolding her in his arms and also kissing her cheek, appreciating the warm greeting from his nieces.

"Let us sit, and you can tell me what you've been up to during my absence."

Eliza poured out, and both girls jabbered away, telling Fox about their latest dance lesson and the gowns which had already been completed for them. He listened to them but continually glanced toward the door, wondering what was taking Delaney so long to arrive.

Tea finally ended, and he told his nieces he had work to do and would see them at dinner.

Making his way to the top floor, Fox entered the schoolroom and saw Delaney with a gown in her lap, her needle and thread moving up and down through it.

"Miss Colebourne? A word, please."

She set aside her sewing and followed him into the corridor, closing the door behind her.

"Why didn't you come to tea?" he asked.

"I needed to finish working on the appliqué of a gown. It is a very delicate job, and I wished to complete it while the light was good, Your Grace."

He frowned. "We are alone, Delaney. There is no reason for you to address me so formally."

Her chin rose a notch, and he saw stubbornness fill her eyes. "There is every reason for me to address you in such a manner. You are my employer. I am your employee."

Fox caught her wrist and dragged her across the hall to an empty bedchamber. Shutting the door, he asked, "What is wrong?"

Her eyes shuttered. "Nothing is wrong, Your Grace. We have merely returned to our usual roles."

He clasped her elbows. "There is nothing usual about us now, Delaney. Things have changed between us. You know that."

Her gaze dropped. "No, they have not."

Fox heard the sadness in her tone, and his grip tightened on her as panic filled him. "What are you not telling me?"

Still looking at the ground, she said, "There is nothing more to say, Your Grace. I will continue working alongside my seamstresses to provide your nieces gowns for the upcoming Season."

He took her chin in one hand, raising it, forcing her to meet his eyes. Gathering his courage, he uttered, "I love you."

She flinched.

"I *love* you," he repeated, saying the words he had kept to himself, hoping if she finally heard them, it would make a difference. "You may not love me—yet—but we will marry. We must after what—"

"We will not wed," she said, looking into his eyes, regret filling hers. "What happened between us is something I will never forget. But I am not going to marry you, Fox. I am never going to marry anyone."

"No!" he hissed. "You must. I love you, Delaney. The girls already adore you. I *need* you."

She blinked. "What you need is to wed a woman who will make for an appropriate Duchess of Abington. That woman is not me."

"I choose *you*."

"And I choose never to wed. I cannot, Fox. I will not. You must respect my wishes."

He jerked her to him, his mouth crashing down on hers. The kiss was brutal, punishing her for her words which had cut him to the quick. She stood stock-still, not responding. He broke the kiss and shook his head, anger and hurt filling him.

"You could have had the world," he said harshly, shaking his head. "You could have had *me*."

Delaney merely looked at him, no emotion on her face.

"Very well," he said, releasing her. "Have it your way, Miss Colebourne. We will not need to speak to one another again."

With that, Fox stormed from the room, humiliated at having laid his soul bare and being rejected. He would avoid Delaney from now on. He would move forward. He was a duke. He could have any woman in society he chose.

Even as he attempted to pick up the pieces of his shattered heart.

CHAPTER NINETEEN

DELANEY WATCHED FOX stride away and fought the urge to call after him. He walked from the room—and out of her life. She knew it was for the best, but she also knew she would never be whole again. The rugged duke had taken her heart with him, leaving her gutted. She would never be the same.

"It is for the best," she said aloud, not believing her empty words, even as a torrent of tears cascaded down her cheeks. Delaney did not try to stop them. She let herself weep for what she had lost. For what could never be. She was an earl's bastard and an outcast, no matter what world she tried to belong to. She would fulfill her duty to Lady Eliza and Lady Grace and then retreat from London to lick her wounds. The thought of opening a new millinery shop in High Wycombe had no appeal to her now, nor did returning to London one day. If she did, she feared she would run straight to Fox's doorstep and collapse upon it. No, her best move now would be to leave this great city and never return.

Still, she had her workers—who had become her friends—to consider. She would not abandon Ruth, Dilly, and Fanny. If they were willing to make the move with her, she would give them a place to live at Chapwell Hall and positions in her new millinery shop. Delaney had actually enjoyed designing dresses for the Foxwell girls and now considered opening a combination of dress shop and millinery. By providing both to clients, it would most likely give all of them plenty to do. Somehow, Delaney knew she would have to find a way to fill the long hours of loneliness which would try to eat away at her.

She dried her tears and waited a few more minutes before returning to the schoolroom.

"You have worked very hard today," she told the three seamstresses. "Why don't we stop a bit early?"

Dilly, with her sharp eyes, studied Delaney and asked, "Are you all right, Miss Colebourne? Has something upset you?"

"I haven't been sleeping well. I am simply overtired. I will see you three in the morning."

She collected her things and left the Abington townhouse, not bothering to hail a hansom cab. Instead, she decided to walk the streets of Mayfair, hoping to find some solace.

A quarter-hour later, she found herself passing the residence of the Duke and Duchess of Westfield. She could use a friend now and decided to call and see if the duchess might be available.

Her knock was answered by a footman, who smiled and said, "Hello, Miss Colebourne. Are you here to see Her Grace?"

"I am. I do not have an appointment with her, however."

The butler appeared in the foyer and said, "Ah, Miss Colebourne. It is good to see you again. Her Grace and Lady Norrie are in her studio. She would be happy to speak with you. May I take you to her?"

"Please do so," she told the butler.

She followed him up the staircase until they reached the top floor of the townhouse and moved down a long corridor. The servant stepped through the open door at its end and said, "Your Grace, Miss Colebourne has come calling."

"Oh, please send her in, Hampton."

The servant turned and waved her in.

Entering the art studio, Delaney caught the whiff of paint and turpentine. She saw the duchess sitting before a canvas, her daughter in her lap. Crossing the room, Delaney went to stand next to them.

The duchess smiled warmly. "I hope you do not mind me not rising to greet you, but you can see that Norrie and I are painting together. Bring a stool over and join us if you would."

She did as asked and sat near the pair. Lady Norrie held a brush in her small, chubby fingers, and her mother guided the babe's hand, moving the brush across the canvas.

"I know most would say Norrie is far too young for me to put a brush in her hand, but I believe if she does possess any artistic talent, it will bloom if encouraged at an early age. I try to spend a few minutes with her in my studio each day, sometimes guiding her hand and other times letting her move the brush freely."

Delaney looked at the child, just over a year old, who had the bright, fiery hair of her mother and large, green eyes.

"Norrie, this is Miss Colebourne, Mama's new friend."

The child looked solemnly at Delaney for a moment and then turned back to the canvas.

"I am glad you came to see me today, Miss Colebourne. I was about to extend another invitation to you to come to tea again. Have you been busy with the Foxwell girls' wardrobes?"

Delaney spent a few minutes describing some of the gowns which had been completed for the girls. The duchess asked several questions regarding the fabrics used and the cut of the gowns.

"I think it marvelous that you are designing all these gowns for them. I may have to engage you to make up some for me next Season."

Tears welled in her eyes, and the duchess leaned over and patted Delaney's hand. "We need to talk."

She nodded. "I would like that."

"Would you hold Norrie a moment?"

The duchess handed her daughter over to Delaney and went and pulled a cord to summon a servant. She then busied herself cleaning the brushes as Delaney drank in the scent of the small child who looked at her with interest. A deep yearning struck her, a pang so sharp and poignant that it caused tears to glide down her cheeks. Lady Norrie reached up and with chubby fingers, touched Delaney's cheek, causing her to laugh.

A servant appeared, and the duchess said, "Please take Norrie to the nursery if you would."

The nursemaid came to Delaney, who reluctantly handed over the sweet bundle. "Goodbye, Lady Norrie," she said, waving at the child.

Norrie smiled, drooling, and wiggled her fingers at Delaney. "Bye-bye."

She choked back a sob as the pair left.

The duchess finished cleaning the brushes and came to Delaney. Taking her elbow, she helped her to rise. "We should go to my sitting room. It is much more comfortable there."

As they turned and headed toward the door, Delaney saw a partially completed canvas on an easel and recognized herself. She halted before it.

"You are painting *me*?"

The duchess looked at the barely begun portrait, which only had part of Delaney's face and hair. "I sketched you after our tea together. I usually do numerous sketches before I paint a subject. Your hair is such a unique color, with so many shades of golds and browns woven together."

"Papa called it caramel," she told the duchess.

"I love playing with paints and developing shades. I would like to officially paint you if you do not mind."

She shrugged. "If you wish to do so you may, but I have nowhere to hang it. And I certainly could not afford your prices."

The duchess waved a hand in the air. "I would not expect you to pay me, Miss Colebourne. The challenge of painting the varying shades within your hair would be payment enough."

They left the art studio and retreated to a cozy sitting room. The duchess closed the door behind them, and they took a seat beside one another.

"Tell me why you are so glum, Miss Colebourne." The duchess frowned. "No, I cannot do this. I am Margaret. Please call me by my Christian name if you would. I so want to be your friend." She clasped Delaney's hand.

"I could use a friend now, Margaret. I hope you would call me Delaney." She paused. "I have made a fool of myself. Over the Duke of Abington."

"Why do you think so?" the duchess asked, concern written on her brow.

"Because I went and lost my heart to him." She burst into tears, and Margaret enveloped her in an embrace, patting Delaney's back as she cried.

It took several minutes until her tears were spent, and she pulled away. "I apologize, Margaret."

"Friends are honest with one another. I am touched that you would show such vulnerability to me." She took both Delaney's hands in hers. "Your feelings are not unrequited. Abington has very strong feelings for you."

"He told you this?" she asked in wonder.

Margaret nodded. "The very first time we met him, he did so," she revealed. "It was the day I came to Delaney's Designs, and he accompanied Daniel to White's. In our carriage, Abington confessed that he wished to make you his duchess."

Fresh tears spilled from her eyes, rolling down her cheeks.

"Why would he have shared such a thing?"

"I think because he loves you, Delaney. And from all these tears, I think you love him, as well."

"He did ask me to marry him," she confided. "But I turned him down."

"What was your reason for doing so?" her friend asked gently.

"Oh, Margaret. I have several reasons. I am an earl's bastard, totally unsuited to become the wife of a duke. I have been in trade for years, which is another strike against me. I could not bear for Polite Society to ostracize Fox—and any children we might have. He is a very good man and deserves a woman who has the proper breeding and background to become the Duchess of Abington."

"You might be surprised to learn this, but society can be quite forgiving of dukes. They seem to be a law unto themselves. If you love him—and he loves you—the *ton* will accept this. Will they gossip about you? Undoubtedly. They still talk about Daniel and me. What is important is what the two of you feel for one another. That is all that matters. Do not let what the *ton* might think influence your decision, Delaney."

"I also have a fear of letting go of all that I have worked so hard for, as well as what Papa bequeathed to me."

Margaret frowned. "What do you mean?"

"If I wed Fox, I would lose everything I own. Even my identity. My millinery and the building it's located in. The estate Papa left to me in his will. Even the large sum of money he bestowed upon me. I would be stripped of everything by English law."

Her friend grew thoughtful. "Love involves a degree of trust, Delaney. If you love your duke enough, you must trust him to do what is best for the both of you. Yes, that might mean him taking on your assets and managing them for you. Or he might wish for you to keep them and spell that out, via the marriage settlements. You should not assume what he will do but instead have an open and honest discussion regarding your property and money and what will happen to it if you wed."

"I do love him, Margaret. More than I thought possible. I turned down his marriage proposal, though. I pushed him away. Hard."

The duchess chuckled. "If he truly loves you, that would not be enough to keep him away. I believe Abington is a very determined man and will not give up on you so easily."

"Oh, but he is very angry with me. We parted on ugly terms just an hour ago. I do not see how he will ever forgive me." New tears ran down her cheeks. "I betrayed him in the worst way."

The duchess' brows arched. "How did you betray him, Delaney?"

She described her recent trip to the country and how she had coupled with Fox at Crosshaven.

"I knew it was wrong to do so because I had no intention of marrying him. He assumed our lovemaking meant we would definitely wed. I used him, Margaret, in a most dreadful manner. I am not sure he even loves me anymore, much less be willing to forgive me."

"Sometimes we do hurt the ones we love—but forgiveness is a powerful part of love. Just because you love him does not mean things will always run smoothly between you two. It is the same for Daniel and me. We love one another with a depth and breadth most lovers never achieve, yet we still argue at times. We are both strong-willed individuals and have learned that there are times we will argue. Times we must compromise. Times we even make up. Give your duke a day or two to allow his temper to cool and then approach him again, Delaney. Tell him what is in your heart. Love does not merely vanish. Abington is hurt, but his love for you is still within him."

"I will take your advice, Margaret. Thank you for seeing me."

"You are welcome here anytime, Delaney. I also want you to reconsider attending the ball Daniel and I are giving to open the Season. It would be nice for you to see your charges dancing in their beautiful gowns and perhaps by then, you and Abington will have made up."

"And if we haven't? Would you still wish for me to attend your ball?"

"I want you in my life, whether you are a duchess or a milliner," declared Margaret. "I hope you feel the same toward me."

"I will consider coming. I still worry about Lord Kinnison and the stir he might cause. I would not want my presence to ruin your ball or detract from Lady Eliza and Lady Grace."

"It wouldn't," the duchess assured her. "Besides, I have no intention of inviting Lord and Lady Kinnison. Let them sit home on the first night of the Season and be miserable."

Delaney took her leave, hailing a hansom cab and returning home. She would do as Margaret suggested and give Fox a few days for his temper to subside. Then she would approach him and see if they might have a future together.

CHAPTER TWENTY

Fox woke in a terrible mood. He had tossed and turned most of the night, frustrated by the situation with Delaney. It was one thing to be stubborn and quite another to be hardheaded. Instead of him trying to change her mind, he had finally realized only she could do that. The more he pushed and tried to manipulate her, the harder she would dig in her heels. What they needed was time and distance.

He would give it to her. To them.

He went to breakfast and buried his nose in the newspaper, glad the girls were not present at the table. While he usually enjoyed their conversations, he savored this morning's peace and quiet.

Driskell brought the mail to him, and Fox paused to go through it. A note from Hodgkins confirmed that Mr. Craft would arrive in London shortly after noon today. Hodgkins would meet the steward's mail coach and bring him directly to the townhouse.

Several invitations were included in the mail, including one from the Duke and Duchess of Westfield. He noted that their ball would open the Season. He thought it good that Grace and Eliza had already met the duchess. It would ease some of their nerves as they attended their first ball. The other invitations all came from names he was unfamiliar with, but they included both him and his nieces. He supposed word had gotten out of the new duke in town and his nieces who would be making their come-outs. From what Westfield had said, he and the girls would be invited to every event held this Season.

Merely because he was a duke.

He doubted they should attend every affair they were invited to, else they would be exhausted by Season's end. If he were on speaking terms with Delaney, he might have showed her the invitations as they came in and asked her which ones would be the ones he should accept. He didn't think it a good idea, though, still wanting to keep his distance from her. Besides, from what Westfield had told him, dukes did not always respond to invitations and either showed up or not. The hostess put on a smile if they appeared and made excuses for them if they did not. What a strange world he was now a part of, so unlike the military, with its precision and attention to detail.

The last bit of correspondence was from Mr. Farmington. He and his assistants had finished up several pieces of Fox's wardrobe and wondered if he could come around for a final fitting today.

Claiming Driskell's attention, he said, "Send Parchmann to Mr. Farmington's shop, and let him know I will come for my fitting in an hour's time. And instruct Parchmann to stay at the shop. I will need his advice."

"Of course, Your Grace." Driskell left the dining room.

Eliza and Grace joined him, ordering their breakfasts. He decided now would be the time to tell them of his plans.

"I will be leaving later today," he informed them.

"Again?" Eliza asked, her exasperation obvious. "Where are you going this time, Uncle Fox?"

"I do not want to neglect my other estates. While I was at least familiar with Crosshaven because I had grown up on the property, I did learn quite a few things about it during my brief stay there. I have yet to see the other four country estates which are my property. I plan to visit them during the next few weeks."

"And leave us here?" Eliza complained.

"You wouldn't want to go anywhere anyway," Grace said airily, buttering her toast points. "You don't even like the country. Besides, we need to stay here and continue our music and dancing lessons, not to mention the daily fittings for our new wardrobes."

"You have to be back in time for the Season, Uncle Fox," Eliza chastised. "If you are not here, then we cannot go. You must escort us."

He chuckled. "I would not abandon my duty to you and your sister. I do not plan to stay at any of my estates for long. I promise to be back in plenty of time to make it to the Duke and Duchess of Westfield's ball."

"They are hosting the first ball this Season?" asked Grace, now interested. "Oh, the duchess was so lovely and friendly to us. She asked us all kinds of questions about ourselves. I truly like her a great deal."

"I do, as well," he seconded. "Now, if you will excuse me, I have a fitting of my own at my tailor's. I know you will want me appropriately dressed if I am to accompany you to events."

"Is Miss Colebourne going with you?" Grace asked. "I know she helped you pick out much of it."

He swallowed, trying to get his emotions under control. "No, it is not necessary for her to accompany me today."

"But she could make certain things fit you well, Uncle Fox," Eliza pointed out.

"Parchmann will be there. He is an expert on everything. Just ask him."

Both girls laughed, and he sighed, hoping no more conversation regarding Delaney would occur.

"When will you leave?" asked Grace.

"Most likely this afternoon. I am interviewing my steward from Surrey to see if he is fit for the same position at Crosshaven."

Eliza's nose crinkled. "We went to the Surrey property once. It was a very small house. I didn't like it."

"I remember Mr. Craft," her sister said. "He was very friend-ly. So was his son."

"Well, this is Mr. Craft's son I will speak with today. Appar-ently, the father has retired, and the son took his place."

"He was very handsome. Remember him, Eliza?" Grace asked.

"Not at all. Why would I recall a steward?"

Grace gave a devilish smile. "Because you said he was hand-some and wished you could kiss him."

"Grace!"

Fox laughed. "There will be no more talk of kissing, either Mr. Craft or anyone else."

"Miss Colebourne has warned us about never being alone with a man. That if we are found that way—especially if we are found kissing—it will mean we must marry him," Grace said solemnly.

"Yes, Miss Colebourne said we would be ruined if we did not marry the fellow. She advised us not to kiss anyone until our wedding day."

He smiled to himself, thinking of the many kisses he and Delaney had shared.

Rising and setting aside his newspaper, Fox said, "Listen to Miss Colebourne. She is a very wise woman. If I do not see you before I leave, I will write to you while I am gone."

Eliza jumped up and hugged Fox tightly. "Try not to be gone too long, Uncle. We will miss you."

Grace joined them and hugged him, as well. "We will miss you, Uncle."

His throat thickened with emotion. "I will miss the two of you, as well."

As he left the breakfast room, he wondered how two young women, strangers to him until only recently, had come to feel like family.

Fox went to his waiting carriage and spent a good hour trying on all manner of items at Farmington's shop, getting Parchmann's approval as he went along. Only minor adjustments were needed on a few items. Farmington assured Fox that within two weeks, he would be able to present the remainder of Fox's wardrobe to him.

"I will see that things are packed up and sent to your townhouse, Your Grace," the tailor told him.

"I will remain behind and supervise the packing," Parchmann said haughtily. "I will also see to having everything pressed once it is delivered, Your Grace. Your shirts from the shirtmaker have arrived, as well."

"Then I will see you later," he told the valet. "But you can wait on pressing all the new clothing. You and I are leaving town for a couple of weeks. We are going to visit my other country estates."

"But what of the Season, Your Grace?" demanded Parchmann.

"We will only stay at each property a night or two. Just enough time for me to speak to the stewards and servants and briefly tour the estates. I know I am to escort my nieces this Season. Lady Eliza reminded me of that at breakfast when I told her of my plans."

"Then I will see to the packing. When do you wish to leave, Your Grace?"

"This afternoon after I speak with Mr. Craft."

Outside the shop, he instructed his driver to head to Bow Street. Something had been nagging at him, and Fox had finally recalled what it was during the hours he'd lain awake last night worrying over Delaney.

Upon arriving, he was taken directly to Mr. Franklin's office.

"Good morning, Your Grace. Are you here for a report?"

"No, Mr. Franklin. I have thought of another matter to take up with you. One regarding a man formerly under my command. A Lieutenant Garrison."

He explained how the soldier had lost his life and wished for Fox to give a message in person to his widow and young boy if and when he ever returned to England.

"I wrote to them in Colchester upon the lieutenant's death," he explained. "I have no idea if they are still in Essex or not. Perhaps once Fulghum is found, you could put the same team of agents on this."

"I can do that, Your Grace, or I can assign someone new to this case."

"I will leave that up to you, Mr. Franklin. The matter is not as pressing as finding my former steward."

He rose and offered his hand. "Thank you for your time."

Leaving Bow Street, Fox returned to the townhouse, avoiding the top floor and Delaney. He spent time in his study until Driskell came and informed him that Mr. Craft had arrived.

"Mr. Craft has gone to wash up and will be here shortly, Your Grace," the butler informed him. "Mr. Hodgkins is here if you have need to see him."

"No, but you may give him this," he said, handing over a letter he'd just finished writing to the solicitor. In it, he informed Hodgkins of the quick visits to his properties and said he would look at the marriage contracts when he returned. Fox wasn't ready to give up on Delaney yet and hoped the settlements could be signed upon his return. The special license he had purchased would be good until the fifth day of the Season. If he hadn't convinced her to marry him by then, he would need to buy a new one.

When Craft arrived, Fox took to him immediately. He guessed there was only a year or two difference in their ages. Craft was intelligent and friendly and answered Fox's questions regarding the Surrey property with ease.

"I would like to offer you the position of steward at Crosshaven, Mr. Craft," he explained. "It is my ducal seat and the largest of my properties."

Craft's eyes gleamed at the thought of the opportunity. "That would be quite a step up for me, Your Grace. I gladly accept."

"I wish to see all my estates and meet the men who manage

them. Would you care to accompany me on my visits? The Season starts in just under three weeks, and I must be back to spend it with my nieces. It would be a fast trip, but I want an idea of what each property looks like so that I have a better idea of my holdings."

Craft smiled and with enthusiasm said, "I would be delighted to come with you, Your Grace."

"We will make Surrey our last stop. That way you can collect your things and go straight to Crosshaven from there. Since I have already visited Crosshaven, I will not need to return to it during this visit."

"I am ready to leave when you are, Your Grace."

"How about now?" Fox countered.

The two men left the study. Driskell lingered nearby, and Fox told the butler to have the carriage brought around and for Parchmann to have his trunk loaded onto it. He excused himself and went to the drawing room, knowing the girls had their weekly pianoforte lessons at this time. He went inside and listened for a moment and then decided not to interrupt. They had already said their goodbyes this morning. No need to go through them again.

Venturing downstairs, he pushed aside thoughts of telling Delaney goodbye. He assumed the girls would eventually tell her where he had gone.

In the foyer, Driskell said, "Your carriage is ready, Your Grace."

Fox went outside and found Craft waiting for him. "After you," he said, allowing the other man to climb into the vehicle.

He glanced up at the top of the house and thought he saw a shadow at the window. He hoped it was Delaney and that she would miss him so much, her teeth might ache. He gave a wave, hoping she was there and saw it. Then he entered the carriage and rapped on the roof, indicating to his coachman to begin.

As they pulled out of the square, he thought of this house as home. Not just because it was designated as his residence.

Because Eliza and Grace were there.

And Delaney.

Settling against the cushions, he looked to his companion. "We have talked about my Surrey estate, Mr. Craft. Tell me something about yourself."

As his steward began to speak, Fox's thoughts drifted to Delaney Colebourne—and how he could get her to accept becoming the Duchess of Abington.

CHAPTER TWENTY-ONE

D ELANEY SET ASIDE the gown she had just finished for Lady Grace, pleased with her efforts. The past two weeks had gone by quickly and yet agonizingly slow at the same time. Fox had been away the entire time, and she had thought about him a great deal, wondering if he still might love her. If he would forgive her for turning down his marriage proposal.

And if he would consider once more to make her his wife when she told him she loved him.

She had joined with Fanny, Dilly, and Ruth each day at the Abington townhouse, sewing for long hours on the gowns for the Foxwell girls. Daily fittings occurred, with small adjustments being made here and there. Eliza and Grace were pleased with the gowns which had been completed. Eliza had even contributed three different designs of her own, two of which had already been made up, one for each girl. The pair constantly chattered about the invitations pouring in and how excited they were to make their debut into Polite Society.

Today, she would stop much earlier than usual because Margaret had invited her, along with Lady Eliza and Lady Grace, to tea.

She had visited three times with her new friend during these past two weeks, agreeing to attend the opening night's ball, whether Fox accepted her apology or not. She wanted to stay for at least one dance and observe her charges on the dance floor in their new gowns on the night of their first ball.

With a week to go before the Season began, she really should start on her own gown. While she had appropriate evening clothes for a dinner or even a night at the theatre, thanks to the outings with Papa, she lacked in possessing a ballgown. Though she would only stay for a short while, Delaney did not want to embarrass Margaret in any way by being underdressed. She would start a gown for herself once she arrived home after tea this afternoon.

Driskell stepped into the schoolroom and cleared his throat. "Miss Colebourne, His Grace's carriage has arrived."

She rose and said, "Thank you for letting me know, Mr. Driskell."

Delaney had already informed her friends she would depart early today, and they wished her well.

Joining Lady Grace and Lady Eliza downstairs, the three of them boarded the Westfield carriage, allowing a footman to hand them up.

The moment the door closed, Lady Eliza squealed in glee. "I cannot believe we are going to tea with the Duchess of Westfield. Oh, isn't this carriage marvelous!"

"It is remarkably like that of Uncle Fox's," Lady Grace point-ed out, grinning. "But I, too, am thrilled that the duchess thought to ask us for tea." She looked to Delaney. "It was very thoughtful of Her Grace to include you, too, Miss Colebourne."

She had not told the girls of her budding friendship with Margaret and now listened as they jabbered about the duchess and the ball she would host on the opening night of the Season.

"I wonder how she will decorate the ballroom," Lady Eliza mused.

Delaney already knew the theme of the ball but kept it to herself, wanting these girls to be surprised.

Minutes later, they arrived at the Westfield townhouse and were taken not to the drawing room but Margaret's sitting room instead.

Grace's eyes grew large, and she slipped her arm through Delaney's, whispering, "It is a great honor to take tea in a private sitting room."

She smiled at the girl. "Her Grace must like you and your sister quite a bit."

The butler announced them, and they swept into the room. Margaret greeted both girls warmly, saving Delaney for last. She smiled brilliantly and enfolded Delaney in her arms. Delaney heard Lady Eliza's gasp and held in her laughter.

Margaret released her and asked, "Won't you all sit?"

They did so, and Lady Grace said, "Thank you for having us to tea this afternoon, Your Grace. It was most thoughtful of you."

Margaret smiled at the girl. "I am eager to hear all about your new wardrobes. Tell me what you will wear to my ball."

As usual, Lady Eliza took the lead, describing her gown in minute detail. When she paused for a breath, Lady Grace interjected, telling about her own gown. Margaret asked the girls several questions and showed a great interest in Lady Eliza having designed gowns they both would wear.

"You must be most talented, my lady," Margaret praised. "I know what high standards Delaney has. If she agreed to allow your designs to be made up, they must be worthy indeed."

Delaney watched as the young ladies' eyes showed their surprise at the Duchess of Westfield having used Delaney's first name. They looked from the duchess to her and back again.

Lady Eliza, ever frank and curious, asked, "You are *friends* with Miss Colebourne?"

"We are becoming fast friends," Margaret confirmed. "Delaney and I have much in common. I only wish she could meet a few of my other close friends, but they are not traveling to town this Season."

"They are missing the Season?" Lady Eliza asked, her shock apparent. "Why would *anyone* want to miss the Season? It is the most wonderful time of year," she declared.

"They all have a very good reason, my lady," the duchess told them. "The Duchess of Linberry had a babe in February, while the Duchesses of Stoneham and Bradford will each deliver a child this month. It is the first for all three of them."

Smiling, Margaret added, "A child is the most glorious thing on earth, my ladies, and well worth missing a Season."

Lady Eliza frowned and then asked, "Do you have any children, Your Grace?"

"I have a daughter. Her name is Lenora, but we fondly call her Norrie. She was a year old in February, and I hope my husband and I will be blessed with more children."

"Is it true that your husband proposed to you in the middle of a ballroom during a waltz?" asked Lady Grace shyly.

Margaret chuckled. "Oh, he did, indeed. Daniel even kissed me in front of the entire *ton*."

Both girls gasped, and Delaney and Margaret laughed aloud.

"That was rather bold of His Grace, wasn't it?" Lady Eliza asked.

"He believed it would take a grand gesture from him in order for me to accept his offer of marriage." The duchess paused, smiling radiantly now. "I was very touched by his actions. We have been happy ever since."

"The newspapers say you are a love match," Lady Grace said.

"We are, my lady. Not every marriage is as fortunate but if I were you, I would hold out for love," Margaret advised.

Lady Grace nodded in agreement. "I hope to find love. My sister thinks me foolish, though."

"The best thing to do," Margaret said, "is to find a decent and kind man. Sometimes, an attraction is instant. Other times, love grows slowly. I hope both of you will find good men and make happy marriages."

For once, Lady Eliza did not go on and on about marrying a wealthy, titled gentleman. Delaney thought perhaps the girl was learning to hold her tongue and be more discreet in her conversation.

"Would you like to see our ballroom?" Margaret asked.

"That would be wonderful, Your Grace," Lady Eliza said.

"We are finished with tea so let us go see it. Some of the decorations are already in place, but the fresh flowers and shrubbery will not be brought in until the morning of the ball next week."

The four went to the ballroom, Margaret elaborating on the theme she had chosen, and then the girls walked about the room in awe, twirling and dancing in its center.

"They are good girls," her friend noted. "Lady Eliza will be a handful, but the right man will bring out the best in her."

"I agree wholeheartedly," Delaney said. "Lady Grace worries me, though. She is desperately wanting to marry for love. She has not seen much of it in her life. Their parents ignored both girls for the most part."

"Well, they turned out quite lovely. I know you have been a good influence upon them and Abington, as well. Has there been any word from him?"

"Lady Grace mentioned yesterday that a letter had arrived from him. He promised he would return in time for your ball next week."

"Speaking of that, Delaney, I want to make certain that you have a beautiful gown to wear for it."

"Oh, I was going to start one for myself tonight."

"You are being worked to the bone as it is," Margaret said. "I want this to be my gift to you. I plan to send the girls home now because my modiste is coming here to measure you and discuss the gown."

Delaney's throat grew thick with tears. "I am touched by such a generous gesture, Margaret, but I cannot have your modiste working on something for me when I am perfectly capable of doing so myself."

"I never said you weren't capable, Delaney Colebourne. But you need a bit of spoiling, in my opinion. No one has done so for you since your father passed. Please, let me do this small thing for you. It would mean a great deal to me."

She knew her friend would be working with the top modiste in town. At least this way, if she were gowned properly, she would not embarrass anyone.

"All right," she agreed.

Her friend embraced her. They waited until the girls returned to them.

"The dance floor gleams," Lady Grace said, awe in her voice. "It is almost slippery because it is so highly polished. I hope I do not fall."

"You won't, my lady," Margaret assured. "I am glad you like my ballroom. Hopefully, having seen it now, you will not be nervous when you arrive here to make your come-out."

"Thank you again for having us to tea this afternoon," Lady Eliza said. "It was thoughtful of you to send your carriage since Uncle Fox is away."

"I enjoyed getting to spend time with the two of you, but I am going to send you home now. I want to keep Delaney with me since we have other things to chat about."

Once more, the young ladies' eyes went wide. Eliza couldn't help but note, "You certainly favor Miss Colebourne."

"I do. I find a kindred spirit in her."

They walked the girls to the carriage and saw them safely inside it before returning to Margaret's sitting room. They chatted for a few minutes until Hampton came and told them the modiste had arrived with her assistant.

"Then show them here," Margaret told the butler.

The modiste swept into the room dramatically, followed meekly by her assistant. She paused in front of Delaney. "Miss Colebourne, I must say it is quite an honor to meet you. I have seen many of your creations worn by my clients. You are nothing short of a genius. It is a shame what happened to you."

"Thank you, Madame, for your compliment," she said.

"Let us sit and discuss the type of gown Miss Colebourne should wear," Margaret suggested.

They did so, each of them tossing out ideas. The modiste

sketched as they spoke and after a few minutes, she held up her drawing.

"It is stunning," Delaney said. "It is hard to think of me wearing something so grand."

"Her Grace wishes for you to look your best, Miss Colebourne. Doing so may help to put Lord Kinnison in his place," the modiste declared.

Delaney did not mention that the Kinnisons would not be attending the ball. She knew many of the couple's friends would be there, though, and wanted to do everything in her power to avoid most of Polite Society if she could. Still, it would be incredible to be gowned in such a creation.

"We should discuss the fabric you will use," Margaret said.

The debate began anew as to what to use for Delaney's gown. They decided on the color, with a darker underskirt.

"Would you care to come to my shop now to examine different choices of material?" Madame asked.

"No, I trust you implicitly, Madame. I am certain Her Grace does, as well."

"Then let me get your measurements, Miss Colebourne."

"That is not necessary. I know them off the top of my head."

The assistant jotted down each measurement Delaney provided, and the modiste said, "Please come to my shop in three days' time. We will do a fitting and see if any adjustments are required. It is a pleasure to work with you, Miss Colebourne. Perhaps I might even talk you into creating a hat for me sometime."

"I would be delighted to do so, Madame. Just let me know what type you might prefer."

The modiste spoke a minute of her preferences, and Delaney decided to make up the hat and bring it to her fitting.

She stayed behind after the modiste and her assistant left, thanking Margaret again for such a generous, elaborate gift.

"I want Abington to see you at your absolute best," her friend declared. "One look at you in this gown, and the duke will know you are duchess material."

CHAPTER TWENTY-TWO

F OX WAS CHAMPING at the bit by the time his carriage reached London. He had visited all his properties with Craft in tow and had gotten to know his new steward quite well over the last few weeks. They had finished up their tour yesterday, with him riding the property in Surrey and having a quick meeting with a few tenants. He had left Craft in Surrey this morning. The steward would spend the next two days training his chosen replacement before leaving for Crosshaven.

During every mile trekked these past three weeks, Fox's thoughts had not strayed far from Delaney. The longer they were apart, the more he missed her and prayed she felt the same. He would call for her the minute he arrived home and make her see they were meant to be together. How he would argue his case, though, had yet to be decided. He had already told her that he loved her. That the girls thought highly of her. His next move would be to clue her in as to what lay in the marriage contracts he'd had Hodgkins draw up before he'd departed from London. If Delaney knew she could keep everything she had worked for and had inherited from her father, perhaps then she might reconsider her position.

If she didn't, he hadn't a clue how to convince her, short of kidnapping and seducing her. As a gentleman, he couldn't consider that alternative.

As a man desperately in love, though, the idea certainly tempted him.

His carriage turned into the square, and his heart beat rapidly as the vehicle slowed and then came to a halt in front of his townhouse. Without waiting for the footman to attend to him, Fox threw open the door and bounded to the pavement.

Driskell awaited him, along with a well-dressed woman he did not recognize. He strode toward them.

"It is good to see you, Your Grace," his butler greeted. "I hope you had a pleasant journey."

"It was time well spent, Driskell." He gazed upon the woman who was tall and lean and had interesting eyes, golden ones rimmed in brown. "And you are?"

"Miss Shelby Slade, Your Grace. I am one of the agents assigned to your case. I arrived a few minutes ago with news for you regarding Fulghum. Mr. Driskell here told me you were expected, and I decided to wait and speak to you in person."

"Did you find Fulghum?" he asked eagerly.

She gave him a look that made him feel small. "Of course, Your Grace. We brought him and his companion in late last night. They are in custody at Bow Street as we speak. Mr. Franklin would like you to come at once and view the case notes before Fulghum is turned over for prosecution."

Fox was torn, wanting to go inside and speak with Delaney, but he knew the Bow Street runners had accomplished the impossible in a short length of time. He was also curious and wanted to confront Fulghum in person.

"Very well, Miss Slade." He looked to Driskell. "Have my things brought in. The horses need watering and rest. Miss Slade and I will hail a hansom cab and go directly to Bow Street now."

Driskell looked conflicted, and Fox asked, "What is it?"

Sheepishly, the butler said, "Lady Eliza will not be happy at you going off again, Your Grace. She and Lady Grace are most eager to see you."

"This matter is too important to wait, Driskell. I will be back in plenty of time to prepare for tonight's ball."

"Yes, Your Grace."

He walked the length of the square with Miss Slade and quickly found a hansom cab.

"Are you working on the other case I brought to Mr. Franklin?" he inquired.

"No, Your Grace. My partner and I have been in search of Fulghum these last few weeks. Mr. Franklin did mention it last night, however. So far, Mrs. Garrison and her boy have not been located."

"You found Fulghum. Would you consider looking for Mrs. Garrison?"

"That would be up to Mr. Franklin. He assigns all agents to the pending cases. You already have someone working on your behalf."

"I want *you*, Miss Slade."

She bowed her head in acknowledgement. "That is kind of you, Your Grace. You can take it up with Mr. Franklin when we reach headquarters."

"Tell me where you found him."

The rest of the trip, Fox listened to the runner explain how Fulghum was tracked down and taken into custody. He admired her ingenuity and doggedness and told her so.

"I would like to award you with some type of bonus, Miss Slade. Your partner, too."

"That is up to you, Your Grace, but know we are amply compensated by the agency."

They arrived at the Bow Street headquarters and Miss Slade led him to a room several doors down from Mr. Franklin's office.

"Fulghum is inside, shackled, and cannot harm you," the agent told him. "Do you wish for me to accompany you when you speak to him?"

"No, you may wait here, Miss Slade. Where is the parlor maid?"

"She is in the next room. I have interviewed her. The only

thing the poor girl is guilty of is letting Fulghum turn her head with empty promises. She is half his age and quite naive. It is obvious that she had nothing to do with the embezzling. That was all Fulghum."

"Then let her go," he advised, placing his hand on the door-knob and turning it.

Entering the room, he saw the former Crosshaven steward sitting in a chair pulled up to a table. Fulghum wore manacles on both his wrists and ankles, and they were connected and fastened to a center ring protruding from the table. A chair was opposite the prisoner and Fox took it.

"You're not another runner," Fulghum said grumpily. "You're far better dressed than them. You must be Abington."

"I am the Duke of Abington. The man you stole from."

Fulghum shrugged. "Not you, exactly. It was from the previous duke. He was a blunderbuss. Never once examined the ledgers from the estate. Never even bothered to meet with me in all the years I served at Crosshaven. I was hired by that solicitor of his and sent my monthly reports to Hodgkins. Abington and his family came to Crosshaven once a year and stayed for only a short time. You think he would show some interest in his estate. No, he was a selfish prick with loads of money. He didn't miss a whit of what I took."

"So, you do admit to embezzlement?"

Again, Fulghum shrugged. "I would consider it more . . . shifting funds around. I was underpaid, as it was. Abington owed me. I labored day and night on his behalf and never once got so much as a single thank you from the man. So what? I took what became a tidy little sum over the years. I worked hard and deserved it."

"And the maid?"

Fulghum snorted. "I've always had an eye for a pretty girl," he admitted. "Told her I was coming into some money and that if she came with me, she'd never have to work a day in her life again. She jumped at the chance to leave Crosshaven with me.

And then she kept whining about her sister being left behind. Truth be told, I was going to cut the chit loose," he said matter-of-factly.

"You are more than a thief," Fox said. "You are cruel, Fulghum. You took what wasn't yours. I have seen the salary sheets and know you made more than a fair living. Try and justify it all you want, but you are a criminal. I plan to see you pay for your crimes."

For the first time, the bravado left the man's eyes. "You don't have to turn me over to the authorities, Your Grace. I did nothing to you. Why don't you let bygones be bygones?"

Anger poured through Fox. "You stole from the Foxwell family, Fulghum. I plan to see you swing at the end of a gibbet."

Fox left the room without another word, ignoring Fulghum's pleas as he closed the door. Miss Slade waited for him.

"I had the maid released, Your Grace. Did you get the answers you were looking for?"

"All I heard were excuses and lies. See that Fulghum is sent immediately to the authorities. Do you know of the agents who were working with the ledgers? Have they prepared their case against Fulghum?"

"Let me take you to Mr. Franklin, Your Grace. He will be able to answer your questions."

They went down the corridor and were soon seated in Franklin's office, Fox asking the runner to remain with them as they talked.

"We have built a strong case against Fulghum, Your Grace. Miss Colebourne's help was invaluable to my agents. Are you ready for him to be prosecuted?"

"Immediately," he said. "I want a swift hammer brought down upon him."

"I will see that he is transferred today. You will be kept apprised of when he goes to trial, but things would move forward more speedily if you spoke to the authorities today and made your wishes known."

Reluctantly, he agreed to do so and then said, "Miss Slade tells me that your runners have been unsuccessful in finding Mrs. Garrison and her son."

Franklin nodded. "That is true, but we are still looking for them."

"I would like Miss Slade and her partner placed on the case. Replace the agents currently assigned to the case," he said firmly.

"Of course, Your Grace. I will do so today."

Fox turned to the runner. "Come and see me the minute you find them, Miss Slade."

"I will, Your Grace. Do not worry. We will find Mrs. Garrison and her son."

Franklin said, "Would you accompany His Grace, Miss Slade, and oversee the prisoner's transfer?"

"Yes, Mr. Franklin. At once."

They rose, and she gave Fox the address where Fulghum would be taken.

"We have a secure vehicle for transporting criminals. If you will follow us, you can speak to the officials regarding Fulghum's case."

"How long will this take?"

"It could be an hour. Possibly two. But once you speak with them, you may not even have to come and testify."

"I will do whatever it takes to see this man locked up or executed."

Fox left the Bow Street headquarters and looked around for a hansom cab.

"Your Grace?"

He turned and saw a young woman about Eliza's age. She was fairly pretty, with brown hair and brown eyes, but she sported a large, discolored bruise on her cheek. He knew exactly who had put that bruise there.

"You must be the parlor maid who ran off with Fulghum."

She nodded, her shame obvious. "I wanted to apologize to you, Your Grace. I'm sorry I up and left with Fulghum. He told me he would buy me pretty clothes. That he would marry me, and I wouldn't have to work for a living anymore. He promised I would have a maid of my own and a butler, and we would live in a fancy house."

She sniffed, tears beginning to stream down her cheeks. "I am so sorry. He lied about everything. He was ugly to me. Hit me. Called me stupid. I think he was ready to cut me loose when those runners showed up." She paused. "I just wanted you to know I'm sorry. I was a fool to believe such fancy lies."

The girl turned and shuffled off glumly. Fox knew she would have a hard time finding a new employer, with no references to share. Most likely, she would turn to a life on the streets and earn her living as a strumpet.

He couldn't let that happen.

"Wait," he called, and she turned. He closed the distance between them. "You made a mistake. A very big mistake. But everyone deserves a second chance. What is your name?"

Her tears flowed freely. "Becky, Your Grace."

"Well, Becky, you didn't steal a farthing from me, did you?"

"No, Your Grace," she blubbered.

"Then it would be wrong to punish you any further. Come home with me now. You can stay in London for a bit. My housekeeper can find something for you to do. Eventually, you can return to Crosshaven and your sister if you'd like."

She fell to her knees and wrapped her arms about his leg. "Oh, thank you. Thank you. Thank you, Your Grace. God bless you."

He took her elbow and guided her to her feet. "Come with me. I will find a hansom cab to take us home."

Her jaw dropped. "I cannot ride with you, Your Grace."

He could see where that might be awkward. "You shall ride with the driver, Becky."

Fox hailed a cab and asked the driver if Becky could ride beside him. He looked a bit puzzled but agreed and took Fox to the address where Fulghum was being taken.

Once they arrived, he paid the driver and said, "Please take Becky to my townhome now." To the maid, he said, "I have business here which might take a few hours. Tell Mrs. Driskell that I have sent you to her and that she is to find a place for you."

"Yes, Your Grace. Thank you ever so much."

Fox went inside and gave the clerk his name, telling him that Bow Street was transferring a prisoner here and that Fox wanted to speak to someone about bringing charges against the man.

"Wait here, Your Grace. Prisoners are brought around back. I'll see if this Fulghum has arrived."

After several minutes, Miss Slade appeared. "Fulghum is in custody. If you would like, I can stay with you and guide you through the process with the magistrate."

"I would very much appreciate that, Miss Slade."

Close to three hours later, they wrapped up their business, and Fox secured a hansom cab for them. He gave the driver both his address and that of Bow Street, having the driver drop him off first and then continue to Bow Street with Miss Slade.

As they parted, the agent told him she would speak to the other runner regarding his progress in finding Mrs. Garrison.

"Don't worry, Your Grace. I am very good at what I do. I will find Mrs. Garrison for you."

"Thank you, Miss Slade."

Wearily, he entered his townhouse, being greeted immediately by Driskell.

"We took in the maid from Crosshaven, Your Grace," the butler said. "Mrs. Driskell found a spot for her in the kitchens."

"Fine. She can remain here or be sent back to Crosshaven when it's convenient. I will leave that up to you and Marsh."

"It is close to dinner, Your Grace. Cook always prepares a light meal to be served earlier than usual during the Season. You will be able to partake of a midnight buffet at the ball. From what I gather, those are quite lavish meals."

"Have a tray sent to my rooms, Driskell. I am in need of a long, hot bath and a bit of quiet. And let my nieces know I am home. For good."

Driskell chuckled. "They will be happy to know so, Your Grace. Lady Eliza's nose was quite out of joint when you arrived earlier and did not come in to say hello."

He roared with laughter.

It was good to finally be home.

CHAPTER TWENTY-THREE

"**Y**OU MUST COME eat with us, Miss Colebourne," Lady Grace encouraged. "Uncle Fox is back. I know he will be happy to see you."

For a moment, Delaney wondered about the girl's comments. Did Grace know of anything that had passed between her and Fox? She decided she was being overly worried.

Her fears were put to rest when Lady Eliza said, "Yes, he will want to know all about our wardrobes. You can tell him what you and the other seamstresses have been working on. But let *me* tell him about my designs," she cautioned. "I will want to show him my sketches, and then he can see the gowns tomorrow."

Delaney didn't think she could eat a bite put before her with Fox sitting at the table. Not wanting to seem churlish, however, she said, "Yes, I will go in to dinner with you. We must let Driskell know so another place can be set."

Once downstairs, she entered the dining room with the young ladies of the house. They paused, and Lady Eliza told the butler that Delaney would be dining with them.

"If you would like, Miss Colebourne, you may sit in His Grace's spot this evening. The place has already been set."

"But isn't His Grace joining us?" she asked.

"No, I am afraid not," Driskell shared.

"Why not?" Lady Eliza demanded.

"His Grace needed rest and a bath after his long journey, my lady," the butler said.

"He got back to town hours ago," the young woman complained. "He could have rested then instead of running off without so much as a hello."

"Yes, but he had important business to attend to since he had been gone from town so long, my lady," Driskell countered. "He only arrived home again moments ago. He will dine in his rooms and bathe and dress in time to escort you and Lady Grace to the ball."

"I will give him a piece of my mind when I see him," Lady Eliza threatened.

Delaney glared at the girl but before she could say anything, Lady Grace spoke up. "You will not do anything of the kind, Eliza. Uncle Fox is being gracious enough to escort us this evening. He has spent a small fortune on each of us with so many gowns being made up for us and dozens and dozens more still to come. He promised he would be here in time, and he is. Stop your complaining and eat."

Eliza's mouth settled in a pout, but she said, "Oh, all right."

Delaney was proud of Lady Grace for taking a stand. She liked how the girl stood by her convictions.

They took their seats at the table and started the meal with a simple broth, followed by fish and vegetables. She found herself being able to eat with Fox not in the room. Delaney had hoped to meet with him privately before tonight's ball, speaking plainly of her feelings for him. She realized now she would not have that opportunity.

Once they finished dinner, she accompanied the girls back upstairs. Hot baths awaited the pair. She made certain their gowns were ready to go and helped the maids in dressing the two. Lady Eliza was still debating on how to wear her hair as Lady Grace's maid arranged her hair artfully. Fanny, Dilly, and Ruth had come downstairs to watch, and Ruth suggested to Lady Eliza how to wear her hair this evening. It surprised Delaney when Ruth's advice was taken.

Pride filled her as the two stood side-by-side, ready for their debuts.

"Don't you look lovely?" Fanny said. "You'll turn every gentleman's head in the ballroom tonight."

Lady Grace smoothed her skirts. "Do you really think so, Fanny?"

"I know so," Fanny said firmly.

"What if no one asks us to dance?" Lady Grace asked worriedly.

"Pish-posh," her sister said. "We are daughters of a duke and very comely. Our dance cards will quickly fill."

Delaney hid her laugh, holding her hand to her mouth and coughing lightly. Lady Eliza certainly did not lack confidence.

Wanting to assure the younger Foxwell sister, she said, "You both are beautiful, kind young ladies. Lady Eliza is right—you will first be judged because you are daughters of a duke—but it will take more than that to find the right husband for you. Remember the things we have talked about, and you will be fine."

"Oh, I do hope at least a few gentlemen will call upon us tomorrow," Lady Grace fretted.

Delaney hoped so, too, because that might be the thing that helped Lady Grace begin to believe in herself.

"Thank you, Miss Colebourne," Lady Eliza said. "Actually, thanks to all of you—Ruth, Fanny, Dilly. We will go into the Westfield ballroom this evening with our heads held high, brimming with confidence, because we know how good we look. You have worked so very hard on our behalves."

She almost burst into tears, so proud this young woman actually thought to acknowledge the seamstresses. Lady Eliza had grown quite a bit since Delaney had come to know her.

"We should get downstairs," Lady Grace said. "Remember how the Duchess of Westfield told us the opening night of the Season sees the streets teeming with carriages."

"Thank you for allowing us to see how you look tonight," Ruth said.

"We will do you and the others proud, Ruth," Lady Eliza responded.

"And you better tell us all about it tomorrow," Dilly added. "I want to hear about the other gowns. Who dances with you. What you ate. Everything!"

The girls left, and Fanny said, "You better hurry, Miss Colebourne. You need to get ready yourself."

Delaney had shared with her friends how the Duchess of Westfield had invited her to the ball, so that she might see the Foxwell girls there. The gown Madame had created for her fit perfectly when she had tried it on, and Madame had it delivered to the Westfields' townhouse. Delaney would now go there and slip into it.

"You're right, Fanny. I will see the three of you tomorrow."

Going down the back staircase, she went through the kitchens and came out the door, climbing the stairs to the pavement. Margaret had wanted to send a carriage for her, but Delaney had said the streets would be too crowded, and it would be easier for her to walk the few blocks.

"Miss Colebourne?"

She recognized one of the Westfield footmen and greeted him.

"Her Grace sent me to walk with you," the servant explained. "She did not want you to be out at night alone."

"That was most thoughtful of her."

"She is a good woman," the footman agreed, looking smart in his fancy livery, most likely reserved for special occasions such as tonight.

The footman walked alongside her, and they arrived at their destination less than ten minutes later. She was glad she had insisted upon walking because the streets were already clogged with numerous carriages and groups of people were entering the townhouse. At least she would not be going through the receiving line. They had both decided it was unnecessary to do so. Delaney would slip into the ballroom just before the dancing began and stay for a dance or two before retiring upstairs and spending the night in one of Margaret's guest bedchambers. Although she wished she could find a few minutes with Fox, she would not take away time from him this evening. This was as much a debut for him as it was for his nieces. Polite Society would be getting their first look at the new Duke of Abington, and she wanted all eyes on him.

Once again, she cut through the kitchens with the footman, parting from him as a maid took over, leading Delaney up the servants' staircase and to the room reserved for her use. She told Delaney that her name was Molly, and she served as Her Grace's lady's maid. Across the bed lay her gown for the evening, a square-necked one of gold, trimmed in lace, with a wide satin ribbon that encircled her just beneath her breasts. The underskirt was a darker gold. It looked like something an angel might wear.

Reaching out, she rubbed the gown between her fingers, delighting in its feel.

"May I help you to dress now, Miss Colebourne? The receiving line has already started."

"I will not be going through it," she told the servant. "We can take our time. I want to look just right."

In case Fox did happen to see her from across the room.

Molly helped remove the gown Delaney wore, as well as her stockings. Margaret had insisted on new silk stockings and dance slippers dyed to match the new gown. Her artist friend had an excellent eye for detail and wanted Delaney to look her absolute best.

"Oh, my earrings," she proclaimed, retrieving her reticule and locating the amber earrings her father had given her. He would be surprised at her even wanting to attend a ball. She only wished he could have seen her in such finery.

"Please sit at the dressing table, Miss Colebourne," the maid instructed. "We need to work on your hair."

It took another half-hour, but Delaney was delighted with the results of using the curling tongs. The maid had swept up Delaney's hair, weaving a wide lace ribbon through it. Soft curls cascaded from it, framing her face.

"Now for a bit of rouge," the maid declared, opening a pot and dipping her finger into it.

"I have never used rouge before."

"We'll just put a dab on each cheek and blend it in. A tiny bit on your lips, too."

By the time the maid finished, Delaney's face was flush with color and her lips a soft cherry.

"No licking them, Miss Colebourne," Molly warned.

Delaney nodded, admiring her image in the mirror. "You have done an outstanding job, Molly. I would love to repay you. Do you like hats?"

"Yes, Miss Colebourne. I do." She laughed. "What woman doesn't like a hat?"

"Tell me a color hat or bonnet you would like, and I will send one around for you tomorrow from my shop."

"Anything blue. It is my favorite color," the maid said.

"Very well. Blue it shall be. Now, if you would help me find my way to the ballroom, I would appreciate it."

The maid took Delaney down two flights of stairs, the noise growing as they drew closer.

"You can leave me here. Thank you for your help in preparing me for my first ball."

"You're welcome, Miss Colebourne."

She stood and watched the last few people make their way through the receiving line. Margaret and Daniel greeted their guests, Daniel handsome in his black evening clothes and Margaret a vision in green, her red hair piled high upon her head.

When the last couple began speaking to the Westfields, Delaney made her way closer, allowing the pair to pass and then greeting her friend.

Margaret gasped. "Oh, Delaney, you look splendid!"

They embraced, and the duke said, "If I weren't a happily married man, Miss Colebourne, I would offer for you on the spot."

She felt her cheeks warm at Westfield's words. "Thank you, Your Grace."

"Come inside with us," Margaret said.

"No, all eyes will be on the door, waiting for the host and hostess to appear. I will come in after you do so that no one will notice me." She hesitated. "He is here?"

"He is. And his nieces look very appealing. Abington will need to order a cane a week in order to beat off the young men." Margaret paused. "Have you spoken to him since his return?"

"No. He arrived home barely in time to bathe and dress for the ball. I have not even seen him."

Her friend took Delaney's hands and squeezed them. "Be sure that he sees you in this gown. You are ravishing tonight."

Margaret kissed her cheek. "I will see you later." She took the arm her husband offered.

Daniel winked at Delaney and then led his wife to the entrance of the ballroom. They paused in the doorway and then went inside.

She waited a full minute before stepping to the entrance, seeing the duke and duchess heading toward the center of the ballroom. The musicians, who had been tuning their instruments, paused, bows in hand. Guests began moving toward the dance floor. Delaney caught sight of Lady Grace stepping out with a tall, auburn-haired gentleman. She couldn't help but smile as she caught sight of the girl's happy face.

Continuing to skim the room, she found Lady Eliza being escorted to the dance floor by a handsome man with dark blonde hair. He bent and said something in Lady Eliza's ear, and the girl beamed up at him.

Delaney moved from the entrance and went to the edge of the ballroom as the musicians set their bows against the strings of their instruments, and the conductor waved his baton. Suddenly the music started up and a lively country dance began. She watched, smiling, seeing the happiness on the faces of both Foxwell girls.

Then she became aware of someone standing behind her. She turned—and gazed up at the Duke of Abington.

He smiled down at her, causing warmth to flood her. "You look breathtaking, Delaney. If I knew how to dance, I would ask you to do so."

"I never learned myself," she admitted. "I saw no reason to do so. Bastard daughters of earls are not usually invited to *ton* balls."

His gaze reached into her soul. His fingers found hers. "And yet here you are, the guest of a duke and duchess."

"Her Grace thought I might wish to see your nieces dancing in my gowns. I only plan to watch for a dance or two."

"Then we shall watch together."

Fox tucked her hand into the crook of his arm. He gave off a tremendous heat, which caused her to grow dizzy. Delaney blinked a few times and even bit down on her tongue, telling herself to faint in front of all these guests would lead to utter humiliation.

When the dance ended, she watched Lady Eliza and Lady Grace leave the dance floor. They were immediately claimed by new partners and led out once again. The dancing commenced, and she sighed.

"They look happy, don't they?" she said.

"They look lovely in your gowns. And yes, they seem very content," Fox agreed. He looked down at her. "May we speak privately? There are things that were left unsaid between us before I left town."

Delaney thought of how she had turned down his marriage proposal and sensed the blush spreading across her cheeks.

"Yes, I believe we do have things to say to one another."

"Shall we stroll on the balcony?" he suggested. "I doubt anyone will be out there this early in the evening."

She nodded, her throat swelling with emotion. She knew in

the next few minutes that her entire future would be decided. It would either be spent loving this man—or she would retire to Chapwell Hall and a life of loneliness.

"Lead the way," Delaney said.

CHAPTER TWENTY-FOUR

F OX LED DELANEY to the other side of the ballroom, and they slipped through a set of opened French doors onto a terrace. After the heat and crowd of the ballroom, the cool, fresh night air felt good to her.

Fox had been right in believing the terrace would be empty. She supposed there would be couples strolling upon it between sets of music and even after tonight's midnight buffet. For now, though, they had it to themselves.

As he moved them slowly down the length of it, Delaney said, "I owe you an apology."

"You have nothing to apologize for, Delaney. I stormed off and sulked as a petulant child might, not the adult I am. I regret my behavior."

Marshaling every ounce of courage she had, she gazed up at him. "And I regret my answer to your question."

She saw the hope that filled his eyes. "Are you saying what I think you are saying?"

"You offered a life to me, Fox. A life with you. I chose not to focus on what was important and instead let the doubts and fears which plagued me stand in our way."

She swallowed, mustering her courage. "But I love you. And I—"

His mouth was on hers, the kiss passionate from the start. He clasped her shoulders, his lips moving against hers, their tongues mating. In that moment, Delaney knew they could conquer anything.

As long as they stood together.

After a long moment, Fox broke the kiss, resting his brow against hers. "I had not given up hope," he admitted. "I was going to offer for you again tonight." He grinned sheepishly. "And every day and night after until I wore down your defenses, and you finally said yes."

Laughter bubbled up from her. "It sounds as if you were treating me as an enemy soldier to be conquered." She touched her fingers to his cheek, caressing it. "I am not your enemy, Fox. I am the woman who will always love you."

This time, she pulled him down for a long, lingering kiss.

When he broke it, he glanced about. "Thank goodness no one saw us."

Disappointment filled her, and she wondered if he truly had meant what he said.

He framed her face with his long fingers and said, "I would not want others to discover us kissing and you feel obligated to marry me, Delaney. I want you to do so because you choose to do so. That you choose to love me."

She relaxed. "I love you more than I ever believed possible, Fox. Although part of me feels you will be making a dreadful mistake by marrying the bastard daughter of an earl, one who is in trade. A part of me, though, simply doesn't care because I love you so much. I know the *ton* can be judgmental, but Margaret assures me that dukes are a law unto themselves. That Polite Society might actually forgive you any transgression—because we are a love match."

He smiled down at her. "We are more than a love match, my sweet. We are a love story for the ages. I love you so very much, Delaney."

He kissed her once more, a kiss full of unspoken promises to her he would keep over the decades. Delaney felt loved.

Cherished. Treasured.

Fox released her and reached inside his coat, pulling out a folded page. Holding it up, he told her, "You are looking at the special license which I purchased after we returned from Crosshaven."

His words stunned her, and she let out a few choice curse words, causing him to burst into laughter. "You have had it all these weeks? Is it even still good?"

"The clerk assured me it would be valid for a month. We still have a few days to put it to good use. I don't want to rush you, however. If you need more time in which to plan our wedding, then I am happy to give it to you. I would buy a hundred special licenses, Delaney. I would wait a thousand years for you. For it is only you for me."

Her heart soared, her happiness now complete. "I want to take advantage of this special license," she told him. "I would marry you tonight, but I doubt a clergyman is present at this ball."

He grinned boyishly. "Would tomorrow be soon enough for you?"

"Tomorrow would be perfect, Fox."

"Then we should go in and share our news with the Duke and Duchess of Westfield. I have a suspicion Her Grace might want to host our wedding breakfast."

He guided her to the French doors once more and just as they reached them, she halted. Gazing up at him, she asked, "Is this truly happening? We are to be wed?"

Fox looked at her solemnly. "We will marry. We will be deliriously happy. We will make for remarkable parents. I have already had a glimpse of what parenting is like, becoming the guardian to Eliza and Grace. I am sorry I missed out on seeing them grow and mature over the years, but we will be able to do so watching our own children."

Delaney had to blink away the tears of happiness filling her eyes. "Thank you for your reassurances."

He lifted her hand to his lips and kissed it tenderly. "Thank you for loving me."

Tucking her arm once more into the crook of his arm, Fox led her into the ballroom. They stood a moment, watching the dancers, and she caught sight of Grace just as the music ended.

"I see the Westfields," Fox said, guiding her through the crowd toward them.

The moment they reached the couple, the duchess exclaimed, "You have done it!"

Westfield looked at his wife and then to them. Grinning, he said, "Yes, it is obvious that you have settled whatever differences you might have had. When is the wedding?"

Delaney laughed. "We were thinking of tomorrow, Your Grace, but are in need of finding an available clergyman. It seems Fox has a special license burning a hole in his pocket and wants to put it to good use before it expires."

The duke said, "Then let us offer our help. We would be happy to host your wedding breakfast."

"It will be very small," Fox said. "I want my nieces there. The Mortons, as well. And Mrs. Damson, Lady Morton's sister." He looked to her.

"I would like my three employees to come, along with my longtime maid. I know they make for unusual guests, but they have been good friends to me."

"Shall we announce your betrothal during the midnight buffet?" Westfield asked. "I would be honored to do so."

Fox looked to her, and Delaney nodded. "Yes, Daniel. Feel free to share our happy news."

Margaret embraced Delaney and whispered in her ear, "You are going to be so happy."

She looked at her friend. "I think we will be."

Turning to Fox, she asked, "Should we prepare Lady Eliza and Lady Grace for this news?"

He shook his head. "No, let them enjoy their fun for now. When the buffet starts, we can pull them aside before the engagement announcement is made."

"I hope they will be accepting of me," she said quietly.

"Those girls think highly of you," Margaret interjected. "I would not worry about that. If you will excuse me, I am going to tell my cook that she has a wedding breakfast to prepare for tomorrow morning. Shall we say eleven o'clock for the ceremony?"

Delaney and Fox agreed, and the duchess excused herself.

Westfield said, "I am off, as well. I need to dash off a quick message to the clergyman who married Margaret and me. I will return soon. In the meantime, enjoy a dance together."

Delaney and Fox glanced to one another and burst out laughing.

After the duke left, Fox said, "Perhaps we should hire the dance master that comes once a week for my nieces. After all, if we are going to partake in the Season each year, I will need to know how to dance with my beloved duchess."

The love for her shining in his eyes let Delaney know how happy they would always be.

The orchestra started up again, and they stood on the sidelines, watching the dancers, enjoying the music. Their hosts rejoined them a short while later, and both confirmed tomorrow's wedding had been arranged.

"If you would like," Margaret said, "we could hold the ceremony in the ballroom. The flowers will still look fresh. It would make for a beautiful setting."

"Wherever you wish us to be," Fox said, "we will be there. I would marry this woman in a ballroom. Outdoors during a rainstorm. In the dead of winter. On the darkest night or the brightest day. My love for her knows no end."

The Westfields beamed at them. "I am glad you admitted your love for one another," the duke said. "I hope you will be as happy as Margaret and I are."

Midnight finally came, and the musicians took a much-needed respite as guests filed into the room where a lavish buffet had been arranged. Margaret insisted that Delaney and Fox join them at the head table.

"That is a lovely offer," Delaney said firmly but politely. "It is unnecessary, however. You are already doing so much for us."

Margaret frowned, clearly puzzled by her refusal. "Why would you not wish to sit with us?"

She drew on a reserve of courage she didn't know she possessed and said, "Your Grace, you must realize how it would reflect upon you and His Grace if I were seated with you. I am not accepted by Polite Society, for reasons you well know. It is one thing for you to be so kind as to host our wedding ceremony and breakfast with a small group in attendance. It is quite another thing for me to boldly sit next to you at the head table at this ball. I fear if I do so, your reputations would be besmirched."

The duchess started to reply, but her husband cut her off. "My duchess has asked for your presence at our table, and that is what she will get. We choose who we are friends with, Miss Colebourne. I do not give a bloody fig what the *ton* will think or say. The two of you are very special to us, and I believe the four of us will be friends for years to come."

The duke smiled. "Besides, you are soon to be a duchess yourself. I already know what a good one you will be. No more nonsense. You are our guests, and we wish for you to dine with us."

Delaney's eyes misted with tears. "You are both so kind and generous. How can I refuse?"

"You can't," said Westfield, grinning at her. "After all, no one can refuse a duke—or a duchess."

Fox smiled at her. "Since you are in good hands, I am off to have a quick word with Grace and Eliza."

He set off across the room and pride swelled within her, knowing this marvelous, rugged man was hers. All hers.

"Shall we go through the buffet together?" Margaret suggested.

"Yes, I would enjoy seeing it. I can also make up a plate for

Fox."

The duke led them to the front of the line, and they went through it together. Delaney had trouble choosing items because the selection was so varied.

Once their plates were filled, they returned to their table, where Fox awaited them, his nieces with him.

Eliza told Delaney, "I knew there was something between the two of you. I told Grace that very thing."

"She did," her sister confirmed, smiling at Delaney. "We are very happy for you, Miss Colebourne."

"Miss Colebourne is far too formal," Eliza declared. "Might we call you Aunt Delaney?" the girl asked.

Delaney's heart warmed at the suggestion. "I would be touched for you to do so, my lady."

"Then you must stop calling us my lady, Aunt Delaney." Eliza threw her arms around Delaney and squeezed her tightly, saying, "Now, Uncle Fox will not have to look for a bride for himself."

Grace came and also embraced Delaney.

"Come, Grace. We must go back to our supper partners. By now, I am certain they have gone through the buffet and are awaiting us."

The two young ladies left, and Fox seated Delaney.

"They took it rather well, I thought," he said.

"I hope they will not be embarrassed by me and my background," she said.

"Nonsense," Margaret said. "By this time tomorrow evening, you will be the Duchess of Abington. After all, those girls are the daughters and nieces of a duke. They are beautiful and friendly. They will have no trouble securing husbands."

Delaney chuckled. "They might have offers, but Fox mostly likely will put any prospective suitor through the wringer."

"Good for you," Westfield said. "I already know it will take an extraordinary man before I send my Norrie off with him."

They enjoyed their meal, and then the duke said, "I see my

ALEXA ASTON

footmen are bringing in the champagne now. Are you ready for us to make the announcement?"

Trepidation filled her. She still worried about how this first engagement of the Season would be received by the *ton*. She nodded, however, as did Fox.

"Then come stand beside my duchess and me," Westfield said.

The four of them rose and went to stand in front of their table as footmen circulated about the room, distributing flutes of champagne. A buzz started, and Delaney felt all eyes upon her.

The duke took his flute and held it high. "I am delighted to announce the betrothal of two dear friends of ours this evening. My duchess and I are pleased to ask you to raise a glass to celebrate the engagement of Nigel Foxwell, Duke of Abington, and Miss Delaney Colebourne."

A stunned silence followed the duke's words, and then chairs scraped against the floor as the guests came to their feet and held their glasses high.

"To Abington and Miss Colebourne," Westfield said, his voice ringing throughout the room.

"Wait!" shouted a voice.

Even though he had not been invited, Delaney watched as her half-brother made his way through the crowd.

Her worst nightmare would play out now.

In front of the entire *ton*.

CHAPTER TWENTY-FIVE

F OX DIDN'T RECOGNIZE the man pushing his way through the standing crowd, but his gut told him exactly who it was.

The Earl of Kinnison.

"Stop this travesty," Kinnison commanded as he reached them, standing mere feet away from Fox and Delaney. "This by-blow of my father's has bewitched you, Abington. The same way her wanton mother did my father. She was a dairy farmer's wife, for God's sake. And this one—she is in trade. *Trade!*"

He took a step forward. "She was—until you bullied Polite Society into casting her into oblivion. All because of your jealousy, Kinnison."

The earl's face reddened. "Why would *I* be jealous of such a bit of muslin?"

Fox's hands fisted at the insult. "Miss Colebourne is no woman of easy virtue. She was a beloved daughter of an earl. Lord Kinnison doted upon her."

"He did!" roared Kinnison. "He ignored me—*ignored me*—his heir. In favor of his love child. I hated him. I hated her and her mother. Do you know he tried to make the bitch his countess? We would have been the laughingstock of the *ton* if he had done so." The earl shook his fist at Delaney. "He gave all his time and attention to you."

"He tried to give it to you, too," Delaney told her angry half-

221

brother. "But you were never interested in him. In the estate. In caring for its tenants. All you wanted to do was drink and gamble with your friends. I loved Papa."

"Don't call him that!" Kinnison demanded. He whirled, looking about the room. "Can't you see what she is?"

Fox said, "Miss Colebourne was a beloved daughter, both of her mother and father. She is a talented milliner and modiste and close friends with the Duchess of Westfield. Most importantly, she is the love of my life. I was raised a gentleman, Kinnison. As a major-general in His Majesty's army, I was taught to treat everyone—particularly women—with respect. My future duchess has my love and my respect. She is full of grace and light. When you denigrated her and forced her clients away, she spoke not a foul word against you. She was a true lady in every sense of the word—and she will make for an outstanding duchess."

He paused, letting his words sink in. "You were not invited tonight for a reason, Kinnison. You are a bitter, stupid fool. I am a duke and outrank you. I will issue the same edict you once did against my beloved." He glanced around the room. "If anyone present publicly acknowledges this man and his countess, as well as his in-laws, then they will receive the cut direct from my duchess and me."

Westfield stepped forward. "And from my duchess and me. We did not invite Lord and Lady Kinnison to our home tonight for a reason. They are a poison which would ooze through those present, tainting everyone they come in contact with."

Fox took up the mantle. "The four of us will not attend any *ton* event in which they are present."

"I also speak for my close friends, the Dukes of Linberry, Bradford, and Stoneham. They will stand with us. Make your choice wisely," Westfield warned the *ton*.

Lord Kinnison's jaw dropped. "You would have us cut from every guest list?" He turned in circles, his eyes pleading with the members of Polite Society who now glared at him.

"You were not invited here this evening," Fox said quietly.

"You are not welcome. Please leave—or His Grace's footmen will see that you do."

He watched as the earl's shoulders slumped in defeat. Slowly, he turned away, shuffling along as a man three times his age. Polite Society watched in fascination as Lady Kinnison, her face stricken with horror, followed him.

Fox slipped an arm about Delaney's waist. "Are you all right?"

She placed a palm against his cheek. "You fought for me. You told the entire *ton* you love me." A slow smile spread across her beautiful face. "Of course, I am all right. I have the love of the most wonderful man in the world and two incredible friends who stood by us."

"We will always stand with you," Margaret said quietly to them.

He sensed the gazes of all the guests on them and nodded at Daniel. "I believe you were about to finish your toast, Your Grace."

His friend flashed a triumphant smile. "I was, Your Grace." Westfield faced his guests and raised his flute again. "To our very good friends who have a deep, abiding love for one another. To Abington and Miss Colebourne."

"To Abington and Miss Colebourne," echoed everyone present in the room.

Fox and Delaney drank a sip of their champagne, and then he took the flute from her hand, setting both down on the table behind them.

Then with the entire *ton* looking on, the Duke of Abington wrapped his arms about his fiancée and proceeded to kiss her senseless.

⤛⤜

DELANEY HAD ALREADY planned to stay the night with the Westfields and kept to that plan. She did not go to bed until almost four o'clock in the morning, as the last of the ball's guests departed. Surprisingly, she had encountered nothing but encouraging words from the many people who made a point to come and congratulate her and Fox on their upcoming vows. Many of these were former clients who begged for her forgiveness, apologizing for abandoning her and giving in to Lord and Lady Kinnison's bullying. She accepted each apology gracefully.

When one former client asked if she would keep designing hats after her marriage, Fox replied before Delaney could, saying how proud he was of her creativity and business acumen and that the woman could count on new hats appearing at the grand reopening of Delaney's Designs next Season.

She pulled aside her new fiancé after that, asking him if he meant what he said. He told her that she had his full support in continuing to run her shop. When she told him running a household would take up a good deal of her time and energy, they agreed on a compromise. Delaney would continue sketching her creations and turn over her drawings to Dilly and Ruth to make up. Fanny would assume a leadership role and manage the store in Delaney's place. They would probably have to hire another milliner and a clerk to assist Fanny if the response was what Delaney thought it would be.

For now, though, her three friends would continue sewing the many gowns for the Foxwell girls. Once the Season ended, they could return to the millinery world and work on building up the inventory for next Season's launch. She couldn't wait to share this with her friends, along with the fact that they would be coming to her wedding today.

She rose when hot water arrived for her bath. Margaret came and sat beside the tub, telling Delaney of everything in motion this morning.

"Mr. Hodgkins arrived with the marriage contracts early this morning. Daniel sent for his solicitor, and the two of them went over the settlements carefully. Fox expects nothing from you,

Delaney. You are to remain totally in control of your possessions. Your estate. Your business. Mr. Hodgkins said he would continue to advise you separately in all matters."

"Am I to sign these before the ceremony?"

"Yes, Daniel advises that you do so. Don't worry about it now, though. You can get to it later. Let me tell you everything else."

Margaret informed Delaney that word had been sent to inform her friends of their invitation to the wedding. Molly, Margaret's lady's maid, had been sent to Delaney's Designs to make certain Mary was apprised of the wedding and to look through Delaney's wardrobe to find something appropriate to serve as her wedding gown.

"Daniel also has lined up a clergyman," Margaret continued. "The ballroom still has all its flowers and greenery."

"How is today's weather?" Delaney asked.

"I have not been outside," her friend said. "Are you worried about rain?"

"It is just that Fox and I declared our love for one another on your terrace. The seeds of our future together were planted there. I wondered if the weather might be good enough to move a few of the flowers and plants onto the terrace and speak our vows there."

Margaret beamed. "That is a lovely idea, Delaney. I will go check on the weather now and if it looks to be good, I will have Hampton supervise moving things outside."

Mary arrived with Molly just as Delaney was drying off.

"We brought two gowns for you, Miss Colebourne," Mary said. "Either one would make for a lovely choice for the ceremony."

The three of them decided upon the dress, and Molly went to press it while Mary helped Delaney into fresh undergarments.

Suddenly, the door burst open, Eliza and Grace rushing in.

"We had to come see if you needed any help, Aunt Delaney," Eliza said. "Uncle Fox is downstairs. He knows not to come up."

"As I dress, you must tell me about your night," she encouraged. "How was your first ball?"

Both girls chatted animatedly, telling her about their different dance partners. Eliza had half a dozen gentlemen she was already interested in, while Grace admitted to liking two bachelors, one fresh out of university and one a few years older.

"We told all of them not to call upon us today," Eliza said airily. "That we would not be at home because our uncle was getting married. I think it made a few of them even more interested, knowing they couldn't call just yet."

"The drawing room was already filling with bouquets when we left to come here," Grace shared. "Both gentlemen I took a fancy to sent beautiful arrangements."

Molly returned with Delaney's gown and helped her into it before beginning to work on styling her hair. She asked more questions of the girls and told them they could tell callers they would receive them tomorrow afternoon.

"Your uncle and I will be on hand each afternoon to chaperone you."

"Won't you go away on a honeymoon?" Eliza asked.

"We can save that for later. It is important for us to be here for the two of you."

"You are very thoughtful, Aunt Delaney," Grace said, leaning down and kissing Delaney's cheek.

Margaret sailed in. "All the guests have arrived, as well as the clergyman. The terrace is brimming with flowers."

"You are marrying outside?" Grace asked. "Oh, I think that is a wonderful idea."

"I think an outdoor wedding will be perfect," Delaney said. She glanced in the mirror and smiled. "Thank you, Molly. I look perfect."

Her friend came and embraced her. "You look like a woman in love. Come, everyone. We should go downstairs."

The duchess sent everyone to the ballroom, while she and Delaney stopped at Westfield's study.

"I will leave you to it," Margaret said. "But don't be long. The guests are waiting, along with a very impatient groom." She kissed Delaney's cheek and left the room.

Mr. Hodgkins told her, "Everything is in good order, Miss Colebourne. His Grace has already signed his portion of the contracts. We are awaiting your signature. The Duke of Westfield will witness it."

She took the offered quill and dipped it into the inkpot, scribbling her name where Hodgkins pointed and setting the quill aside.

"Is that it?" she asked.

Her solicitor smiled. "It is, Miss Colebourne. I wish you a happy day."

"May I escort you to your groom?" the duke asked, his eyes twinkling.

"I would like that very much, Your Grace."

As he led her to the ballroom, he said, "I would like it if you would address me as Daniel. I know you already call Margaret by her given name."

"You have been a good friend to Fox, Daniel. I would be happy to honor your request."

He offered her his arm. "Let's get you married."

They moved across the ballroom and to the open French doors. She spied a string quartet. They began to play as she and Daniel stepped from the ballroom onto the terrace, which was a kaleidoscope of colors, thanks to the flowers and greenery decorating it. She knew others were present.

But Delaney only had eyes for Fox.

Her groom locked eyes with her, and Delaney swallowed at the intensity of his gaze. She and the duke moved to Fox, who took her hand and laced his fingers through hers.

"I thought you would never get here," he murmured.

"You look like a fox who's gained access to the henhouse," she teased. "I would swear you were about to gobble me up."

He smiled wolfishly at her. "Oh, I plan to feast on you later, my love."

Delancy cursed under her breath. Her groom laughed aloud.

Together, they faced a slightly bewildered clergyman and Fox said, "What are you waiting for? We are ready to be wed now."

"Of course, Your Grace." Clearing his throat, he began. "Dearly beloved . . ."

She didn't hear much of what the clergyman said. What she was aware of was the spice of Fox's cologne. The warmth of his fingers against hers. The swarm of butterflies that beat rapidly in her belly.

Her groom turned her so they faced one another, and he repeated the minister's words, promising to love, honor, and cherish her forever. Delaney repeated them to him, their gazes never wavering.

When the clergyman pronounced them man and wife, he had barely gotten the final word out of his mouth when Fox grabbed her and gave her a long, deep kiss. He broke it. Grinned at her. Then kissed her again.

"There is a wedding breakfast, Abington," Daniel said loudly.

Fox lifted his lips from hers and swore under his breath. She laughed. "I must be rubbing off on you."

"I suppose we should go celebrate with our friends," he said grumpily.

"We will only be there an hour or two. Then we will have the rest of the day with one another."

He cupped her cheeks. "No, the rest of our lives." He kissed her lightly. "Let's go see what is for breakfast."

They went to a dining room, beautifully decorated with more flowers that she assumed were used at last night's ball. She met Lord and Lady Morton, along with Mrs. Damson, and liked the three of them quite a bit. She remembered Lady Morton had previously been a client of hers, and Delaney was touched when the countess apologized for abandoning her.

"No apology is necessary, Lady Morton," Delaney assured her. "I am glad to renew our acquaintance. It is lovely to meet your sister."

"I only recently met your husband, Your Grace," Mrs. Damson said. "He made quite an impression upon me, however. You are a most fortunate woman."

"Most would believe me fortunate to become a duchess," she told the widow. "I know I am fortunate because I have the love of a wonderful man."

Once they finished dining, Margaret told them, "Daniel and I will be calling for Lady Eliza and Lady Grace this evening. They will be under our care as we escort them to tonight's ball. That will give the two of you some private time together."

"Thank you," Delaney said, taking her friend's hand and squeezing it.

"Speaking of private time," Fox said, rising and bringing Delaney to her feet. He looked out at their guests. "Her Grace and I will bid you farewell now." He looked to his nieces. "The Duke and Duchess of Westfield will escort you two to tonight's affair. But Delaney and I will see you tomorrow afternoon. I have been informed that our drawing room will be crawling with callers."

Grace and Eliza came and kissed her cheeks. "We will see you tomorrow, Aunt Delaney," Grace said.

"Do not let Uncle Fox embarrass us tomorrow when our suitors call," Eliza said.

Delaney laughed. "I will keep him well in hand," she promised.

They went out to their carriage, and her new husband handed her up. He climbed in after her and pulled her onto his lap.

"I plan to kiss you the entire way home, Your Grace," he promised, his voice husky.

"I plan to let you, Your Grace," she retorted. "And then I will ravish you once we get home."

Fox cocked one eyebrow. "I thought I was in charge of ravishing."

"I believe that is something we might do together."

Her husband was laughing as he kissed her, and Delaney knew their lives would be full of love and laughter throughout the coming years.

EPILOGUE

London—Two months later . . .

D ELANEY AWOKE TO a delicious kiss and romp in bed with her handsome duke. The past weeks had been nothing short of amazing. Her organizational skills, along with Mrs. Driskell's knowledge of the household, had led to a happy relationship between her and the housekeeper. She had also hired an additional seamstress to take her place in the schoolroom since Fox did not want his wife's days tied up with a needle and thread in her hands. The new seamstress, a friend of Dilly's, was quick and efficient. Gowns were being completed at a rapid pace. Delaney had taken a second trip with Fanny and the girls to the fabric stores shortly after her marriage, looking at materials for the second and final round of gowns to be completed, five of the designs ones Eliza had created.

The seamstresses had also started on a wardrobe for Delaney. While some of her current gowns could be worn to various events, she definitely lacked in ballgowns. She insisted upon designing her own wardrobe, knowing what would best flatter her figure. Her collection of gowns now grew, and she had received numerous compliments. When she told others they were of her own design, women clamored for her to create gowns for them. She was taking it into consideration, expanding

Delaney's Designs from strictly hats to all wardrobe needs of ladies.

Both girls had accepted Delaney with open arms, and she already felt motherly toward them. She and Fox had been kept busy not only with the busy schedule of social affairs to attend but also being present while suitors called upon Eliza and Grace. The pair proved to be quite popular, and she hoped they would both find their future husbands during this Season. If not, she and Fox would look forward to helping as much as they could in steering the girls to the right gentlemen in the future.

Her husband kissed her deeply and then said, "I suppose we should go down to breakfast. What are our plans for the day?"

She ran her fingers through his dark hair. "You will be happy to know we will not be at home this afternoon."

"Good," he said gruffly. "No addlebrained men mooning over the girls. And no drawing room stuffed to the gills with flowers. I am tired of the scent of roses."

"Well, you might not escape the roses, Your Grace. We will not be home because we have a garden party to attend. Most likely, the garden will be full of roses."

He gave her a wicked smile. "We could always find a private path in the garden, Your Grace. I would be happy to steal a few kisses from you along the way."

She laughed and kissed him soundly, tossing back the bedclothes and reaching for her dressing gown. "I will see you at breakfast."

Delaney went through his dressing room and bathing chamber, which connected to her own set of the same. She arrived in her bedchamber, which she only used for dressing. Her nights were spent in her duke's arms in their shared bed.

Ringing for Mary, she set out the gown she wished to wear this morning. Mary had agreed to come and take care of Delaney as she always had, delighted that she no longer had to also cook and clean.

Once she was ready, Delaney went down to the breakfast

room. Fox was already there. Grace and Eliza no longer came down to breakfast. They preferred taking their morning meal in bed in their rooms. She didn't mind because it gave her extra time with her husband.

They went through the post and discussed a few events reported in the newspapers. As they finished breakfast, Driskell spoke to a footman who appeared. The butler came to them.

"Your Grace, there is a Miss Slade here to see you."

"Have her taken to my study. We will be there in a few minutes."

Fox had shared with Delaney the work Miss Slade did on behalf of Bow Street and how the runner and her partner had located his thieving steward. She wondered if Miss Slade's visit was to update Fox on the upcoming case being brought to trial.

As he escorted her to his study, he said, "Miss Slade has also been working on locating someone else for me. A Mrs. Garrison."

"Who is that?" she asked, curious because she had never heard the woman's name mentioned.

"I always wrote to the wives and mothers of men lost in battle who were under my command. Mrs. Garrison's husband, a lieutenant, was the last man who served under me that died before I left the army. I wrote to her in Colchester."

"If your letter informed her of her husband's death and was sent to her address, then why do you have Miss Slade trying to find her?"

"Because of a promise I made to Lieutenant Garrison."

They reached the study and went inside. Fox introduced Delaney to Miss Slade, a tall, lean woman with lively, interesting eyes.

"This is my wife, Miss Slade. You may speak freely in front of her. Please, have a seat."

The agent did and then said, "We have located Mrs. Garrison and her boy, Your Grace. She has been in London for some time now."

"Where?" Fox asked.

ALEXA ASTON

"Mrs. Garrison had been living with her parents in Colchester at the address you wrote to her. Both died suddenly, about the time her husband's mother asked her to come and live with her and her second husband. Things did not work out," the runner said. "Their servants were tightlipped for the most part, but a scullery maid spilled all to me. Apparently, the mother-in-law is quite controlling. She didn't really want Mrs. Garrison there. She only asked her daughter-in-law to come so the grandson would be under her roof. Mrs. Garrison was being treated little better than a servant, and she decided to up and leave."

"How terrible," Delaney said. "What is she doing now?"

"She is working as a laundress, Your Grace. The hours are long and the work is rough, but it is something she can do from home. Her boy is now three and children that age need constant supervision."

"Did you speak with her?" Fox pressed.

"I did not, Your Grace. I thought I should come and report to you personally before making contact with Mrs. Garrison."

"Take us to her now, Miss Slade," he said.

Fox rang for Driskell and asked for the carriage to be readied. As they waited, the Bow Street runner told Delaney about a few of her most recent cases.

"You lead a fascinating life, Miss Slade," she said.

"It is a busy one," the agent said. "Fascinating may be giving me too much credit."

They went outside, and Miss Slade gave the coachman the address. Inside the carriage, Fox said, "I want to help Mrs. Garrison. Do you have any ideas how we can do so, my love?"

"If she is talented with a needle, I could always use her at Delaney's Designs," she suggested. "She could even sew from home if she chose."

"Then we should offer her that opportunity," he said.

They arrived at the tenement, located in a very poor section of town, and entered the shabby building. A rat scurried across the floor. The smell of urine permeated the structure.

234

"Mrs. Garrison is on the top floor," Miss Slade said.

They mounted the stairs, working their way up six flights. Miss Slade rapped at the door and said, "Mrs. Garrison? It is Miss Slade here to see you, along with the Duke and Duchess of Abington."

Delaney heard footsteps. "Please do not continue to harass me," a voice said. "Go away."

Fox stepped closer. "Mrs. Garrison, I am Abington now—but once upon a time, I was Major-General Foxwell. You should recognize the name because I wrote to you of your husband's death."

A long pause occurred, followed by the turning of a lock. The door swung open, and Delaney saw a tired woman with dark circles under her eyes. The strong smell of lye clung to her.

"Your Grace?" she asked, looking Fox up and down.

"Yes, Mrs. Garrison. Might we come in?"

The woman winced. "There is nowhere for you to sit, I am afraid."

"We can stand. Please?" he asked softly.

She moved aside, allowing them entrance. As she did, Delaney saw a small boy holding on to her skirts.

"Hello," she said, kneeling. "I am Delaney. Who are you?"

He eyed her with suspicion. "Will."

Mrs. Garrison shut the door. "My husband was William. I named Will after his father."

The single room was cramped. A bed was the only place to sit. Several tubs were filled with water and clothing was in stacks throughout the room.

"I am sorry things are so crowded. I am a laundress now," the woman explained. "Why have you come, Your Grace?"

"Because your husband asked me to," Fox said solemnly. "I was with him during his last few minutes on this earth. He asked when the war was over that I come to you, Mrs. Garrison. Lieutenant Garrison was distraught because he had never seen his child. He knew he was dying and never would see his boy or you again."

Tears filled the widow's face. "That was my William," she said softly.

"I promised him I would visit with you and tell you of how courageous he had been on the battlefield." Fox paused. "It wasn't what he wanted, Mrs. Garrison. He told me that wasn't important. His last words are burned into my memory."

Taking the woman's hands in his, Fox said, "Lieutenant Garrison said all you need to say is that I love them. That they were in my thoughts always, especially at the very end."

Mrs. Garrison burst into tears. She collapsed into a heap on the floor. Her arms went about her boy, and she held him tightly as she wept.

Fox frowned, looking unsure. Delaney said quietly, "Let her cry. She needs to have this release."

After a few minutes, the widow dried her tears. She pushed herself to her feet, sweeping up her little boy. He, too, had begun to cry as his mother did and now wiped at his eyes.

"Thank you, Major-General. I mean, Your Grace. You do not know how much comfort that brings me. I loved William with all my heart. I will do everything in my power to keep his memory alive for Will. I appreciate you taking the time to locate me and share William's final words with me."

"Mrs. Garrison, I want to do more than that," Fox said. He looked to Delaney.

"Mrs. Garrison, might I ask what you did before your marriage?"

The widow looked at her. "I worked in my uncle's store. I waited on customers and kept the ledgers. Helped order supplies. That kind of thing. I met William while working there."

"Could you not return to your uncle?" she asked.

"He died shortly after my marriage to William. My aunt sold the shop and moved to the country to be with her sister." She paused. "My parents, too, have passed."

Knowing she wanted to help this woman, Delaney said, "I

own a millinery shop."

"Oh, I used to help my mother make hats," Mrs. Garrison said, wiping away her tears with the back of her hand.

"Do you sew?"

The widow looked puzzled. "Yes, Your Grace. Why?"

"I could use another seamstress now. And eventually another milliner." She smiled. "Especially one who might be able to keep my books."

Delaney explained about her shop and how it was temporarily closed as her employees worked on supplying new wardrobes for the duke's nieces and her.

"Would you be interested in coming to work for me? I lived above my shop before I married His Grace and the rooms now stand vacant. You could move into them and sew there. No rent would be required and I offer a decent, living wage to my workers."

Mrs. Garrison burst into tears. "Oh, Your Grace, I don't know what to say. This would be a godsend. I live in fear of Will being bitten by a rat and getting sick and dying."

She placed a hand on the widow's arm. "I can assure you that you will not have that problem if you accept the job and move to my old rooms."

The woman burst into tears again, as did the boy. Delaney picked him up and comforted him, calming the child as his mother tried to get hold of herself. Will finally squirmed so much that she set him down, and he ran back to his mother.

Mrs. Garrison took Delaney's hands and kissed them and then turned to Fox and did the same. "You are saving our lives, Your Graces."

"Return these clothes to their owners, Mrs. Garrison," Fox said. "I will have a wagon sent within the hour to take you and your things to your new home."

"And I will come around tomorrow morning and see that you are settled in nicely," Delaney promised. "We can talk more at that time about what you will be doing."

"Bless you," Mrs. Garrison said. "Bless you all."

They left the widow's building, returning to the ducal carriage.

Miss Slade beamed. "You have done a good thing, Your Grace. You have saved two lives. And Mrs. Garrison is left with the memory of how her husband treasured her until his end." She paused. "Mr. Franklin will send the final bill to you, Your Grace. Go ahead and have the carriage stop here. I have another case to begin and am close to where I need to interview a subject."

Fox rapped on the roof and the carriage pulled to the curb. "Thank you, Miss Slade. You have helped me not once, but twice. I will sing your praises to all I can."

"All in day's work, Your Grace." Miss Slade opened the carriage door and hopped to the street below.

Delaney saw Fox withdraw something from his pocket. He reached out, handing it to the runner.

"What I promised you earlier, Miss Slade."

The investigator accepted it with a brisk nod. "Good day." She shut the vehicle's door and told the coachman to continue.

"What was that about?" she asked curiously.

"I promised Miss Slade a bonus for her efforts regarding my case. I found her to be most competent and extremely professional. I believe in rewarding someone for making such an extraordinary effort."

As it had before—and she knew it would many times in the future—her heart melted at the generosity Fox showed toward others.

"I like your Miss Slade," Delaney told him.

His brows shot up. "She is not exactly my Miss Slade."

"No, but I like her all the same." Delaney rested her head against his shoulder. "And I like that we will be helping Mrs. Garrison and Will start a new life."

Fox took her hand in his and kissed it tenderly. "I am happy we could help her." He kissed her softly. "I also like the life we are building together."

Delaney decided the time was right to tell him. "Our life is going to change. Quite a bit, in fact." She paused, anticipating his reaction. "You see, there will be three of us come next January. I think I became with child on our wedding day."

"Are you joking?" he asked, taking her face in hands. "No, of course, you aren't. This is marvelous, Delaney. The best possible news ever. Ever!"

He smothered her with kisses, and she began to laugh as he pulled her onto his lap.

"I have a wife who is perfect for me—and now we will have a child together. What will we name her?"

"Or him. It could be a boy, Fox. Your heir."

"Or it could be a girl with caramel hair and a quick wit. Son or daughter, it does not matter. I only know that we will shower our child in love."

Delaney sighed. "I do love you, Your Grace."

Fox smiled. "I love you more, Your Grace."

And he kissed her the entire way home, just to let her know how much he did.

About the Author

Award-winning and internationally bestselling author Alexa Aston's historical romances use history as a backdrop to place her characters in extraordinary circumstances, where their intense desire for one another grows into the treasured gift of love.

She is the author of Regency and Medieval romance, including: Dukes of Distinction; Soldiers & Soulmates; The St. Clairs; The King's Cousins; and The Knights of Honor.

A native Texan, Alexa lives with her husband in a Dallas suburb, where she eats her fair share of dark chocolate and plots out stories while she walks every morning. She enjoys a good Netflix binge; travel; seafood; and can't get enough of *Survivor* or *The Crown*.

Printed in the USA
CPSIA information can be obtained
at www.ICGtesting.com
LVHW052039300723
753623LV00015B/586